# THE RAMADAN DRUMMER

a novel by

Randolph Splitter

**pandamoon**
publishing

www.pandamoonpublishing.com

Jacket design and illustrations © Pandamoon Publishing
Art Direction and Cover by Don Kramer: Pandamoon Publishing
Editing by Zara Kramer and Rachel Schoenbauer: Pandamoon Publishing

Pandamoon Publishing and the portrayal of a panda and a moon are registered trademarks of Pandamoon Publishing.

Library of Congress Cataloging-in-Publication Data is on file at the Library of Congress, Washington, DC

Edition: 1, version 1.01 2019
ISBN-13: 978-1-945502-78-1

# Critical Reviews

A good writer captures the reader's attention in the opening paragraphs. Randolph Splitter's book *The Ramadan Drummer* does just that.... The story does more to paint a picture of what happens when cultures meet, when daily life is a challenge, and when social pressures force people of all ages into making difficult choices. Having participated in Palestinian Jewish dialogue for many years, I appreciate Splitter's ability to illustrate through story the difficulty of engaging in relationships with people whose story we haven't heard.... the book challenged me to ponder my own personal choices and how I choose to conduct my own life. —**Libby Traubman, co-founder of the 26-year-old *Jewish-Palestinian Living Room Dialogue***

Randolph Splitter's The Ramadan Drummer opens as a conventional (but compelling) mystery. A three-year-old boy is shot during a fair in the neighborhood of Little Mecca. Who done it? Why? Readers will want to know. At the same time, Splitter's mystery goes much deeper. In his novel, he explores questions of faith and fanaticism—and of love's ability to transcend both. There are no easy answers here, and this is to Splitter's credit. The book soars because of its honest engagement with human complexity. —**Mark Brazaitis, author of many books of fiction and poetry, including *The River of Lost Voices: Stories from Guatemala, Julia & Rodrigo,* and *Truth Poker.***

The Ramadan Drummer is an ingenious detective novel set in the contact zone of cultures in an unnamed American city, where violence is always possible but where humanity endures. Splitter tackles the great issues of our time with wit and vision, and I couldn't put this novel down. —**Elizabeth Mckenzie, author of *Stop That Girl, MacGregor Tells the World,* and *The Portable Veblen.***

# Dedication

For Jenny, Jocelyn, and Margo, and in memory of Ron and Merle

"More than 100 million women are missing."
—Amartya Sen, Nobel Prize-winning economist

"If you prick us, do we not bleed?"
—*Merchant of Venice*, 3.1

# THE RAMADAN DRUMMER

# August: Shots Ring Out

Hundreds streamed into Lincoln Park on that warm summer night. The children ran to the face-painting booths or to the Ferris wheel that had been erected in a grassy meadow that had probably once been a cornfield. Twenty-somethings gravitated toward the temporary stage where a Lebanese pop singer was going to perform. Young mothers in colorful headscarves pushed their strollers around the park, in no hurry to get anywhere. Hungry visitors munched on popcorn or dripping ice cream cones or juicy *shawarma* stuffed inside pita bread. Others stopped at the many booths arrayed along the park's south side, where representatives of health food stores, Islamic bookstores, car dealerships whose salesmen claimed to speak Spanish and Arabic, martial arts schools, afterschool recreational programs, *halal* butcher shops, Islamic educational workshops, and zero-interest Islamic loan societies touted their products and services.

But at the eastern edge of the park, near the children's playground, members of a self-styled "Christian" organization held up signs that read "Keep the Christ in Christmas," "Say No To Sharia," and "Sand Niggers Go Home!" The men wore white shirts and narrow black ties, while the pale-faced women battled the heat in long dresses, thick socks, and blocky shoes. They directed a steady stream of verbal abuse at the fairgoers, but a phalanx of police officers kept them far enough away that most people didn't even know they were there.

The park was located in Terre Nouveau (locally pronounced "Terra Novo"), a mid-sized American city with a large Arab and Muslim population concentrated in a neighborhood known, either affectionately or derisively, as Little Mecca.

Pakistani-born, British-educated Dr. Ali and his family mingled with the other visitors to the summer fair. Since he was a long-time fixture in the community and a respected physician, he wore an expensive suit and a striped silk tie. He liked to give a good impression. His wife Mariam, her head bare, wore a simple, modest, but tasteful lilac blouse and matching skirt. Accomplished in her own right, she had studied South Asian history at university until meeting her future husband and was now serving her third term on the city council.

People greeted them in English, Urdu, or Arabic.

"*As-salamu alaikum,*" said the more traditional-minded.

"*Wa alaikum as-salaam.*"

Their son Farid, a year or two out of high school, spotted a booth that sold raffle tickets for a brand-new car and bought one. He worked part-time at a Toys 'R' Us and took classes at the local community college. Auto tech, American History, "developmental" English—though he had been born and raised in the States.

"You think you can win a fancy car without paying for it?" his father chided him.

"I might get lucky," said Farid, shrugging.

"Leave the boy alone," said Mariam, nudging her husband. "He's a hard worker."

Dr. Ali grunted. Farid drifted off to the tent where the singer was about to perform.

A few months before, the Ali family had moved from a squat, stucco eyesore in Little Mecca to a more elegant and spacious house in the hills, and now their fourteen-year-old daughter Yasmin, fresh from middle school in the old neighborhood, was suddenly surrounded by a gaggle of squealing girls from her new school. It was like bumping into a wasps' nest except that the wasps seemed friendly.

"Mom, can I hang out with my friends?" she asked.

Mariam looked to her husband, but Yasmin, not waiting for an answer, was already gone.

"What's got into that child?" said Ali, querulously.

But the mood was festive. A near-full moon hung high in the sky. Fireflies danced in the night air. Mariam held onto her husband's arm.

"Hey, Doc," said a balding man in shorts and shirtsleeves, accompanied by a willowy woman half a head taller than he was. It was one of his poker-playing buddies from the occasional Thursday-night game, a smart card player and, reputedly, a decent surgeon.

The women nodded to each other.

They could hear the electronic buzz of the singer's band, muffled by the tent's thick canvas and the distance. It sounded like flies just learning how to play the violin. Suddenly a series of short, sharp noises like rocks glancing off the face of a cliff rang out. Ali, his wife, and their friends exchanged nervous glances. Others craned their necks this way and that, trying to determine the source of the noises. Face-painters paused mid-stroke. The Ferris wheel seemed to hang in mid-air. "Gunshots," said someone and the idea spread like wildfire. Mariam gripped her husband's arm even more tightly. The sound of shots being fired was succeeded by the wail of police sirens.

"Yasmin! Farid! Where are they?" Mariam cried.

Suddenly their son popped up beside them, his face drained of color.

"Farid!" Ali barked while clapping his son on the shoulder. "Go find your sister!"

At the same time, the doctor hurried off in the direction of the grassy meadow toward which scores of other fairgoers seemed to be streaming.

"Where are you going?" said his wife, but he didn't stop to answer.

In a minute, he arrived at the spot where others had gathered. People were running in every direction. Everyone was talking at once.

"Let me in," he said. "I'm a doctor."

A young child with big brown eyes was lying on the grass, a twenty-something man cradling his head. The child was breathing heavily but not crying.

"Are you the boy's father?"

The man nodded.

Dr. Ali knelt down and looked into the boy's eyes. They seemed healthy and alert.

"Are you okay?" he asked the boy, who couldn't have been more than three years old.

The boy moved his head a little, as if nodding.

Ali examined the boy's left shoulder. A hole had been ripped in his T-shirt, but there was little blood. The situation was different in the boy's leg, which was bleeding significantly, the flesh torn like raw meat grilling on a fire. After a moment's hesitation, the doctor undid his silk tie and knotted it around the leg to staunch the bleeding. He patted the boy's ankle and started to say something to the father.

It was then that the police arrived.

\* \* \*

"So the boy isn't Muslim," police detective Ezra Kaufmann said the next day in the cramped, paper-strewn office of his boss, Captain Aimee Schroeder, an imposing woman whose uniform was just a little too small for her broad shoulders and expanding midriff. The walls were covered with framed certificates, photographs, even newspaper clippings. There was a window or two in there somewhere.

The child's father turned out to be an Indian food cart vendor, who had taken his son to the fair in order to entertain the boy and give his wife a few hours' rest. The child was taken to the hospital as the police swarmed over the park, demanded to see people's drivers' licenses or immigration papers, and carted off hapless fairgoers who had shown up in shorts and skirts and flip-flops and sandals, sans documentation.

Captain Schroeder shook her head. "Either the bullet was intended for someone else or the assailant thought the father was Muslim or—well, the fact of the matter is we just don't know. It's your job to find out." She nodded to the third person in the small office, a short, slight, thirty-something police officer who had apparently been working on community outreach for the last two years. "Yours and Sgt. Khoury's."

Kaufmann and Khoury looked at each other. Kaufmann, a veteran of the force who had been promoted to detective five or six years earlier, preferred to operate by himself. Not that he had anything against the other man, but he didn't like explaining his hunches or dealing with someone else's bad decisions. It was hard enough having to report to his higher-ups.

"I talked to several of the picketers," said Sgt. Khoury. "They have an alibi, of course, since they were carrying signs and parading around in full view of our guys."

The captain swiveled on her squeaky chair. "I spoke to Officer Torino, the head of the security detail. He confirmed that the picketers stayed behind the line we set up. The group was hostile, but it appears it didn't get beyond shouts and signs."

"Didn't the group's head—what's his name?—have a gun?"

Schroeder nodded. "Jeff Hampton. A loaded gun, too, but he had a valid permit. He grudgingly consented to having the weapon tested, and our tests showed that it hadn't been fired any time recently."

"Well, the picketers could have been working with someone else," said Sgt. Khoury. "An accomplice."

"It could have been someone they don't even know," said Kaufmann. "Their presence may have inspired some lone crazy to put their ideas into action."

The captain, who happened to be African American, picked up the thread. "The election campaign gets ugly. The hate groups get bigger and more brazen. The crazies come out of the woodwork. And they all decide to come here, where the inhabitants speak Arabic and there are two Muslims on the city council. We're like catnip to bigots."

Detective Kaufmann spoke up. "Wasn't there some bad blood between the two high schools last spring?"

One of them, Terre Rouge, was situated in the flatlands where the city originated and had a high proportion of Muslim students. The other high school, called Terre Noire, on the edge of the wealthier hills, was newer, more affluent, and more "white," with a smattering of second- and third-generation Chinese and Japanese Americans. Despite his modest detective's salary and the basic, two-

4

bedroom, wood-frame house they lived in—a house which badly needed a new coat of paint—his teenage son Jonathan, by a quirk of districting, attended the latter. It was true that the "Terre Rouge" soil was reddish, but by now most of it was covered by concrete and asphalt. The names derived from the early incursions of French trappers and fur traders, a legacy that survived even after the French themselves were pushed out by the English.

"Graffiti, fistfights, name-calling," said Khoury. "A couple of guys from the Noire baseball team pulled off a girl's headscarf and called her—"

"Towel-head?" said the detective. "*Hajji?*"

"Something like that."

"So," said Kaufmann, "it could have been some kid from the high school."

"Which?" said the captain.

"Which kid?"

"No, which high school."

Kaufmann raised his eyebrows. "Why would Muslim kids want to shoot up a Muslim summer fair?"

"Maybe they were shooting at the picketers," suggested Sgt. Khoury. "Or maybe they wanted folks to think that the Christians were doing the shooting. Anything's possible."

The captain exhaled loudly. "Okay, guys, get going. The press wants to know what happened. The city council is meeting tomorrow night. The Chief is breathing down my neck. I'm expecting results."

The detective and his new partner stood up. "So how's the boy doing?" asked Kaufmann.

"Hanging in there," said Khoury.

\* \* \*

While his partner was following up on some of the tips that had already been called into the department's hot line, the detective himself was pacing the section of the park where the protesters had been picketing. The sky was a dull gray, and an on-and-off drizzle had turned the grass wet and slick. Yellow police tape cordoned off this corner of the park, and the department's small, underfunded Forensics team had already been over it. They hadn't found the bullets that had struck the boy or any spent shells. Or, for that matter, the weapon in question. Most witnesses—not the right word, maybe, since no one claimed to have seen anything—said they had heard two shots, but some said there were three or even more.

The children's play area was empty now. Kaufmann crunched his way across the wood-chip ground cover and sat down on one of the kid-sized swings. As he went over the potentially relevant elements in his mind—the popular singer, the various hawkers and vendors, the face-painters, the Ferris wheel, the anti-Islamic protestors, the police officers assigned to keep the peace—he slowly rocked back and forth on the swing. He remembered his wife pushing Jonathan in a swing just like that years ago. Tentatively at first, then higher. When Jonathan was older, when he was able to propel himself, he liked to kick up his heels and point them at the sky. And that memory triggered a later one of him shooting baskets with his son at a school playground. Jonathan was never very good at basketball—not quick enough—but (over his mom's objections) he put on the pads and tried out for the high school football team. He wasn't that good in football either, but he was strong and doggedly persistent, more or less like Kaufmann himself.

Wait a minute. The Ferris wheel. Couldn't someone have fired shots from one of the hanging cars? He sprinted over to the big wheel, which sat motionless in the meadow, its power turned off, like an abandoned space ship. Did the Forensics guys check out all the cars? Kaufmann dug out his phone and called Ted Rudnitsky, the long-time head of the team who evidently knew something about fingerprints, spatter patterns, ballistics, and DNA. But Rudnitsky didn't answer and the detective left a message.

\* \* \*

The next day, Kaufmann and his partner sat in the back of a modest Middle Eastern restaurant, sharing a quick meal of hummus, eggplant, warm pita bread, and tepid, sweet-sour lemonade. The tables were made of Formica and the seats were covered in plastic, but the food wasn't bad.

Khoury was explaining how the tips he had pursued hadn't panned out.

"One guy said he saw someone with a gun, but then he admitted it was far off and the gun could have been a cell phone. A woman who bought a raffle ticket complained that the raffle was called off and she hadn't gotten her money back. Someone who wasn't at the park claimed that the whole thing was a hoax, that there hadn't been any shooting, and that the Muslims might not be so lucky the next time."

"Jesus."

"Exactly." The sergeant ate a black olive and spit out the pit. "Have you talked to Mehta?" The food cart vendor.

Kaufmann shook his head. "Not really. He's pretty freaked out by what happened. Doesn't leave his apartment except to visit his son. He and his wife."

Khoury nodded. After nibbling on some pita and hummus, he continued, "So what now, boss?"

Kaufmann bristled at the word "boss," but wasn't ready to be on a first-name basis with the sergeant. What was his first name anyway?

"We need to talk to the picketers again." They were told to stay in town, but it wasn't clear the police had any legal authority to enforce that.

Khoury nodded again, then mentioned the city council meeting later that evening.

The detective frowned. The idea of listening to political posturing and public "comments" made him feel sick to his stomach. He had already had enough of that during the current election campaign. "You think we're going to pick up clues at a city council meeting?"

"No, but it's always good to keep one's hand on the community pulse."

"You go. I'll track down some of those 'Christian' folks. Go over it one more time."

"Okay, boss. I'll fill you in later."

\* \* \*

When he got home, it was almost seven o'clock. He retrieved the mail, dropped his keys on the hall table, and helped himself to a beer from the fridge. For a moment, his mind drifted off and he forgot what he was thinking about. Right. The shooting of a three-year-old boy. But where was Jonathan? It was still the middle of summer, so he wasn't in school. Why wasn't he home yet?

Kaufmann grabbed his phone and texted his son. It was a simple message: **Where r u? Dad.**

What was the point of cell phones, he wondered, if nobody actually talked on them? Poor Bell or Edison or whoever it was who had invented the telephone must have been wondering the same thing. Bell's day had come and gone.

He sat down again and took another sip of the cold, refreshingly bitter beer. But there on the kitchen table, under the salt shaker, was a note from Jonathan. "Hey Dad," it said, "don't forget I'm at football practice. Later, J."

Oh, right. The team was beginning to practice now, in the summer, before school started. And after practice, some of the guys would go out for pizza. He picked up his phone again and tapped in the number he had been given for Hampton, the leader of the "Christian" group. After four rings, a man picked up and grunted a greeting. So this telephone device worked after all.

"Mr. Hampton? This is Ezra Kaufmann, Detective Kaufmann, of the Terre Nouveau Police."

"Yeah?"

"I'd like to talk. Is this a good time?"

A pause. "I already spoke to you guys. Nothing more to say."

"I understand. But I have a few more questions. Have you had dinner yet?"

Some muffled whispers in the background.

"Or a drink. How about we meet for a drink at the Harvest Grill? It's a tavern off of Dufresne Street."

Did these self-styled "Christians" drink? What kind of Christians were they, anyway?

"Okay. Harvest Grill. Seven-thirty."

\* \* \*

Farid and his friend Tariq were smoking cigarettes during the ten-minute break in the middle of their three-and-a-half-hour marathon summer session class. The young, bearded professor was trying to coax or drag them through three or four centuries of American history in six weeks while everyone else was barbecuing hot dogs or catching the last rays at the lake, but at least he gave them a short break now and then. Smoking was prohibited on the community college campus, except for the asphalt border zones between the parking lots and the rest of the campus. Between classes, and during breaks, the border zones were dense with smoke and populated with nicotine addicts who spent their free time sucking burning tobacco and coughing, staring past each other like already-dead zombies.

Actually, Farid wasn't smoking. He just paced the asphalt with his friend, watching him take deep breaths and blow out dirty air.

"Did you understand that Presley versus Jefferson shit?" Tariq said between puffs. Since he was tall and thin like a scarecrow and wore a red cloth *kufi* that topped his scrawny head like a tuft of scarlet plumage, he reminded Farid of the Sesame Street character Big Bird.

"Plessy," said Farid.

"What?" said the other, coughing.

"Plessy v. Ferguson. Yeah, I mean, what didn't you get?"

"I didn't get how the Supreme Court could say that blacks had to ride in separate railroad cars."

"Well, it was a long time ago, brother. Ku Klux Klan and all that."

"Yeah, but it was the fucking Supreme Court. And slavery was, like, over."

Farid shrugged. Yes, slavery was over. Still…

"Besides," Tariq continued, "this Presley guy, the plaintiff, was seven eights white. I mean, he was probably whiter than you are."

Farid said nothing. Tariq el-Malek, born Timothy Morrison, had converted to Islam eighteen months earlier and was as pale as a Ku Klux Klan member's sheet.

"Just kidding," added Tariq. "I mean, if it was women I could understand. Separate cars for women. Separate accommodations. Back of the bus."

Farid looked at his friend. "What are you talking about?"

Tariq tossed his cigarette to the asphalt, rubbed it in with his sneaker, and laughed. "Just messing with you, brother."

"C'mon, let's go back. I'm getting cold out here."

They were wearing T-shirts and threadbare jeans, and after the day's showers the air was cool.

"I don't know, man. Two more hours of that shit?"

"This stuff is important. There's a midterm next week."

"It's all in the book. Let's go to a movie."

Farid hesitated.

"C'mon. It's on me."

Farid laughed. "And what about the fifty bucks you owe me?"

"*Inshallah*, I'll pay you back, brother. *Inshallah*."

* * *

The Harvest Grill, closer to the downtown police headquarters than to the motel where the leader of the "Christian" group was evidently staying, was half-empty on that weekday night, but the patrons who were there made up in noise what they lacked in actual numbers. It was dark inside, but Hampton, sitting at the bar in his trademark white shirt and black string tie, made color vision irrelevant.

"Mr. Hampton," said the detective as he slid onto the seat next to him.

The bartender, a woman with a tattoo on her left arm, asked what he wanted.

"I'll have what he's having." Which looked like a bourbon on the rocks.

"We already told the police everything we know," said Hampton, who had short bristly hair, a narrow, block-like face, and a compact, wiry-looking body.

"I appreciate that," said Kaufmann. "But maybe you can tell me what you guys, well, believe in."

The man took a sip of his bourbon and turned to face the detective. "We believe in Jesus. We believe in freedom. We believe in America."

"Does that include American Muslims?"

"We got no problem with law-abiding, peace-loving Islamic people, but they cross the line when they start telling us what to do and how to think."

The bartender brought his drink.

"And where do you see that happening, Mr. Hampton?"

He slapped his palm on the bar. "Right here."

Kaufmann tasted his drink. It was quite strong. "Here?"

"Yesterday, Detective, I was woken up by a goddamn Moslem prayer call. Right here in an American city. Or what used to be an American city."

Kaufmann sighed. "You talk about freedom. Freedom of speech, freedom of the press, freedom of religion…"

"You've got to be kidding, Detective. Over there, they murder Christians and other Moslems that don't make the grade. Chop their heads off. They say it's in the Koran. Then they take the women as sex slaves because that's in the Koran too."

Hampton finished his drink and ordered another.

"So," Kaufmann continued, "you believe in fighting fire with fire?"

"Jesus said he didn't come to bring peace. He came with a sword."

"Or a gun?"

"Listen, Detective, we like to choose our battles. We had a permit to carry a gun, and we had a permit to picket. We're sorry the boy was shot."

"You mean you didn't intend to shoot him?"

The man started in on his second drink. Or was it his third?

The light in the bar was feeble, but Kaufmann tried to look him in the eye. "Why do you carry a gun?"

"I could ask you the same question, Officer."

Kaufmann sipped his bourbon. "As a detective, I don't normally carry a weapon."

Hampton took a long drink, then coughed. "I guess you're depending on guys like us to defend you."

Another customer sat down near them and ordered a single-malt scotch on the rocks.

"So why—"

"To protect my family. To exercise my God-given, constitutional right. To defend myself if the government tries to take it away from me."

"So you carry a gun to make sure nobody takes it away from you?"

Hampton just shrugged.

Kaufmann continued, "How big is your group?"

"Bigger than a breadbox, but not as big as a battleship."

"How many members does it have?"

"Do you want to see our tax returns?"

"You're based in Texas, aren't you?"

"No. My wife and I live in Day Shoots." A small town less than a hundred miles away. "We've got members all over, but we're not based anywhere."

"Do you have followers? Sympathizers? Individuals who aren't officially part of your organization but might, let's say, be inspired to take action."

The man took another drink and squinted at Kaufmann out of the corner of his eye. "Why? Do you know someone who might be interested?"

* * *

City Hall, next door to police headquarters, was sleeker and more modern than the law enforcement structure. Sergeant Khoury stood in the back of a wood-paneled conference room and scribbled a few notes while a man in a black baseball cap took his turn at the microphone.

"Why are the police hassling young men leaving the mosque," the man wanted to know, "while crazy people with guns are shooting innocent children in public parks?" He spoke with the hint of an accent.

"Mosques are not on the agenda," one of the councilmen murmured into his own mic.

"But shooting children is, isn't it?"

The councilman sighed.

Councilwoman Ali, wearing pale pink face powder and a dark tailored suit that made her seem older than she probably was, picked up the slack. "The shooting of Pankaj Mehta is a tragedy," she said, "but our small and understaffed police department is doing an excellent job with very limited resources. They're tracking down numerous leads and questioning dozens of witnesses."

Khoury noticed Captain Schroeder slipping out of the room. She seemed to be fidgeting with her tight collar.

"Limited resources?" said a gray-haired man in plaid suspenders. "Property taxes are already through the roof."

"The city budget is not on the agenda, either," said the first councilman, wearily.

"Stop telling us what is and isn't on the agenda," the man in the baseball cap protested.

"The horse is out of the barn," added the man in the suspenders. "The kid's already been shot."

Murmurs of agreement rippled through the audience.

11

Sergeant Khoury felt someone standing at his elbow and turned to see who it was. "Hey, boss, I thought you didn't like city council meetings."

"Well," said the detective, "I had a drink with Jesus' right-hand man and I figured I was ready for anything."

"You didn't miss much."

"What about the word on the street? The pulse of the city?"

The sergeant held up his narrow-ruled spiral notebook and said, "I'm taking the pulse, but it's feeble. No one knows what to think or who to blame. Whether it was a terrorist act or some random event…"

Kaufmann shook his head. "You're a detective now. There are no random events."

"Thanks, boss. I'll keep that in mind."

The detective noticed two uniformed cops monitoring the meeting. One was Torino, the twenty-year veteran who had been on security detail at the park. He stood up straight and did his best to look alert. The other, a husky, cabbage-faced rookie named Richmond or Richter, whose puffy features suggested he drank three or four beers each night, looked as if he wanted one now. Kaufmann had passed him in the corridors of the police building, but they had never actually met.

His eye chanced upon a thirty-seven or maybe thirty-eight-year-old woman in a lavender headscarf. She was taking notes in a notebook just like his partner's. He nodded toward her and asked Khoury if he knew who she was.

"Yeah. Aisha Hassan. She covers community affairs for the *Register-Guardian*."

"Hmm. I guess her finger is on the pulse of the city too."

* * *

The movie, a buddy film about two soldiers who don't know the war is over, was not as good as it sounded, and Farid wanted to leave before the two recruits even figured it out.

"What's your hurry, brother?" said his friend. "The night is young."

"I have to get up early to go to work," said Farid.

"Chill, man. You work too hard." Tariq was munching on a giant container of popcorn.

"That's not what my father thinks."

"Your dad is old school. Like my stepdad."

Farid stood up, prompting some hoots from people behind him.

"All right, brother. I'll give you a ride."

The two of them trudged up the aisle. Tariq's motorcycle was parked on a nearby side street, and Farid climbed on behind him. The drizzle had started again, and gray clouds blocked whatever stars might have dotted the night sky. Tariq turned on the ignition and revved the motor. Farid held onto his waist, and soon they were speeding through the slick streets.

"I can't believe it," Tariq shouted over the noise of the engine and the wind.

"What?"

"I can't believe they shot a little kid in broad daylight. I mean, it could've been my little brother. Or yours."

"Yeah, but it wasn't broad daylight. It was almost dusk."

"Fucking close enough," countered Tariq. "I can't believe they fucking shot a little kid at a friendly neighborhood community fair and fucking got away with it."

Drops of water from the trees above fell on Farid's head. He wasn't wearing a helmet. "Not yet," he pointed out. "They haven't gotten away with it yet."

Tariq half-turned around to look at him. "Yeah, right. You think they're gonna catch the asshole?"

"Maybe. The police—well, they know what they're doing."

"Fucking police don't have nothing better to do than chase Muslims around and ask for their green cards."

Farid didn't say anything. Now he was tired and wanted to go to sleep.

"Hey, brother, I got an idea."

His friend seemed to be waiting, so Farid said, "What?"

"We start our own self-defense force. Take matters into our own hands."

"Huh?"

"Yeah, walk the streets, patrol the park, guard the mosque. Like the Black Panthers or the vigilante dudes in those old westerns."

Farid laughed. "You and who else?"

"You, brother. You."

Farid snorted through his nose. "Okay. You, me, and who else?"

Tariq didn't respond, so Farid watched the streetlamps and the traffic lights whiz by.

"Turn here," he said finally.

"You live up in the hills, man?"

"Yeah, my family moved a few months ago. My dad cashed in on some real estate deals or something."

"Fuck," said Tariq. "My stepdad kicked me out of the house when I was sixteen."

Now he was twenty-three, several years older than Farid but still apparently trying to figure out what he was supposed to be doing with his life. Having met him one day at an Islamic bookstore, Farid had convinced Tariq, a high school dropout, to take a class or two at the community college, where there were no entrance requirements. The conversion to Islam had marked a turning point, and he prayed five times a day, but otherwise he seemed to be drifting.

"Sorry, brother," said Farid, adding, "I didn't mean to throw dirt on your self-defense force. It sounds like a good idea."

* * *

The cluster of food carts was close enough to the police station that the detective could walk there. Salvadoran tamales wrapped in banana leaves, Thai curry dishes, hot pita pockets stuffed with spit-roasted lamb, peanut butter avocado and bacon sandwiches, and slurpy-spicy Japanese ramen bowls vied for the customers' attention. But Kaufmann's attention was focused on the samosa stand where Arvind Mehta had gone back to work. He showed Mehta his badge, and the slender man—looking older than his twenty-eight or thirty years—agreed to sit down with him at a nearby redwood table while his co-worker dished out samosas on his own.

"You doing okay?" the detective asked him.

The man nodded, but his deep brown eyes looked troubled.

"How is your son doing?"

"He's still in the ICU, but I hope the doctors will get him out of there soon."

"How about your wife?"

A long pause. Then: "It's difficult for her."

"I understand. I'm sorry, but I have to ask you a few more questions."

"I already told the first policeman—I don't remember anything. I don't remember whether I was holding Pankaj's hand or carrying him on my shoulders. I don't know which direction the shots came from. All I remember is Pankaj lying on the ground at my feet, people swarming around us, sirens screaming."

The Forensics team had speculated that the bullet that passed through the boy's right side came from a lightweight, lower-caliber pistol, one that was probably easy to conceal, but they couldn't be sure. A sweep of the Ferris wheel had turned up no trace of a weapon, shells, or gunshot residue.

"So why did you take your son to the park?"

"My wife was tired out from her job—she's a health aide—and from taking care of Pankaj, so I thought I'd give her a break. I'd heard there was face-painting, fun rides, what have you, and I thought Pankaj would like that."

Nearby, a couple of office workers were digging into their rice bowls. Kaufmann could smell the spices in the curry.

"But you're not a Muslim."

Mehta shook his head. "No. I didn't know it was a Muslim event. I thought it was for everybody."

A *hijab*-wearing woman with dark eyebrows and dark eyes sat down next to them. It was the reporter from the local paper.

"It was," she confirmed. "For everybody."

The food cart man looked confused.

"I'm Aisha Hassan, from the *Register-Guardian*."

Mehta glanced back at the samosa stand. "I have to get back to work."

Kaufmann handed the young man a card. "If anything else occurs to you, Mr. Mehta, don't hesitate to call me." The man nodded. "And if there's anything I can do to help—"

"Thank you, Detective. I still don't understand why…" His voice trailed off. "I mean, I listen to the news. I know people are upset about refugees, immigration, what have you. But a park? A summer fair? A three-year-old child?"

The reporter jumped in. "I just wanted to ask you, Mr. Mehta, if you passed the line of picketers on your way into the park."

Kaufmann started walking away.

"No, I didn't know about them until I watched the television later."

"And did you see anything else? Anything unusual or unexpected?"

"No." He shook his head. "I'm sorry, I really have to get back." He got to his feet.

"Nothing?"

"Only—"

"What?"

"The face-painters." The detective turned to listen. "All the children were thrilled by the face-painters, and Pankaj was very pleased with the tiger stripes they put on his face."

"Yes," said the reporter, "I was there myself. My daughter got a flower on her cheek."

"But," said Mehta, "one man started arguing with them."

The detective took a few steps back to the table. "What were they arguing about?"

Mehta shrugged. "I'm not sure. I was too far away."

The reporter continued, "What did he look like—the man who was arguing?"

Mehta thought for a minute. "Like I said, I was far away. But he looked thin, like he never got enough to eat. Tall, thin, young. That's about all I could tell."

"Young?" said the detective. "How young?"

"I don't know. Twenty, twenty-one—something like that."

Kaufmann and Hassan exchanged glances. Then she turned back to the food cart vendor.

"Thank you," she said, handing him her own card. "You've been very helpful."

* * *

The *Masjid al-Salaam*, or Mosque of Peace, was a single-story, cement-block building in a commercial stretch of strip malls and car repair shops. A small parking lot separated the mosque from the street. Since there was no identifying signage on or in front of the building—a deliberate security feature—you wouldn't know it was a mosque unless you were already informed.

Three young men paced the sidewalk in front of the parking lot: Tariq with his red head covering and black tennis shoes, his shorter, plumper friend Farid, and Kadiye, an even younger recent arrival from somewhere like Yemen or Somalia whom Tariq had managed to recruit. The sun had just passed its zenith, and the temperature was soaring. Cars entered the parking lot and pedestrians streamed toward the mosque for Friday prayers.

"*As-salamu alaikum,*" a man said to Tariq.

"*Wa alaikum as-salaam.*"

Here they were guarding the *masjid*, thought Farid, yet his friend preferred to pray by himself and rarely set foot in the mosque. He seemed to practice a kind of do-it-yourself Islam. Yet it was better to pray, even alone, Farid concluded, than to turn away from Allah.

A few minutes later Tariq decided that they needed to split up. Farid would cover the back of the building, and Kadiye would monitor the visitors getting out of their cars.

"How do we know—" asked the youngster. "How do we know which ones are friends and which ones enemies? Or FBI?"

Tariq pondered the question. "The suspicious ones—bring them to me."

# Mid-September, Thursday: Ftirling

*Rachel? Alive? As he cleared the coffee cups and other breakfast dishes from the kitchen table, he saw his wife getting ready to go off to her job as a social worker, pushing back her chair, picking up her tote bag brimming with papers, saying something to him which he could not hear. He took a long, uncertain look at her and thought, should I tell her? But tell her what? The truth being that she had cancer or rather that she had had cancer and now she was, in fact, dead. Or was she? The clear evidence in front of his own eyes said no. She was back from the dead. It made no sense. It was a miracle. But there it was. In fact, he had found himself in the same situation numerous times since she had died. No point in telling her. Just hold his tongue and hope for the best.*

Kaufmann opened his eyes. Outside, far away, someone seemed to be playing a drum. A late-night jazz hound just emerging from a club? An early riser practicing for the noontime drumming circle in the park? He closed his eyes and tried to go back to sleep.

* * *

A few hours later, the clock radio switched on. Kaufmann turned over in bed, the same queen bed which he and Rachel had shared for many years but which he now slept in, on the same side as before, alone. The light was filtering through the blinds, the broken slat still broken, the blinds still slightly askew.

There was a knock at the door.

"Hey, Dad, can you take me to school? I'm running late."

His sixteen-year-old son Jonathan stood in the doorway, already dressed in baggy jeans and a neo-punk-band T-shirt. He had a mop of curly hair and no desire to comb it.

Kaufmann wished he had time to make himself some strong coffee, read the sports page, and avoid thinking about more serious things. Maybe even stop at the gym. But no matter. It was good to spend some time with his son, especially now.

"Sure. Just give me ten minutes."

In fact, it took him twelve minutes to wash his face, brush his teeth, stare at his own unruly hair, and swallow some pills. The forty-year-old face that stared back at him in the mirror looked older than he remembered though younger than he actually felt—the untrimmed eyebrows taking off in all directions, the three-day beard ready for a shave. He put on some random, mismatched clothes and stepped out the door.

"How are your classes going?" he asked his son on their way to the car. It was September, the mornings turning cool.

Jonathan was listening to something on his music player and didn't hear. Kaufmann tapped him on the shoulder.

"I said, how's school?"

Jonathan pulled the buds out of his ears and shrugged.

"Got any good teachers this year?"

His son dropped his pack in the back seat and climbed into their much-traveled Toyota sedan, which was almost as old as he was. Then he mumbled something incomprehensible.

They snaked through residential streets, paused briefly at stop signs, turned onto a larger road that was quickly filling up with traffic.

"What were you listening to?"

"Uhh, it's Not Rocket Science."

"I know it's not rocket science, Jonathan. I'm just curious."

"No, Dad," he replied, as if explaining rocket science to an idiot. "It's the name of a band. Not Rocket Science. A punk-metal group from England. You wouldn't like them."

Jonathan used to be a happy kid, Kaufmann recalled, singing in the shower or just bursting spontaneously into song while skipping through the house. But the songs he listened to now had no melody, and he didn't sing along.

Kaufmann pulled into the crowded parking lot of a dazzling, two-story, stone-and-glass building adjacent to grassy playing fields. Young men and women were climbing out of late-model cars and hurrying up the cement steps of the school's main entrance.

"You need a ride home?"

Jonathan shook his head.

"Practice?"

A second- or third-string running back on the football team, he wasn't big enough or fast enough to start, but the coach sometimes used him in spot situations.

"Nope. I mean, yeah, there's practice, but I'm skipping it."

"How come?"

"Rehearsal."

"Rehearsal?"

"*Merchant of Venice*. Shakespeare. Remember?"

Oh, right. Jonathan had been juggling football and drama, as if he couldn't decide what he really wanted to do. He wished his son would pick one thing and stick to it, maybe even get good at it.

"Which reminds me," said Jonathan. "Have you thought about what I asked you?"

"Uh, you asked me something?"

"A car. You said you would think about buying me a car. A good used car."

"Mnn, well, I *am* thinking about it. You haven't taken your driver's test yet. And I said if you earned enough money on your own, I might match your contribution."

"So? Will you? Match my contribution?"

Other cars were honking behind them.

"Jonathan, do we have to talk about this now?"

His son shook his head, stuck the little plastic buds back in his ears, and marched off.

"Hey, wait!" Kaufmann called after him. He wanted to remind him that tonight was the beginning of Rosh Hashanah, the Jewish New Year.

But Jonathan had already gone.

\* \* \*

Jonathan was heading down the hall between classes when he overhead two senior girls saying something about a list.

"Yeah, she's on it," said one.

"You serious?"

"Yeah, she's cool."

They were standing in front of one of their lockers, depositing their books and checking their makeup, but he was soon out of hearing range. A stream of students swirled around him, shouting, texting, talking. In the confusion, he practically bumped into his friend Zach, a skinny kid with brown skin, jet-black hair, and a small stud in one ear. Half-black, half-Japanese, and half something else, he liked to joke.

They gave each other a three-part dap handshake.

"Hey, man."

"Hey. What's up?"

"You hear about the party at Allison's house this weekend?"

Jonathan shook his head.

"Her parents are out of town. Everybody's going."

"Everybody?"

"Come on. It'll be a blast."

The bell rang, and the students remaining in the hallway hurried to class.

\* \* \*

The police headquarters was a 1970s architectural dinosaur with windows that didn't open, walls that looked like accordion pleats, and a fading reddish-orange paint job. The structure had been unsuccessfully remodeled in the 1990s, and two bond measures aiming to finance a new building had been soundly defeated in more recent years. Trying to ignore the headache that had been pressing on his eyes from the inside, Detective Kaufmann nodded to the duty sergeant and the mousy-looking woman scurrying behind him, a civilian whose job seemed to be to construct a filing system so byzantine that no one would ever find anything.

His own office was a windowless hole-in-the-wall that had formerly housed a Xerox machine and several giant boxes of pencils. Sergeant Khoury was already there, drinking coffee out of a paper cup.

"Don't you ever sleep?" the detective asked him.

"Sure, sometimes. I find that I need less sleep than most people."

Kaufmann collapsed into a shaky chair. "So—what did you hear?"

Several weeks after the shooting, Pankaj had gone home from the hospital, but their investigation had stalled. The anti-Muslim picketers had left town. A search of police databases had turned up a few hits—a DWI, an alimony dispute, a bar fight—but nothing major. Conversations with several face-painters led them to doubt the food vendor's perceptions. Two of them had no recollection of anyone complaining, and the third vaguely recalled someone saying something about Islamic beliefs though he didn't remember what he looked like. The reporter Aisha Hassan alluded to the man who supposedly didn't like face-painters in one of her articles, but no one came forward with any more information. To make matters worse, a series of editorials elsewhere in the paper had been criticizing the police department for bungling the investigation.

The detective and his partner had a meeting the next day with Captain Schroeder, and Kaufmann was not looking forward to it. For now, they were getting back to basics, visiting the two high schools, talking to teachers and students. Tracing the hostility that had grown up between them in the last few years.

"The Terre Noire principal," said Khoury, "claims it's just normal school rivalry, nothing serious."

"What do the kids say?"

"They say it started with Rouge. That some Rouge guys beat up a Noire kid after a baseball game, and that Rouge boys were, like, harassing Noire girls. Catcalling or whatever."

Of course, he could have asked his son, and he had. Jonathan had said pretty much the same thing, but he admitted that it went both ways.

"So," Kaufmann continued, "what did the Rouge kids say?"

"They say the graffiti has gotten nastier in the last year, and the teachers agree. They also say that Noire boys harass Rouge girls who wear the *hijab*. I asked the students about the baseball game incident. Almost no one had heard of it."

"Not surprising."

"But one young woman said she heard about it from her brother, who told her the boy from Noire was looking for a dealer who would sell him some hash." The sergeant took a drink of his coffee.

Kaufmann's eyebrows went up. "Drugs? In Little Mecca?"

"The local kids told him to get lost. He wouldn't take no for an answer. Evidently punches were thrown."

"Is there a police report on that?"

Khoury shook his head. "If there is, I can't find it."

Maybe the clerk behind the front desk had hidden it somewhere.

"I think I'll talk to the brother," said the detective. "See if he has any details or knows anyone who was involved." He realized they were grasping at straws. What did this mostly forgotten incident have to do with the shooting at the park? But what else could they do?

"Let me do that, boss."

"Khoury, don't call me boss."

The sergeant seemed to be caught off guard. "No problem, sir. I just thought you might want to see the football practice at Rouge High."

"Football practice? Why?" He had a sudden vision of his son carrying the ball across the goal line.

"They're doing it at night. After dark."

"Huh? Why?"

"Because it's Ramadan. Usually Ramadan falls during the summer, but this time it's at the beginning of the school year. A lot of the football players are Muslim, and they can't eat or drink during the day."

"Isn't that a bit extreme? When do these kids sleep?"

"Didn't you already ask me that, sir?"

Kaufmann heard himself grunting in reply.

"Anyway, it's cooler at night, and the players can drink water during practice. I'm sure you'll find it interesting."

\* \* \*

The seats in the dimly-lit auditorium were empty except for a few students who had nothing better to do than watch the rehearsal, play games on their smart phones, or sleep. Or all those things at once. The crew members fiddled with the sets, the lights, and the curtains while the actors, including Jonathan and Zach, rehearsed in their school clothes. The school's drama teacher, Mr. Blankenship, looked on.

They were starting again from the beginning. Antonio, the depressed merchant of the title, voiced the opening lines of the play:

*In sooth, I know not why I am so sad:*
*It wearies me; you say it wearies you;*
*But how I caught it, found it, or came by it,*
*What stuff 'tis made of, whereof it is born,*
*I am to learn;*
*And such a want-wit sadness makes of me,*
*That I have much ado to know myself.*

His friends tried to cheer him up or at least figure out why he was so depressed. It wasn't love, he assured them, and it wasn't anxiety about his high-seas trading ventures. Then what was it? But he didn't know any more than they did.

"Okay, good," said Mr. Blankenship, stepping onto the stage among the cast members. A large, pink-faced man who looked a bit like a panting Saint Bernard, he wore a black sweatshirt, black pants, and white tennis shoes, with a silver whistle around his neck. "But something is missing."

"I know it's still rusty," said Nadim, the boy who played Antonio.

22

The original idea was for a joint production of the two high schools. That plan fell through, but two students from Terre Rouge—Nadim and Olivia, who played Shylock's wayward daughter Jessica—had joined the cast of the play.

"No, it's not that," said the teacher. "You're doing a great job of looking depressed." Jonathan wondered whether that was a backhanded compliment. "But we have no clue why Antonio is so sad. What's your motivation? What's the subtext?"

"But," Nadim complained, "he doesn't know either. That's the first thing he says."

In fact, thought Jonathan, it was the very first line of the play, as though a couple of scenes were missing.

"And," said someone else, "his friends have no clue either."

The teacher resumed, "Maybe there are clues elsewhere in the play, in what other people say about Antonio or what he does. Don't take things for granted. Read between the lines."

"But Mr. Blankenship," Zach protested, "the play opens in a week." And he played the pivotal role of Shylock, the Jewish moneylender.

"That's why I'm bringing it up," the teacher said, half-smiling. "You guys are doing great. You've got your lines down cold. Your blocks. Your beats. But this play is tricky."

"Why don't you just tell us?"

"Thank you, Jonathan, but that wouldn't be much of a learning experience, would it? Besides, I don't know. There are lots of possibilities."

Learning experience. Fuck. They were supposed to act in a play by Shakespeare and figure out the subtext too? Football was easier. "Maybe he woke up on the wrong side of bed," he muttered. "Maybe he had a fight with his wife."

In the background, the crew continued to move heavy scenery and shout instructions to each other.

"Okay, places everyone," said Mr. Blankenship. "Let's take it from the top."

No one seemed to be paying any attention to what he said until Olivia, who played his love interest in the play, the woman he ran off with, remarked, "Uh, he doesn't have a wife, does he?"

The drama teacher started to reply, but angry words burst out of Jonathan's brain before he could stop himself. "How the hell should I know? Should I check the fucking marriage records?"

Olivia flinched. She looked at him as if he was the biggest asshole in the school. Zach stared at him as if he thought he needed to see a counselor, fast. Becky, the young woman who played the refined and intelligent heroine Portia, seemed to view him with a mixture of bewilderment and concern. Shit, what had gotten into him?

Mr. Blankenship turned to him and said, "Why don't you take a break, son? We don't need you in this scene."

* * *

The detective arrived home around six o'clock in the evening. The modest two-bedroom cottage that he and Jonathan inhabited, partly damaged in the last big storm, was located in an unevenly middle-class neighborhood at the base of the foothills that overlooked the city. Well-kept bungalows jostled for space with their down-at-the-heels counterparts. Some lawns were freshly mown; others (like theirs) were full of weeds. Maybe he and Jonathan could locate the gardening tools one day and dig up some of the thistles, crabgrass, and other invaders.

There was still plenty of daylight left as he collected the mail from the box out front. Some bills, some catalogs, some police journals, a magazine addressed to his late wife, various pieces of junk mail.

He tossed the junk mail into the recycled paper bin and glanced at the catalogs. Stuck between two of them was a small, hand-addressed envelope. He left it on the table while he sliced a tomato and reheated some leftover pasta. Soon it was almost seven. When was the last time he and Jonathan had eaten dinner together?

While eating, he opened the envelope. The letter, written on pastel stationery, emitted a faint but pleasing scent. *Dear Detective Kaufmann*, it began.

> *I hope you don't think I'm being presumptuous. I don't usually flirt with gentlemen I don't know very well, but I decided to make an exception. Maybe ftirling* [he looked twice at the unusual spelling] *is the wrong word. I know you've been going through a rough patch, and I thought you could use some cheering up—maybe take a little time out, meet for coffee or something. How about 10 o'clock Saturday morning? The Starbucks near the police station?*

There was no signature and no return address. What the hell was that all about? Rough patch? Gentlemen I don't know very well? *Ftirling*? Well, yes, it was the wrong word. Was it Norwegian or something? A Freudian slip? Was that perfume he smelled on the paper? Pale pink stationery. Who wrote letters nowadays? Maybe it was a strategy to preserve the writer's anonymity. He realized that the best response would be to toss the letter into the recycling bin, but his investigative instinct was to trace it to its source. He took a deep breath, tucked the letter back in its envelope, and slipped the envelope into a kitchen drawer next to the paper napkins and the coffee filters.

∗ ∗ ∗

The temperature had dropped by the time he reached the playing field. Floodlights cut through the night, and the coaches yelled instructions as the players bounced off one another in full-contact drills. Some of them were scrimmaging, while others were practicing on the sidelines. It was almost eleven o'clock.

"Hut-hut-hut," called the quarterback, taking the ball from the center and dropping back to throw a pass. The receiver crossed over the middle, but the passer, under pressure from the defense, overthrew him.

The coach, dressed in an extra-large short-sleeve sweatshirt and XXL-sized baggy shorts despite the cold, like a walking advertisement for big-and-tall clothing, was making periodic notes on a clipboard.

"Excuse me. I'm Detective Ezra Kaufmann of the Terre Nouveau Police."

The big man eyed him warily. "Anything the matter, Detective?"

"No, I'd just like to watch your practice if you don't mind."

The man frowned.

"You know," Kaufmann added, "we want to establish good relations with the community. The churches, the mosques, the shops, the schools."

The man's face softened.

Nearby, several linemen, looking like larger-than-life GI Joe dolls in their shoulder pads, smashed into each other and grunted, while another player tossed perfectly spiraled passes to a teammate forty yards away.

The detective asked the coach what his name was.

"Bill Syed. I went to this high school, and now I teach social studies and coach football."

"So how do the kids feel about the nighttime practices?"

"Why don't you ask them?"

Kaufmann approached a wiry young student doing stretching exercises on the sidelines.

"It's cool," said the young man, who gave his name as Mo Sanders. "If we were practicing in the heat of the day, with no water, half of us'd be dead by now."

"How about you?" he asked one of the massive linemen.

"For me it's simple. I love football and I love Islam. This way I can honor both."

Kaufmann turned back to the coach. "You ever get any complaints? From the kids or their parents?"

Coach Syed nodded. "Sure, sometimes. But they know that being on a football team requires commitment. And sacrifice. Just like their religion."

"What about kids who aren't Muslim? How do they feel about practicing in the middle of the night?"

The coach blew his whistle and called over one of the other players, a running back who was jogging backwards as part of a drill.

"Jeff, this is Detective Kaufmann. Nothing to worry about. He just wants to know what you think about holding practices at eleven or twelve at night."

The kid hesitated for a moment. "I'm tired in the morning, but I'm learning how to schedule the other things I need to do. Like my chores and my homework. And if it helps the rest of the guys, I'm okay with it."

"You're not Muslim?"

"No, sir. I'm Christian. Go to church every Sunday and Bible study every Thursday afternoon."

Coach Syed nodded at the young man, who trotted back to the field.

"So when does practice end?"

"About two or three in the morning. We give 'em bananas and juice and send 'em off to do their own things. Some of them go to a coffee shop for breakfast; others go home to sleep."

Kaufmann thanked the coach and headed back to his car. So this is high school football in America, he said to himself. No angry demonstrators, no epithets, no gunshots. At least not tonight.

\* \* \*

It was past midnight and the house was dark when the detective got home. He turned the key gently in the lock, slipped off his shoes, and tiptoed softly across the floor. But when he started climbing the stairs, he tripped on some books.

"Dammit!" he muttered, trying to stifle a cry of pain.

As his eyes grew accustomed to the darkness, he shoved the books out of the way and continued up the stairs.

A hoarse, sleepy voice mumbled, "What time is it?"

"Late," said Kaufmann. "Go back to sleep."

"Time for school?"

Kaufmann hobbled into the doorway of his son's room.

"No. Go back to sleep."

Jonathan sat up in bed, his hair sticking out in odd directions as if it were some kind of fright wig.

"Where were you?"

"Football practice."

Lying there in the shadows, Jonathan blinked a few times as if trying to make sense of the words. "Wait. What did you say?"

"Listen, Jonathan, have you thought about tomorrow?"

His son rubbed his eyes. "Tomorrow? What about tomorrow?"

"Remember? It's Rosh Hashanah. You said you might come to services with me."

"Tomorrow? I've got school."

"Jonathan, it's a special day. Can't you miss one day of school to do something, well, spiritual?"

Jonathan closed his eyes and opened them again. "But Dad, I've got a math test, a drama rehearsal, an important history class I can't miss. And—and since when are you into that spiritual bullshit?"

"It's not bullshit." He hesitated. "Not really. And it's especially worthwhile now."

"Now? Why now?"

Kaufmann didn't bother to answer. The tussle with his son caused his thoughts to drift to the day, around this time of the year, when he had told his father he was quitting law school. His dad was a lawyer, so the expectation was that young Ezra would carry on the tradition. The buttoned-down corporate attorney couldn't believe that he would want to leave law school, but what he really couldn't fathom was the idea that he wanted to become a policeman. The law was an honorable profession, his father had said, meaning (he supposed) you could make money and wear a suit, while police work was some kind of semiskilled labor, akin to picking up garbage or sweeping the street. Somebody had to do it, but why him? Why waste his education?

Yes, it was dangerous and dirty—and it had its share of boring paperwork—but at least some of it was real. As a kid who read a lot, played as much chess as football, and did well in school, he wanted to get his hands dirty. His math teacher mom worried about his safety, but she seemed to understand. Back in Russia or Galicia or wherever it was, at least one of his father's ancestors was a rabbi. Or was it his mother's? Did the rabbi study the Talmud the way his father studied his law books, as a lifeless, abstract puzzle with no connection to the real world? Or did he get his hands dirty?

Jonathan took a deep breath. "Look, Dad, you can do whatever you want, but I'm not into that crap. I don't even believe in God."

"Jonathan, it's not about belief. Whether you believe or not doesn't change anything."

"What do you *mean*?" he almost screamed. "If I don't believe in God, what's the point of lighting the candles or keeping kosher or going to temple or doing any of the other stupid, superstitious crap that religious people do? Am I supposed to just, well, lie? Fake it? Go through the fucking motions?"

"It's not that simple, Jonathan. God doesn't care whether you believe in him—or her, or whatever. At least, I wouldn't count on it. But keeping in touch with whatever's out there might help you to deal with Mom's death."

Jonathan stuck the pillow over his head and muttered something unintelligible.

"What?" Kaufmann asked his son.

He took the pillow off. "I said, yeah, Dad, like it's helped you so much."

# Friday: Prayers

*He was walking along a winding, dusty road, trying to reach a small village, maybe his father's village, the one his father always spoke about with such bitter longing, the one he and his family were forced to flee. Yes, that made sense, because in the dream, Jamal, like his father at the time, seemed to be a child. He began to hear a loud drumbeat that sounded like firecrackers or maybe gunfire, but he didn't know where it was coming from and he was scared. He wanted to hide but the road was completely open and there was no place to hide, so he just ran ahead, hoping to reach the village before the bullets reached him, but then the road disappeared and he forgot about the village but the drumbeat got louder and—*

He opened his eyes and realized that the drumbeat really was the beat of a drum. It was coming from outside his window. He woke up and saw the cold blue numbers on the alarm clock—4:31—and he remembered that it was Ramadan and that someone, some guy from the *masjid* or whoever it was, was raising a racket in order to wake everybody up for the pre-dawn *suhoor* meal.

People did things like that for each other in Little Mecca. These days the main street in their part of town looked a lot like Main Street in any American town, with auto parts shops and fast food restaurants and discount drugstores, except that the Kragen and McDonalds and Walgreens outlets had signs in Arabic as well as English. In nearby strip malls and side streets one could also find *halal* butcher shops, Middle Eastern markets, an Islamic bookstore, and two or three cafés where one could drink thick, bittersweet Turkish coffee, eat dense, honeyed confections, and smoke a scented *nargil.* One could hear the recorded voice of a *muezzin* calling the faithful to prayer five times a day. One was likely to be awakened early during Ramadan whether one wanted to get up in the dark or sleep till noon. The drummer woke up everybody within shouting distance. It didn't matter if one was a Muslim or not, if one believed or didn't believe. In this they were all alike.

Jamal muttered a mild curse, turned over in bed, and tried to go back to sleep.

\* \* \*

Aisha heard the drumming too. The sound reminded her of her last visit to her parents' house in East Jerusalem. Her mother, a pastry maker who sold her flaky treats to local stores and restaurants, had given birth to six children. One had gotten married; another had moved out on his own. Three were at home, the oldest an engineering graduate who was still trying to find work and the two youngest more or less underfoot. Her father, who owned a juice bar in the Old City, hid behind his daily newspaper and did his best to ignore the rest of the family, except when they were helping out in the café. Or during Ramadan, when he roused the others before daylight for food and prayer. But now Aisha just stayed in bed and tried to sleep. She wondered what mixed messages she was handing down to her increasingly Americanized daughter.

\* \* \*

The drumming started early that morning, but Farid didn't hear it in their new house, which was high up in the hills and too far from the old neighborhood for the sound to carry. Even so, he was already awake and dressed. Not to mention hungry. Yasmin and the rest of her friends had escaped unharmed on the night of the shooting, having been flirting with some boys behind the tent while the boys sneaked cigarettes. Their parents were relieved, but last night it had been almost ten o'clock by the time Yasmin had gotten home—on a school night—and their dad had yelled at her. The trouble, he thought, was that Dad didn't follow through. Yasmin had always been his favorite, and he was letting her get away with murder. Their mom had tried to smooth things over, but some things couldn't be smoothed over.

He entered Yasmin's darkened bedroom without knocking, pulled up the blanket at the end of the bed, and shook her feet.

"Argh. Don't do that."

"Wake up, dogface. Time for breakfast."

"No, it isn't. It's the middle of the night."

"It will be light soon."

"Argh. In a minute."

"Time to eat, slowpoke."

Yasmin didn't answer.

He left the room, went out to the kitchen, and helped his mother prepare breakfast. This seemed to be her happiest time, the early morning hours during

Ramadan when both her children were around, the family was observing their religion together, and she didn't have to worry about shrinking budgets and burgeoning citizen complaints.

A few minutes later he asked her if he should wake his sister again.

"I guess so. Poor sleepyhead. She must be tired."

Farid opened the door, grabbed a pillow, and threw it at his sister. "Get up already!"

"Go 'way!"

"We're all waiting on you."

"Five minutes. Just five minutes more."

Farid pulled the blinds up with a jerk. Of course it was still dark out, but there was enough light for him to perceive the room's garishly pink walls and the childish stuffed animals lounging at the edge of the bed. An owl and a monkey, strange bedfellows.

"Dad's gonna kill you," he warned.

"Let him try," she mumbled from under her pillow.

"Don't push him," Farid warned again. He pulled the blanket down as roughly as he had pulled the blinds, revealing floral-print pajamas from which her colt-like wrists and ankles poked out.

Five minutes later, Yasmin shut herself in the bathroom and emerged with her face washed and her hair more or less brushed.

Sitting back in a retro-futuristic bone-white kitchen chair, their father muttered, "Yasmin, this has got to stop."

Their mother was still making breakfast.

"I'm up. It's dark outside. What's the problem?"

"Do you know how late you were out last night?"

Yasmin didn't answer.

"Your behavior is unacceptable. We can't let you go on like this."

Yasmin shifted uneasily in her seat.

Their mother murmured, "Not now, Ahmed. Time for *suhoor.*"

"I have a position in the community. If I can't control my own daughter, why should anyone listen to me?"

"She wants to be friends with the other girls. There's nothing wrong with that, and if people see we're just like everyone else, well, so much the better."

Their father shook his head, while their mother placed the food and drinks on the round kitchen table. They and Farid ate eggs, cheese, and several thick slices of bread to tide them over till the evening. Yasmin complained she was too tired to eat, but she nibbled her way through a piece of toast and drained a glass of orange juice.

She seemed about to close her eyes or go back to bed, whichever came first, but her father announced, "I think it's time we sent you back home."

"Ahmed."

"I'm serious. She needs to learn some sense."

Farid chimed in. "That's a good idea, Father. She's out of control."

"Shut up, asshole!" his sister whispered under her breath.

"Make me," said Farid.

"Children," their mom said, trying to make peace.

"I'm going back to sleep," said Yasmin, pushing her chair back.

Farid caught her arm and forced her to sit down.

Their father continued, "Remember the cousins you used to play with?"

"You mean the girl who made fun of my clothes and the boy who kept pulling my bathing suit down?"

"He didn't mean it. He was only five."

"They start early over there."

"They will be nice to you now. Your aunt and uncle will take care of you, make sure you're on the right path."

"This is crazy," said Yasmin. "I'm not going."

"*Inshallah*, when the time comes, they will find you a husband."

"Omigod!" she screamed and ran back into her room.

"Ahmed," said their mother, "you're scaring the girl."

"I know," he replied, shaking his head. Farid wasn't sure what he meant by that.

* * *

A couple of hours later Jamal tumbled out of bed, put on his slippers, and padded into the apartment's tiny kitchen. His cat, Muhammad, looked up at him and squawked piteously. Ramadan or not, daylight or not, Muhammad wanted his breakfast. Jamal had never been sure whether this Muhammad was a Muslim. Better to pray than to sleep, the saying went. Better to feed Muhammad than to ask himself questions he couldn't answer.

He placed the cat's bowl on the floor, and Muhammad stuck his face in it and started eating.

* * *

His first passenger that crisp but sunny fall morning was a quiet, dark-haired woman who was wearing a simple headscarf. Her scarf covered most of her thick, shiny hair but left a few strands undone, as if by accident. Jamal suspected that it wasn't by accident and that it indicated a desire to reveal her beauty, assert her independence, or tease her more conservative friends.

Somewhere between the woman's house and her downtown destination, traffic slowed and ground to a halt.

"What's happening?" the woman said.

Jamal glanced back at her and shrugged. As they inched forward, he made out two young men on the sidewalk questioning pedestrians. Evidently many drivers were slowing down to watch.

One of the young men, shivering slightly in the morning chill, his scratchy beard barely hiding his still childlike face, appeared to be asking a stout, middle-aged man a question.

"What business is it of yours?" said the older man, puffing his chest out.

The other young man, tall and thin, his head topped by a knitted red *kufi*, was seeking to examine the contents of a woman's purse. The woman, her head covered like his passenger's, clutched her purse and kept on walking.

Jamal leaned on his horn.

"What are they doing?" said the woman in the back seat.

"Causing trouble."

"Can't you take another route? I'm meeting someone, and I don't want to be late."

Her voice was throaty and resonant like an alto saxophone, but her question annoyed him.

"Sorry," he growled. "I drive a taxi, not a helicopter."

In a few minutes, the bottleneck eased and traffic started to flow again.

He dropped the woman off in front of a downtown shop and hastily drove away, worn-out shock absorbers doing little to soften the bumps. In the rearview mirror, he noticed that she did not enter the shop after all. She walked down the block, and when she reached the corner she took off her headscarf, slipped it into her purse, and shook her hair free in the brisk morning breeze.

\* \* \*

The morning services were held in a church, not a synagogue, because the congregation was too small or too poor to have a building of its own. The once-glimpsed wooden depiction of a wan and haggard Jesus hanging from the cross was hidden by a cloth, and the stained-glass windows were covered as well.

The Torah reading that morning recounted the birth of Isaac, after God's miraculous intervention, when the patriarch Abraham was a hundred years old and his wife Sarah ninety. (Kaufmann wondered why no one in Jewish or Christian circles ever commented on the resemblance to the miraculous conception of the baby Jesus.) But after giving birth, Sarah was suspicious of Isaac's half-brother Ishmael, the son of Abraham and Sarah's servant Hagar, and worried that he would claim a share of the inheritance. So she persuaded her husband to throw them out of the household and let them fend for themselves in the desert.

Kaufmann looked up at the pulpit, where the Torah scroll was spread open. The congregational elder chanting the sacred words didn't seem to pay much attention to the story he was telling. Nor did the men and women in the pews, who were following along in their prayer books, either in translation or the original Hebrew.

When their water ran out, Hagar in despair separated herself from her child because she didn't want to see him die. But God had other ideas. He rescued them and promised her that Ishmael's descendants would (like Isaac's) become a great nation, a nation later identified with the Arabs. Was that a happy ending? Or just a mixed message. He wondered what the Qur'an had to say about that story.

Between one Torah passage and the next, members of the congregation gathered around the pulpit for a special blessing. Often these blessings were prayers for healing, but this one was to ease the grief of those who had lost loved ones. Kaufmann approached the pulpit. He and the others raised their *tallesim*, spread the prayer shawls over each other's heads, and repeated the rabbi's words. Was God listening?

When he returned to his seat, he flipped ahead in the prayer book to the Torah reading for the next day, the one in which God commands Abraham to sacrifice his son Isaac. Of course, it's only a test, and God calls it off at the last minute, supplying a ram to take Isaac's place. But what would be going through little Isaac's mind as his father tied him up and prepared to, well, kill him? Or Abraham's mind? Or God's? Talk about mixed messages. Despite the last-minute reprieve, wasn't it just a story about unquestioning obedience to authority? As a police officer, he worried about other cops abusing their authority. As a father—a now-single parent—he worried about what the hell he was supposed to be doing in that role. Wasn't the Christian story of God sacrificing his son Jesus just another variation on the old theme? In that version, there is no intermediary between son and father-God, just a father demanding sacrifice and obedience from his son, though the son seems to do it willingly, even lovingly, not exactly for his divine father's sake but for the sake of his fellow human beings. Still, a loving father would never have asked.

During a lull in the five-hour service, some people slipped outside to smoke or chat. The detective followed. The women gathered in small knots to trade advice about their children or make plans for the weekend. Some of the men sneaked around the corner to make a call on their cell phones. A few kids noisily kicked a ball against a wall until an old man in a knitted *kipa* told them to knock it off. Kaufmann took out his own phone and checked his voice mail. There was a message from Jonathan's school, another from Captain Schroeder asking for an update on the investigation, and a third from…Aisha Hassan. The reporter. They had exchanged phone numbers after running into each other several times following the shooting in the park. She was asking him to meet her the following day at the Al-Salaam mosque for Friday prayers, saying it might help him to learn more about Islam and the Muslim community.

Hmm, he thought, praying in a mosque on Rosh Hashanah—what a concept—and went back inside the church.

* * *

Brodsky's aging taxicab sat motionless next to the curb like a tired draft horse that needed to rest. He scrubbed its scratched and dented fenders with warm soap and water (procured from a nearby laundromat) until the surface gleamed, scratches and all. Brodsky too looked like an aging workhorse, with lines around his eyes and strands of gray in his once-dark hair.

His dog Anton, with shaggy brown hair that hadn't been brushed in months, half-slept on the sidewalk, soaking up the morning sun and keeping one eye open to watch his master wash the car.

"Taking break, Anton?" the man said to the dog. "Is only few month, and here we are washing car and breathing morning air like nothing happen."

Anton opened his eye wider and yawned.

For all intents and purposes, Brodsky was homeless. He lived out of his cab—not really his, since it was leased from the company—in a rundown, semi-industrial part of the city. Warehouses with broken windows vied for space with automobile repair shops, self-serve laundromats, and cave-like dive bars. Some of the homeless, especially the alcoholics, the drug addicts, and the mentally ill, slept in doorways and begged for change on street corners, but the others, the ones who had lost their jobs or were just down on their luck, like Brodsky, camped in their vehicles, took refuge in the park a few blocks away, or just kept on moving.

Now Brodsky rinsed his car and patted it dry. He turned to the napping dog.

"Wake up, Anton. Time to play."

He found an old tennis ball in the back seat of the cab and tossed it down the block, though it hardly bounced. Suddenly awake, Anton raced after it, sprinted back with the ball in his mouth, and dropped it at his master's feet, his tail wagging. Brodsky threw it again.

\* \* \*

Aisha walked up the residential street and stopped in front of a narrow, wooden, single-story house with fading paint and broken concrete steps that led up to a sagging porch. Despite the house's shaky condition, the people who lived there did not look happy to be leaving it. While her photographer colleague snapped photos, Aisha watched the father, who was thin like the three skinny children—all, it seemed, under the age of five—carting boxes and chairs out to a U-Haul truck. He was being helped by a slightly older man, probably his brother, who had thinner hair but otherwise looked just like him. The mother, shorter and plumper, with large, dark eyes and an off-white kerchief wrapped around her head, was keeping tabs on the three kids, who were running back and forth over the patchy front lawn and shooting each other with black plastic water pistols.

Rundown apartments, vacant lots, and broken windows were common in this part of the city. Housing prices had recovered, but some neighborhoods were doing better than others.

"Sameh!" the mother yelled. "Don't hit your brother."

Sameh didn't seem to hear his mother, but he turned his attention to his little sister and squirted her in the face with a burst of water. She started crying and ran to her mother as fast as her two little legs could take her. The mother picked her up and held her against her chest.

Aisha approached the father.

"Do you have a few minutes to talk?" she asked the man. "I'm a reporter for the *Register-Guardian*."

The two brothers deposited a large, heavy box in the back of the truck. The day was still cool and comfortable, but the sun was out and the air was becoming warmer. The older brother wiped his forehead with a handkerchief and went back inside.

"Talk? About what?" said the younger man, who wore jeans, tennis shoes, and a ratty sweatshirt. He spoke with the trace of an accent.

"About your house. The foreclosure."

"It's not my house anymore. Belongs to the bank."

"Did you try to work out a deal with them? Postpone payments? Restructure the loan?"

The man shrugged.

Aisha took out her notebook and jotted down some notes. The photographer, Joe Quigley, an old-timer with a lined, craggy face, three cameras looped over his neck, and several pockets stuffed with miscellaneous equipment, took a picture of the young father.

"How long have you lived here?" asked the reporter.

"Sorry, I have things to do," he said, walking back inside.

The boy called Sameh, as wild and playful as a puppy, ran up to Aisha and pointed his pistol in her face. Neither one said anything. It was a standoff.

"Sameh," called his mother, "come back here." She was sitting on the porch with the little girl in her lap.

Joe snapped a photo of the boy with the gun. Aisha thought he might change his target and squirt the cameraman instead, but he held steady, with his eyes fixed on her and his water gun aimed squarely at her forehead.

"Hi," she said, in an especially friendly voice, and the little guy dropped his water pistol and ran after his three-year-old brother, who was now sitting in the dirt and pulling out fistfuls of grass.

In a few minutes, the two brothers emerged from the house, straining under the weight of an ancient armoire that had probably been in the family for generations.

She asked them if they needed any help.

Breathing hard, the younger one looked at her as if trying to figure out whether she was serious, then shook his head. "You can talk to my wife if you want."

The brothers rested the armoire on the curb for a precious moment and then lifted it into the back of the U-Haul. The younger one walked back inside while the older one stood at the curb catching his breath.

"You fellows brothers?" Aisha asked him.

The older man waved his hand dismissively. "Who are you?"

"I work for the paper."

"They just lost their house. Can't you leave them alone?"

"I want to tell your story, let our readers know what's happening."

"Happening?" said the man, raising his voice. "What's happening is that honest, hard-working people are getting robbed." He started speaking faster. Aisha took it all down. "I drive a truck, deliver soft drinks to Mom and Pop stores. Whatever savings Mom and Pop have is wiped out, business is down, so they don't need the same number cases of soda pop any more. I get fewer deliveries and meanwhile my rent goes up. What am I s'pose to do?"

"What about your brother?"

"My brother? He's fucked." He appeared to take notice of Aisha's *hijab* and half-apologized for his language. "Excuse me, but he's fucked. Even with an engineering degree, he's fucked. Got a job fixing bridges for the city, checking their stability, making sure they don't collapse too often, you know what I mean? Good job, good money, just a small kickback to the city council guy's nephew, you follow?" Aisha understood. Her own brother was an engineer, and he couldn't get a job. Corruption was a problem almost everywhere. "Married, two kids, then three, not enough room in the old third-floor walkup. Time to move out, move up. Home prices shooting skyward, but still time to get into the fucking market. Fixer-upper, needs lots of work. Who cares? You can flip the house for double the price. But then the city's laying off workers and the house is under water. No one's watching the bridges, and no one's paying my brother to keep his fucking fixer-upper of a house afloat, you know what I'm saying? My brother goes down to the bank, and they won't talk to him. Say it's not their concern no more. They don't have the mortgage. The fuckers sold the fucking mortgage to someone else."

"Hmm, I see. I'm sorry."

The man's moustache twitched with anger.

"A few months ago, somebody sent a letter. First one letter, then another and another. The bastards threatened to call the cops, change the locks, throw him and the wife and the kids out on the street. What can they do?"

"Ask the city councilman for help?"

The older brother laughed. "You won't believe it, but that is exactly what he did."

"And?"

"And the asshole acted like he never heard of him."

Aisha wrote it all down in her notebook, minus the strong language.

\* \* \*

Some of the city's once-rundown neighborhoods were gentrifying. Jamal parked his taxi and entered a café in one of those neighborhoods, where check-cashing businesses and tattoo parlors had given way to art galleries, clothing boutiques, and trendy new restaurants. The café's decor was simple but elegant—a few tables, some bentwood chairs, a marble-topped counter. The coffee was good and the cookies were homemade. Classical music was playing in the background.

Jamal glanced at the patrons scattered around the café but saw no sign of the friend he was supposed to meet. The sun was rising in the sky, but it didn't matter since he no longer observed the Ramadan fast. He decided to order a coffee and one of those twice-cooked Italian cookies that were kept in cylindrical glass jars like cigars. He sat down at a small table, opened up a well-worn black "marble" notebook, and wrote down something about the mysteriously beautiful passenger who had started his day.

The notebook was a journal of sorts, in which he scribbled down observations, reminders, advice to himself, shopping lists, fragments of dialogue, stray lines that might turn into poems. The journal had started when he was a teenager in the refugee camp and—unless he wanted to scrawl graffiti on the concrete walls—he had nowhere else to put what was on his mind. Sometimes he pasted in pictures from newspapers or magazines, post cards he had received from friends and relatives back home, used theater tickets and bus transfers, what have you. He even copied down song lyrics he liked. The notebook was filled to bursting now, and soon he would have to get a new one.

Jamal's friend arrived a few minutes after the hour. The two men gave each other a hug, and the other man ordered a coffee.

Jamal jumped right in.

"My kitchen is big," he pointed out, like a real estate agent. "I have a double bed, and there is a lot of light in the mornings."

It was a spartan one-bedroom apartment in the heart of Little Mecca, but the light was good and Jamal knew that as an art person—he helped manage a gallery—Henry liked light. Of course Henry knew all about it. He had spent a lot of time there.

"We've been through that already," said his friend. "I told you, I don't want to move. I'm happy where I am, and I wouldn't feel comfortable in a neighborhood like yours. I mean, I know that's harsh, but…"

Besides sweeping the floor, changing the light bulbs, and helping to hang the paintings, the tall, blond jack-of-all-trades sometimes had a hand in curating the exhibits. But he made less money working in the gallery than Jamal did driving a cab.

"What about the falafel stands, the kebab emporiums, the honey pastries?" Jamal paused, taking a bite out of his chocolate hazelnut *biscotto* and thinking of the things that made Little Mecca special. "The lemon trees. You love the scent of lemon blossoms."

"Lemon trees?" Henry drank some of his coffee and put the cup down on the saucer. "Since when do lemon trees grow this far north?"

"There's one lemon tree in the empty lot behind my building," said Jamal. "You've seen it. I don't know how it survives, but it does. Like me."

"The lemon trees, the gossip, the furtive glances. How can you stand it? If your neighbors—at least some of them—knew what we were up to, we would be stoned to death."

"Don't be so melodramatic."

"It would cross their minds, Jamal, and you know it."

"Listen, Henry." Jamal put his hand on the table. "I want you to move in with me. It has nothing to do with light or sun or lemon trees or even neighbors. I just want to share my life with you."

Henry's tone changed. "I can't do that, Jamal. It's not going to happen."

"What? What do you mean?" Jamal felt the color draining out of his face.

"Haven't you noticed? We can't wait to see each other, and when we finally find ourselves in the same room, all we do is argue."

"Everybody argues. The man in the street goes home and argues with his wife. The man's first wife argues with the second." Jamal laughed.

"Not a recipe for happiness."

Jamal reached across the table and grabbed Henry's hand. "I argue because I want to hold onto you. I love you, Henry."

"You know I love you too, Jamal, but, well, nothing lasts forever."

"Okay, don't move in with me. It's not the end of the world."

Henry slowly released his hand.

"You don't understand, Jamal. It's just not working anymore."

Jamal's head was swimming.

"But Henry—"

"I'm sorry. I have to go."

Henry stood up. Jamal was on the verge of stopping him, of putting his arms around him and giving him one last embrace. But Henry walked away, and Jamal let him go.

\* \* \*

Kaufmann bent down, untied his shoelaces, and placed his clunky shoes on the floor next to a wildly diverse assortment of oxfords, sandals, boots, and athletic shoes. Together with twenty or thirty other men—their faces white and black and every shade in between—he entered the prayer hall of the mosque. The women, congregating at the back of the room behind a semi-transparent partition, seemed serious and focused like the men, but every so often one whispered to another and half-suppressed a laugh. In contrast to the men, their heads were covered. He looked to see if Ms. Hassan was among them, but he couldn't spot her.

There were no pews or chairs, just a broad stretch of wall-to-wall carpet. The faithful sat on the carpet, and the imam, a large black man who wore colorful robes and a round, white prayer cap, stood facing them from behind a lectern. After exchanging greetings in Arabic with the worshippers, he launched into his weekly sermon.

"My fellow Muslims," he began, with what sounded like a French accent, "as we pray and fast during the holy month of Ramadan, we look inward and ask ourselves how we can become better Muslims, how we can become closer to Allah and less distracted by the demands of modern life. Soon, at the start of the *jumu'ah* prayer, as you know, we will recite the first *sura* from the Qur'an, beginning '*Bissmilah irra'hman irra'heem…*' With these verses we are asking God to guide us on the right path. The true Islamic path. Not, says the *sura*, the path of those who have angered Allah, nor the path of those who have gone astray.

"Now what does that mean—those who have angered Allah, those who have gone astray? Does it mean those who have violated the commandment to pray five times a day, or to abstain from drinking alcohol, or to give alms to those in need? Perhaps so. Does it refer to those who pray three times a day but not five? Perhaps. Who refrain from drinking alcohol but not always? Who give alms but so little that they don't even notice what they have given? Perhaps.

"Maybe it refers to apostates, those who have turned their backs on Islam. Maybe it means other branches of Islam, although of course the other branches of Islam think *we've* gone astray, and in any case the *sura* was revealed to the Prophet Muhammad, peace be upon him, before Islam split into different branches."

The detective was standing at the side of the prayer hall. His mind was already starting to wander, though the worshippers sitting or kneeling in front of him seemed to be having no problem remaining in an uncomfortable position or paying rapt attention to the imam's sermon.

"What about the phrases 'angered Allah' and 'gone astray'? Is one just a stronger way of saying the other? Do those phrases refer to different groups of people and different paths? In fact, some commentators claim that the first phrase—those who have angered Allah—refers to the Jews and the second phrase—those who have gone astray—refers to the Christians."

A few of the men listening whispered under their breaths. Kaufmann was starting to feel a little uncomfortable.

"Of course, even if true, that would mean the Jews and Christians of that era—for example, the Jews of Medina and the Christians of Najran—not their coreligionists today. Muhammad, peace be upon him, and his early followers naturally sought to distinguish their beliefs from the tenets of other religions, even as they embraced Jewish and Christian prophets such as Ibrahim, Moses, and Jesus and sought to convince the Jews and Christians around them to accept the revelations of Allah and follow the one true path."

*Really?* thought the detective. *Is that what happened?*

"What would Muhammad, peace be upon him, say today? Would he say that it was the Jews and Christians who had gone astray—or the self-proclaimed Muslims who don't practice the Islamic virtues of peace and charity and murder their fellow Muslims in the name of Allah?"

More whispers. Kaufmann turned his head to see if he could find Aisha in the rear of the hall, behind the screen, and this time he did. The two of them exchanged quick glances, and the detective turned back to see the imam stepping out from behind the lectern. He resumed his preaching without any barrier between him and his audience.

"My friends, let me tell you a little story that may have some bearing on your understanding—or at least my understanding—of this *sura*. "As most of you know, I was born in Africa. My father was a *shaykh* and his father before him. I grew up attending a humble mosque and studying with the local *shaykhs*, including my father and grandfather.". I learned a great deal, but I wanted to broaden my horizons, so I went to Paris to study not just Islam but what my teachers called comparative religion. My study of other religions did not shake my faith in Allah, the all-merciful, but it did open my eyes. I learned, I discovered—in fact, it had the force of a revelation for me—that there is no one true path." Now the congregation was buzzing. "I learned that many paths lead to Allah, that only Allah knows which paths are right and which paths are wrong."

A man in the crowd said something which the detective couldn't make out.

The imam continued, "In fact, when I graduated from the university with my degree in comparative religion, I decided to join a convent." Some people laughed, especially some of the women, and the genial imam laughed too. Kaufmann didn't know what to think. "I know it sounds strange, but I was in France, which is a predominantly Catholic country, and I wanted to experience first-hand what sincere believers of other religions were experiencing. So I found a convent out in the country and went up to the woman in charge, the Mother Superior. 'Sister,' I said to her, 'would it be possible for me to join your order?' Picture the situation: a large African man wearing traditional Islamic robes, asking to join a convent. Of course the Mother Superior looked at me as if I were crazy—and maybe I was— and then she pointed to the women who were walking through the courtyard or tending the garden. 'Look at them,' she said. 'Women. We're all women here. This is not a place for men.'

"So I looked around and saw all the women whom I had already seen, but I also noticed someone else, an older man who was raking the soil of the vegetable beds. 'What about him?' I said. 'He's a man.' She looked at him. She looked at me. 'Him?' she said. 'He's the gardener.'"

The worshippers burst out laughing, and the imam joined them. When the laughter died down, he went on, "For a moment I was stymied. But then I said, 'That's okay. I'll be his assistant.'"

Everybody started laughing and talking at once, and it took a few moments for the noise to die down. The imam retired to a nearby chair. The detective walked a few paces, stretched his legs, then leaned back against the wall.

The Friday service was not what he had expected at all. Although he had been to several mosques and had lived in a city with a large Muslim population for many years, he still didn't know much about Islam. He had expected formal Arabic prayers, row upon row of men prostrating themselves, women hiding behind veils. Instead he got this imam. Not an austere Middle Eastern imam, but a thoughtful, open-minded West African who could laugh at himself and could hold his audience in the palm of his hand. His sermon was a lot livelier than anything the local rabbi had come up with.

After a few minutes, the imam took the floor once more.

"Yes, it's a funny story," he said, "but it has a serious point. It turns out that I did join the convent, if not the order. I stayed there for a year and a day. I became the gardener's assistant and helped him, along with the nuns, to take care of the vegetables, the flowers, the hedges, and the fruit trees. I also participated in the nuns' prayers and in their daily routine, and I learned that their faith was sincere, their spiritual experience was deep, and their path—well, their path was as good a path as any."

The end of the sermon led to the beginning of formal prayers, and soon the imam was facing east, toward Mecca, leading the rest of the congregation in the recitation of the first *sura* and the prayers that followed. The worshippers bowed and lowered their heads to the floor.

\* \* \*

The call came in from the dispatcher to pick up someone from Terre Noire High School at the base of the foothills. A teacher whose car had broken down, Brodsky presumed. It was mid-afternoon and school must have just gotten out. But when he arrived on the scene, with teenagers newly released for the weekend swarming over the parking lot like flies, he found two young girls standing on the steps waiting for him.

"You call taxi?" he inquired.

The older one, plumper and taller than the other, said, "Right," and climbed into the backseat. The other one, a small wisp of a girl who looked barely old enough to go to high school, slipped in after her. Anton, nestled on the floor of the front passenger seat, lifted his head to look.

"Where you want to go?" asked Brodsky.

The older girl mentioned the name of a department store downtown. "I'm giving a party," she explained, "and we need new dresses."

The cabbie took off. The dog put his head down and went back to sleep.

After a while the older girl asked him, "Do you always take your dog with you?"

Brodsky nodded and said, "Anton good dog. He won't bother you."

"That's okay. I like dogs."

"We used to have a dog," said the younger, smaller girl. "We had to give her up when we moved."

Driving through the busy downtown streets, Brodsky looked in the rearview mirror. "Your parents give you money for to buy dresses?" he asked them.

The older girl took out her credit card and waved it in the air. "I've got something better than money," she said, laughing.

The idea of buying things for one's children had struck a nerve, and he started to say, "My son—"

"Oh, look," said the older girl. "We're already here."

She paid the tab with her credit card, and Brodsky let them off in front of the department store.

* * *

"So what did you think?" the reporter asked him as they stood in the plain, unadorned lobby of the mosque. She was wearing a summery lemon-yellow dress—the weather was changing but, technically, it was still summer—and a matching scarf.

"Well, I didn't understand the prayers, but the imam's sermon was amazing. I mean, joining a convent—not something I would have expected."

She smiled. "Yes, he's an amazing man. Humble, good-natured, open-minded. We're working with him to create a space for women to pray on their own."

"Wonderful." As the worshippers streamed around them on their way out of the mosque, he added, "Have you heard anything more about the guy who was—or might have been—arguing with those face-painters?"

She shook her head. "*Heard anything, might have been*—journalists try to avoid basing anything on such shaky foundations."

"Cops too. Just thought I'd ask."

"But I think I know what he was arguing about."

Kaufmann looked at her. "Really?"

"In Islam, the depiction of animate beings—human or animal—is *haram*. Forbidden. That's why traditional Islamic art is abstract, based on repeated patterns or calligraphy. Some people think the prohibition includes painting animal likenesses on human beings' faces."

"Painting kids' faces is forbidden?"

"Some people think so."

A young man in a hurry brushed past the detective, who turned back to Aisha. "Maybe we should sit down, grab a bite to eat, talk about the case."

She smiled again. "Sorry, it's Ramadan."

"Of course. I forgot."

A man in a dark suit, white shirt, and maroon-colored tie, his black moustache flecked with gray, walked by. Aisha stopped him.

"Excuse me, Dr. Ali. I'd like you to meet Detective Kaufmann. Dr. Ali is the president of the mosque."

The two men shook hands.

"A pleasure to meet you," said the doctor.

"Likewise."

"You are a…police officer?"

Kaufmann nodded.

"Well," said Dr. Ali, glancing at the reporter, then back at the detective, "I hope you enjoyed the *jumu'ah* service."

"Yes, I did. I especially appreciated the imam's sermon."

"You're welcome to join us tonight when we break the fast. It's Ramadan, you know, and we fast each day until the sun sets."

"Yes, well, thank you, but, uh, my son has a football game and I'd really like—"

"Of course. Another time."

The two of them were left standing after Dr. Ali had departed.

"Well," said the detective after an awkward pause, "thank you for inviting me, Ms. Hassan."

"Call me Aisha."

They shook hands.

"Oh, sorry, do you mind if I shake your hand?" He glanced at her headscarf. "I don't really know what's appropriate."

She smiled. "No, I don't mind. I'm a reporter, you know. I get around."

Kaufmann nodded. "One thing I wanted to ask you. Why is your paper giving us such a hard time?"

"Us?"

"The police. It's not as if we're sitting on our hands."

"The police were already at the scene, but they couldn't prevent the shooting. It's been over a month since then, and the police have no leads. No wonder—"

"Who says we have no leads?"

"Well, do you?"

"I could ask you the same question."

"We don't have the resources you do, Detective Kaufmann."

He took a deep breath. "Call me Ezra."

\* \* \*

Kaufmann and Khoury huddled in Captain Schroeder's cramped quarters like unruly students sent to the principal's office.

"This investigation has dragged on way too long," the captain was saying. She leaned back so far in her squeaky chair Kaufmann worried she might tip over. "We're lucky the kid is out of the hospital, but the public wants closure. As I'm sure you know, the paper has been raking us over the coals."

"Well—" the detective started to say.

"The delayed response at the scene, the botched forensics, the wild goose chase of going after the right-wing Christian group."

"None of those things are even true," Kaufmann protested.

Schroeder threw up her hands. "Does it matter?"

Sergeant Khoury cleared his throat.

"What?" barked their boss.

"I did some research on the influx of Arabs and Muslims into this area."

Schroeder shook the cobwebs out of her head, as if she was having trouble understanding what Khoury was getting at.

"I know it seems like I'm going far afield, but the anti-Islamic sentiment appears to be getting worse and it might pay to find out how it started."

"Started? How did the troubles between the Israelis and Palestinians get started? Or the North and the South? Or the Yankees and the Red Sox?"

"The earliest Arab immigrants to the region were mostly Christians from the Ottoman-ruled province of greater Syria. They came as peddlers, grocers, and laborers and later opened stores of their own. Old-timers say that the early immigrants got along fine with their American-born neighbors. The Arabs sold kitchen and farm supplies to the farmers, often on credit, and the farmers bought more things after the harvest came in."

The captain looked at her watch. "Are you giving me a history lesson, Sergeant Khoury?"

The sergeant seemed to squirm a little on his rickety chair. "Well, one of those early peddlers was my great-grandfather."

"Hmm," said the captain.

Kaufmann glanced over at his partner.

Schroeder drummed her fingers on the desk. "So what happened?"

"After the Second World War, more Syrian, Lebanese, and Palestinian Arabs settled there, many gaining work in the booming industrial plants and factories nearby. Some people worried that they were taking jobs away from the natives."

"Like the Mexicans in other parts of the country," said their boss.

"Right," said Khoury. "Besides, the early immigrants were Christian, like my family, and the locals had less trouble accepting them. In recent years, most of the newcomers have been Muslim. They were driven by upheavals in Lebanon, Palestine, and Syria, as well as Bosnia, Afghanistan, Pakistan, Iraq, Sudan, Yemen, Somalia, and a host of other hot spots. Now it's Syria again. Refugees have been streaming into Europe, some came to the U.S., and a few of them have managed to reach this city. After 9-11, with the success of Al Qaeda, the rise of ISIS, and the proliferation of fundamentalist terrorism, everyone's on edge."

"And some people blame it on all Muslims, even the ones fleeing from the violence."

"Exactly," said the sergeant.

Captain Schroeder took out her cellphone, checked something on it, then turned back to Sergeant Khoury. "Thanks for the history lesson, but how does that help us solve this case?"

"The two high schools weren't always at each other's throats. In the beginning, there weren't even two schools. Rouge came first, and Noire was built when the city became more, uh, stratified, with wealthier families moving into the hills. Now, a lot of the students at Noire—and a lot of their parents—barely know any Muslims."

"Are you serious?"

The sergeant nodded. "So when they think of Islam, they think of the crazies they see in the news media. The fundamentalists, the extremists, and the terrorists."

The captain sat back and exhaled. "The bottom line is that you've made no progress in the case and you're back to square one."

"Captain—" Kaufmann started to say, but Schroeder held up her hand.

"Look, we just want to find out who fired those shots. I'll give you guys two more weeks. After that time, I'm turning it over to detectives with a different game plan."

* * *

About a half hour before game time, the coaches gathered the players together for a pep talk.

"These guys are big, they're strong, they're well-coached, and they expect to win," said Coach Lowry in his familiar booming baritone. A large man who had set now-broken records in college, he stalked the locker room in his trademark canary-yellow cardigan and high-water khaki chinos. "In other words, they're ripe for a fall."

The half-dressed players—sitting on benches, stretching their legs, putting on their pads, tying their shoelaces—laughed.

"But in order to win, we've got to play like we played in practice. Hard. But smart. Keep your eyes open. Think." Some of the guys were nodding. "But don't think too much. Don't second-guess yourself. At this point, everything should be instinctive. Just do what you know how to do."

Jonathan felt his head spinning. Hard, but smart. Think, but not too much. How much thinking was too much? He supposed it was like acting. You just tried to be the guy you were playing. By opening night, it was too late to think about it. If he got into the game, he would just inhabit the part of a running back. He would *be* a running back, and his tacklers would fall by the wayside.

The stands were packed, and the home team fans greeted the players with a rousing cheer. While the quarterback tossed a football on the sidelines, the cheerleaders ran through their routines on the field. Jonathan, sitting at the end of the bench, watched them. He and the rest of the team were weighed down with heavy equipment and covered head to toe, but the girls, he noticed, not for the first time, were bare from thigh to ankle and hardly weighed down by anything. It dawned on him that he and they were both part of the performance, though the costumes were different. He wondered whether the Terre Rouge team across town had cheerleaders and whether, as good Muslims, they were covered from head to toe like the football players.

The game started with a soaring kickoff downfield. Every time the home team completed a pass or ran for significant yardage, most of the spectators yelled and cheered. But despite some promising possessions, the team couldn't advance to the end zone, and the first half turned out to be a defensive battle with both sides making little headway. Jonathan never entered the game. He and the others returned to the locker room with the score tied 3-3.

\* \* \*

When the sun went down, Farid and his friend grabbed some kebabs at a fast food stand.

"How come you never gain weight?" wondered Farid, who was plump like his parents.

"High energy," said his friend while wolfing down a piece of charred lamb. "I burn it off."

After eating, they climbed onto Tariq's motorcycle. Farid held onto the other's stomach as the bike zipped through the streets and alleys of Little Mecca. Though he no longer lived in the neighborhood, Farid returned there often. The Muslim butcher shops, Islamic bookstores, and old-fashioned hookah parlors—not to mention the *halal* McDonalds—appealed to him even though he had been born in America and had a passing familiarity with things like BLT sandwiches and internet porn. He knew that one was a bulwark against the other.

"Hey! Look at that girl!" shouted Tariq.

He slowed down, veered toward the sidewalk, and started following a young woman who was walking down the street.

"Hey! Pretty lady! Why are you wearing pink tennis shoes? You think it's okay to wear hot pink shoes that make people look at your feet?"

In addition to a self-defense force that would protect the community against direct attacks, Tariq seemed interested in warding off more subtle threats. The woman, an attractive twenty-something with a bare head and snug jeans, continued walking. Tariq, following her on the purring bike, kept up a running commentary.

"Pretty lady! You think it's okay to wear tight pants that show off your body?"

The woman speeded up.

"Are you married, lady? What does your husband think? Maybe your husband should give you the beating you deserve, pretty lady."

49

"Forget about it," said Farid. "Leave her alone."

"Bitch," muttered Tariq as he switched off the bike's motor and stopped at the side of the street. He scratched his week-old beard, which was growing rougher by the day.

"You can't chase down every girl in tight jeans, brother."

Tariq turned around to look at him. "Why not?"

Farid threw up his hands. "You're out of your mind, man."

Tariq took a deep breath and laughed. "You're right, little brother. All this fasting—it makes me crazy sometimes."

"So what do we do now?"

"Hey," said his friend, "I got something to show you."

He dug his smartphone out of his pocket, poked a few buttons, and handed the phone to Farid. The screen showed a photo of a smiling young woman, auburn-haired, green-eyed, the light bouncing off her shiny white teeth. She was very pretty.

"There's more. Keep scrolling."

Farid flipped through several more photos of the same woman, showing her variously in powder blue jeans, pink-striped short shorts, and a long navy skirt.

"Who is she?" he said.

"My girlfriend."

The traffic was picking up, and Farid shouted over the noise. "Girlfriend? I didn't know you had a girlfriend."

Tariq shook his head back and forth. "She split with me after I converted. Couldn't handle it."

Farid handed the phone back to its owner. "Sorry, man. Islam is a big commitment."

"A blessing, brother. Islam is a blessing."

* * *

By the time Kaufmann arrived at the school, the game was half over and the score was tied. It was only 3-3, but the second half of the game was very different from the first. The opposing team scored two touchdowns in quick succession, the home squad managed a field goal, and the other team was threatening once more.

Jonathan sat on the bench, his helmet cradled in his lap. Kaufmann wondered whether the coach was punishing him for missing practices. Mr. Lowry didn't seem to have much appreciation for Shakespeare. Then again, the drama teacher, Mr. Blankenship, couldn't seem to understand why Jonathan missed rehearsals for football drills. He had almost cut him from the show until Jonathan promised to practice his scenes with his friends in the cast. Football, Shakespeare; Shakespeare, football. The miscomprehension reminded Kaufmann of his disagreement with his father over law school. Lawyer, policeman; policeman, lawyer. Butcher, baker, candlestick maker.

A cheer went up from the fans on the other side of the field. The opposing team had scored again.

Coach Lowry bellowed in the direction of the bench, though Kaufmann couldn't make out what he was saying.

Jonathan rammed his helmet onto his head and ran onto the field for the kickoff return. The other team lined up across the field like a wide formation of migrating birds. Jonathan and another receiver hung back near their own goal line. The kicker took several quick steps, picked up speed, and kicked the ball far downfield. For a moment, it floated between him and his teammate. After glancing quickly at fellow receiver, Jonathan ran toward the ball and caught it at the seventeen-yard line. Immediately, three potential tacklers bore down on him. He circled back behind his blockers and tried to turn upfield, but he didn't get very far before someone seized his ankle and dragged him to the ground. Another player from the other team jumped on top of him, and the referee blew the play dead.

Jonathan picked himself up and trotted, a bit unsteadily, off the field. As far as his father could tell, Coach Lowry didn't say anything to him. He ripped off his helmet, took a swig of Gatorade, and resumed his place at the end of bench.

He didn't return to the game, and despite a late comeback, the home team lost by seventeen points.

* * *

After he had showered and dressed, Jonathan caught up with Zach in the parking lot. It was mostly empty by that time, but there were still a few knots of high schoolers discreetly drinking, flirting, and doing their best to make the night last longer. Four or five guys had taken their shirts off, though the temperature had dipped into the forties, and were smoking cigarettes in an effort to ward off the cold. Jonathan recognized one of them as a teammate who had been injured in preseason and was out for the rest of the year.

He glanced around for his dad, but if he had come there was no sign of him.

Zach was leaning against his car, chatting with a couple of girls that Jonathan didn't know. The girls were younger than they were, probably freshmen.

"Hey, Jonathan," Zach said as he approached, "this is Courtney." He indicated a girl wearing a lot of makeup and a red or pink cotton sweater, its color hard to determine in the semidarkness.

"Hey," said Courtney, who seemed to be consuming something stronger than Dr. Pepper.

"I'm Yasmin," said the other girl in a soft voice. She was wearing a baggy sweatshirt, but she looked small and slight.

"She's new here," her friend explained.

"Where you from?" said Jonathan.

"Just across town. My family moved for the schools."

"You'll like it," Zach promised. "Noire is cool."

"That's what I told her," said Courtney with a firm shake of her chin. "We've got school spirit."

"It's not just spirit. There's AP classes, Chinese and Spanish programs, Drama Club."

Yasmin nodded. "That's what my dad said. My old school didn't even have enough money for Arabic classes."

Zach opened his palms apologetically. "Sorry, we don't have them either."

"Do you speak Arabic?" Jonathan asked.

"Not really. My parents speak Urdu. But I'm taking Spanish now."

He took a closer look at her. She was pretty in a middle school, tweener kind of way. Couldn't be more than fourteen.

Courtney asked them if they were coming to the party Saturday night.

"What party?" asked Jonathan. "We weren't invited."

"Everybody's invited. Allison won't mind."

"Cool," said Zach.

∗ ∗ ∗

The detective drove his car out of the parking lot and through a neighborhood of tree-lined, moonlit streets. The leaves were beginning to fall from the trees, and the wind was picking them up and scattering them here and there. He turned onto a bustling block of shops and restaurants and stopped at a red light. After a minute, the light turned green, and he started up again.

Across the street, a woman about his age was strolling by herself in the shadows. She was wearing a headscarf and a dress that looked oddly familiar. A few strands of dark curly hair had escaped the scarf and were fluttering slightly in the breeze. Although she was alone, she didn't attract attention. She clung to the inner portion of the sidewalk, away from the streetlights, peering into store windows even though most of the stores were closed for the night and there wasn't much to see.

She seemed thin, maybe too thin, and in the dim light her face looked chalky-gray. Her pale, drawn face made her look unhealthy, as if she had been ill, had received debilitating treatment, had not been able to eat much, had lost weight. In short, she looked like Rachel. His dead wife. What was she doing here? And why was she wearing a headscarf?

He rolled down his window, but some other pedestrians blocked his view and by the time they passed she was gone. He quickly pulled into a parking space and jumped out of the car. He looked up and down the block, but there was no sign of her. He ventured into the side streets and narrow alleys where stray dogs wandered and young men smoked, but—nothing. She seemed to have disappeared.

# Saturday: Party

*At first the ominous rumblings sounded far away, but the flashes that followed lit up the night sky. Gradually the head-splitting thunderclaps came closer. He knew it was God talking to him. He couldn't see the nameless, ineffable Being, but he knew it was Him. What was God trying to tell him? That He was angry at him? That went without saying. That something bad would happen if he didn't make amends. In fact, it had already happened.*

*But now he found himself in a dark cave, lit only by a smoky fire. A giant was tending to the fire, feeding it sticks and dry twigs. Of course the giant was gigantic, but, what was more, he had only one eye, like that scary monster in the* Odyssey. *Despite the fact that he was a cop—yes, even in the dream he knew he was a policeman—his heart pounded and his hands trembled. The one-eyed giant, he realized, was God. More bad things were going to happen, and one of them was that the one-eyed God-giant was going to pick him up in his giant hand, shove him into his mouth, crunch his bones in his teeth, and eat him.*

Kaufmann struggled to open his eyes. He was still asleep, but he knew that if he opened his eyes he would wake up and the bad dream would be over. His eyelids fluttered. The one-eyed God-giant thundered at him. He opened his eyes and peered at the dim walls of his bedroom, his heart still thudding. The thunder was softer and less ominous now, more like drumming, as if God were leading a marching band.

Why had he been dreaming about an angry, bloodthirsty God? Oh, right. The Torah readings about Abraham, Ishmael, and Isaac. He knew it wasn't all like that. Many times, in fact, the ancient Israelites affirmed the need to love the stranger, for the reason that they had once been strangers in Egypt. But the Torah had been written down at different times, by different people. It wasn't surprising that it contained mixed messages.

After tossing and turning for another twenty minutes he gave up, got out of bed, went to the bathroom, and washed his face. Then he made himself a small pot of coffee. While it was brewing, he checked on Jonathan. He was still asleep, so he decided to go to the gym as soon as he had had his coffee.

Still groggy from his encounter with the one-eyed giant, he found the corner where the free weights were laid out, added a few 25-pound plates to the bar, and started lifting. Since he had become a detective, probably no one cared whether he kept in shape, but he liked the physical strain on his muscles, the reminder that his body was still there. Whatever else it was doing, the workout took his mind off—well, all the things he tended to think about when he couldn't make them go away. Other people, including a lot of cops, used alcohol for the same purpose. He wondered how successful they were.

* * *

It was raining out as he drove from the gym to the coffee bar, but it was only a shower and he was confident the sun would make an appearance later in the day. When he entered the café, no one looked up. Several customers were tapping away at their laptops. A businesslike older woman was sipping a latte. A younger woman in more casual clothes was chatting animatedly with a smartly-dressed man.

The sound system was playing a pleasant pop song sung by someone he couldn't identify. The aroma of the morning brews tickled his nose.

The mysterious woman he was supposed to meet said she didn't usually flirt with strangers. *Love the stranger, for you were strangers once…* Just then a beautiful woman in a stylish rain slicker pushed open the door, shook out her umbrella, and looked around the room. She walked toward the counter and joined the ever-lengthening line.

The detective decided to get into line behind her.

The woman's luxurious blonde hair hung halfway down her neck. He stood behind her in the coffee line looking alternately at her hair and the list of exotic coffees posted on a sign behind the counter. The fresh scent of the woman's perfume mingled with the deep, winey aroma of the coffee being served that day.

His heart began to beat faster.

Perhaps sensing his eyes on the back of her head, the woman turned around. They stood there peering into each other's faces for a long second.

"Are you—"

"Ashley!" the young man behind the counter called out. "Double shot of espresso for Ashley."

The woman blinked or batted her eyelashes or did whatever it was she was doing with her eyes.

"I, uh, was supposed to meet someone here this morning. It wasn't you, was it?"

She smiled and shook her head. "No, sorry. Not me."

He turned around and stumbled hastily out the door. The sun was already breaking through the clouds, and gradually the pounding of his heart began to subside.

\* \* \*

Opening night was less than a week away, and Mr. Blankenship had ordered a pull-out-all-the-stops Saturday rehearsal. This one would be a technical run-through, with full lighting, music, and scene changes. Jonathan played Lorenzo, the Christian man that Shylock's daughter—disguised as a boy—runs off with, prompting the moneylender to utter the famous lament "My ducats! My daughter!" Would he really say that? Wasn't it just a caricature of a greedy Jew? Jonathan wondered what his own father would say if he ran away from home. He would love to go somewhere like Alaska or Tahiti where he could yell if he wanted to, cry if he wanted to, pound his head against a wall if he really wanted to, which he did, but something told him that his dad might want to do the same. Maybe they should run away together.

But running away with Becky appealed to him more.

Onstage, he flirted with Jessica, Shylock's daughter, but the rest of the time he had his eye on Portia. Her narrow waist, her rounded breasts, her warm smile. She had sat near him and Zach in math class last year, one vertex of a lopsided triangle. Zach told jokes, Jonathan tried to top him, and she laughed at whatever they said.

"Places, everyone," said Mr. Blankenship.

The lights went down, the spots came on. The rehearsal started. "In sooth I know not why I am so sad."

Later, the sad merchant appeals to Shylock for a loan. The Jewish moneylender, clearly wounded, complains about the treatment he has received from the merchant in the past but offers to lend him the money. At a price, a "forfeit," if the money isn't repaid on time. A "merry sport," the moneylender calls it. A joke. A pound of flesh "to be cut off and taken in what part of your body pleaseth me."

Standing in the wings, watching Zach and the other actors say their lines, Jonathan was struck all over again by the crazy extremes of the characters' words and actions. Mr. Blankenship had provided some of the historical background. (It was high school, he pointed out, and they were supposed to be learning something.) In medieval England, Jews—who could not join the artisan guilds or own land— had filled the role of moneylenders because Christians were forbidden to lend money at interest. Resentment followed. Eventually, Jews were no longer allowed to be moneylenders, were required to wear identifying badges, and, finally, were expelled from England, two hundred years before they were expelled from Spain. What a miserable history.

So did Shakespeare even know any Jews? Well, their teacher explained, a few hundred *marranos* or *conversos*, Spanish and Portuguese Jews who had been forced to convert to Christianity but may have maintained some Jewish traditions in secret, had settled in England. One of them, Roderigo Lopez, had even become Queen Elizabeth's physician. Unfortunately, he was suspected of trying to poison her and publicly executed for treason. The physician protested his innocence, but he was hanged, "drawn," and quartered, amid outpourings of anti-Jewish sentiment. (The thought of it sent a chill up Jonathan's spine.) Surely Shakespeare would have heard of this event, perhaps even seen it.

"One more thing," Mr. Blankenship had said. Ever since the time of Henry VIII, England had been torn by religious conflict. Henry and his daughter Elizabeth had turned the country Protestant, but some former Catholics were suspected of clinging to their old traditions, just like the *conversos*. "Shakespeare's family," said Mr. Blankenship, "may have been among them!" So, despite all the anti-Jewish stereotyping, did Shakespeare identify with Shylock and use him to expose the religious intolerance of the English Protestants?

Jonathan watched the drama unfold. Bassanio, the merchant's young friend, was skeptical and warned him against the deal, but Antonio decided there was "much kindness in the Jew." After all, his ships would return in plenty of time, and he would have no trouble paying back the loan.

\* \* \*

"Coffee? Tea?"

They were sitting in the imam's book-lined office, and the genial man was offering him something to drink.

"But it's Ramadan," said Kaufmann.

"The coffee is not for me," said the imam, smiling. "It's for my honored guest."

"Thank you, no. I'm fine."

"I'm so glad you were able to come to Friday prayers. I wish more members of the broader community would share our observances. We have no secrets, and you are always welcome."

The volumes on the shelves included commentaries on the Qur'an, histories of Islam, as well as books on Gandhi and the Dalai Lama. A photo on the wall captured the imam as he coached a youth soccer team.

"Thank you again, sir."

"Please—call me Ousmane."

"Ousmane, I wanted to talk to you about something that happened—or might have happened—at the summer fair, before the shooting."

The imam leaned forward.

"Mr. Mehta, the father of the boy who was shot, says he heard someone arguing with the face-painters."

"Arguing?"

"That's what he says. I guess some Muslims feel that face-painting, at least the depiction of animal faces, violates the prohibition against creating representations of living beings."

The imam nodded. "Yes, though I don't agree. I certainly don't think we should stifle children's joy in innocent pursuits."

"Well, Mr. Mehta thinks the man was tall and thin, and young, but the one face-painter who remembers anything about a possible disagreement can't recall what the person looked like."

"So there might not have been an argument after all?"

"We're not sure, sir—Ousmane—but we wonder whether you know any member of the mosque, of your congregation, who fits that description. A strict interpreter of Islamic beliefs, about twenty years old."

The imam sat back in his padded chair. Finally, he acknowledged it was possible. "There are many young men who tend to be strict, even rigid, in their views. Especially recent immigrants from some of the more traditional countries."

"Tall? Thin?"

The imam shook his head. "Not really. Wait—there is one. But he's still in high school. About six-feet-three or -four, very skinny, about half my girth." He laughed. "I think he plays basketball."

"What's his name?"

"Haroun Malouf. Lives with his stepmother. His father died soon after they arrived in this country."

Kaufmann took down the information. "Do you happen to have their phone number?"

"I'll ask my secretary."

The detective stood up, as did the imam.

"Detective Kaufmann—Ezra—surely you're not suggesting that he might have shot the boy?"

"I'm not suggesting anything, Ousmane. But I'm not ruling anything out."

\* \* \*

There were not very many bars in Little Mecca, let alone gay ones, but Jamal knew a place across town near the art gallery where Henry worked. In fact, that was where he had met him a year or so before.

Called The Sportsmen's Club, it was a dark but stylish watering hole decorated with a plethora of mirrors and potted plants. An ancient, foot-thick television set with poor reception was always threatening to tumble onto the bartender or the patrons seated on the sleek, tightly-spaced bar stools, but no one seemed to mind. The TV was inevitably tuned to a baseball or football game.

Jamal ordered some kind of newfangled cocktail with grassy herbs and two different kinds of liquor. Settling into a chair near the back, he nursed the drink and eyed the other customers, mostly but not exclusively male, who seemed to range widely in age and background. A cab driver like him could find himself next to an art aficionado like Henry, a computer whiz next to a dropout, an immigrant factory worker next to a businessman whose family had been in the country for many generations.

On that night Henry, drinking with a bunch of his art world buddies, had noticed the notebook Jamal was scribbling in and asked him if he was working on a novel. Just taking notes, Jamal had told him, not wanting to use the pretentious word *poetry*. But this brief conversation led to a conversation about writing and art and an exchange of phone numbers.

Now no one bothered him, and he just glanced back and forth between the ballgame and a book of Walt Whitman's poetry. Jamal had long ago come to terms with his own sexuality—hadn't he?—but Whitman's boundless optimism, his frankness about physical affection, and his sense of connection with everyone around him were a blast of fresh air. In the more backward parts of the Arab world, where women were forced to hide behind veils or thick walls, male homosexuals were either passed around as sexual favors—or punished. Even killed.

Once, when he was fifteen or sixteen, he had met a boy in the refugee camp where he and his family lived. For some reason, they hit it off. They studied together, smoked cigarettes together, kicked around a soccer ball together, watched television together on the tiny black and white set in his parents' cramped and dusty living room. One day the friend said he wasn't feeling well. The boy's parents sent Jamal home. He thought that was the end of their friendship, but it turned out he just wasn't feeling well. They continued to hang out together after school, so much so that the other kids teased them when they saw them together—and if they saw one without the other. Where's so-and-so, they would ask, as if they were joined at the hip.

One day the boy went fishing in the Mediterranean, and of course he went along. They didn't catch any fish, but the day was hot and eventually they stripped naked and swam in the blue water. One thing led to another. The boy was quiet on the way home.

A few weeks later, the young men around the camp were practicing with their AK-47s. The Lebanese civil war was still raging, and the Palestinians from the refugee camp were fighting alongside one of the Lebanese militias. He had no interest in fighting, but his friend was there and he showed up like everyone else. Someone threw a stone at him and said, "What are you doing here, *Luti?*" a derogatory term that meant, roughly, sodomite. "We don't need perverts in this fight." Most of the guys paid no attention, but one or two joined the jeering and threw a few more stones at him. He kept on marching, but then his friend joined the chorus and threw his own stone. After which Jamal grabbed his friend and wrestled him to the ground. It felt like the time at the beach, with the wrestling, the heavy breathing, the sweating, but he was angry and hit his friend in the face and the stomach until someone pulled him off. After that, there was nothing to do but go home, and that really was the end of their friendship.

In America it was different, or at least in Whitman's version of America, where driving a cab was just as honorable as writing poetry, where young men lay down in grassy meadows and embraced, and where the grass growing on graves signaled that even death was just a part of the amazing, eternal energy-stream of life.

Whitman had probably played baseball too. One of the teams on the television scored a few runs. The crowd inside the electronic box cheered, but the smaller crowd inside the tavern paid no attention.

Jamal went back to the bar and ordered another drink.

"Bad day?" asked the bartender, mixing it. His sleeves were rolled up, revealing a complicated tattoo.

"No. Yes. How do you know?"

"Because you're sitting by yourself, staring into your drink, and, uh, looking like you've got no place to go."

"Hmm," said Jamal, stung by the diagnosis. "I didn't know it was so obvious."

"Not to mention the fact that you're on your third drink."

"Third? I've had only one so far."

"Not by my count."

But he slid the honey-colored concoction over to him anyway.

Jamal took it and retreated to his tiny table. Yes, it had been a bad day and a worse night. He was torn between wanting to burn down Henry's gallery and wanting to get down on his knees and beg him to return. It felt like the desperate period of time when his marriage was falling apart, except then he understood the reason for it and almost sympathized with his wife.

A few tables over, a couple of fine-looking fellows drinking red wine with their hamburgers were clinking glasses. Maybe it was their anniversary.

* * *

Some restaurants in Little Mecca served alcohol, and Farid and Tariq had found one. A Lebanese establishment that featured falafel, hummus, mashed eggplant, and skewered lamb, the place was dark and quiet, even on a Saturday night. Some kind of Middle Eastern music was playing in the background, and cigarette smoke (though not permitted) was drifting in from somewhere. Despite the Islamic prohibition on drinking alcohol, Tariq was on his third Budweiser, Farid still nursing his first.

"My dad yells at her," said Farid, referring to his sister, "but she just ignores him."

Tariq's eyes opened wide. "Really?"

Farid nodded.

"What about your mother? She lay down the law?"

"You kidding? She just tries to keep the peace."

Tariq drank some more of his Bud. "Wish my mother would have done that. It would've saved me a lot of beatings."

"Your dad beat you?"

Tariq shook his head. "Not my dad. He split when I was three years old. I never saw him again. After that, there were a lot of boyfriends, a lot of strange guys showing up at the breakfast table. They took her to the movies, bought her jewelry, went off on vacations with her."

"Where were you in all this?"

Tariq shrugged. "Don't really know. I remember staying home and watching television."

Farid took another sip. "The beatings?"

"My mom married one of them. Least I think they got married. For some reason, the dude didn't like me. Maybe I just got in the way. When he tripped over a scooter or the TV was too loud or I didn't finish my dinner, he would just lay into me with a belt."

Farid squirmed. He didn't really like hearing that sort of thing. But curiosity got the better of him. Tariq's family made his seem like the Brady Bunch.

"So what did your mom do?"

"Hide in their bedroom and shut the door."

"That sucks," said Farid. "Listen, I need to take a piss."

The music was louder in the restroom, and the cloudy mirror made his face look out of focus. When he returned, his friend was working on another Budweiser and scrolling through his cellphone.

"Did I show you these pictures of my ex?"

Farid looked at him questioningly. "Yeah, brother. Last night, remember?"

"Oh, right," he said, but he showed him another photo anyway. This one showed Tariq and his girlfriend together, at the beach, their arms around each other, smiling, drenched with sun. The girl was wearing a skimpy bikini.

"You were okay with that, then?"

"With what?"

"The bikini, the skin, the nakedness."

Tariq shrugged again. "That was before I embraced Allah."

"So she didn't want to make the journey with you?"

Tariq stared into his beer for a long time, then shook his head. "That and the drugs."

"Drugs? What are you talking about?"

"Not meth, coke, any of that shit. I'm talking about OxyContin."

"Isn't that, like, a pain reliever?"

"Right."

"So were you, like, in pain?"

Tariq sighed. "It's a long story. Wanna 'nother beer?"

Farid shook his head.

\* \* \*

Yasmin was upstairs getting dressed for a party while he and his wife were finishing their dinner in the dining room.

"The girl is too young for parties," said the doctor.

"Nothing will happen," said Mariam. "I talked to the parents. No alcohol, no kissing, no dark corners."

"High school—it's a big step."

"It is," said Mariam, sipping a glass of white wine, "but if we've brought her up right there shouldn't be any problem. She's like a baby bird, a sparrow. She can't fly yet, but she can take baby steps. We have to let her."

"You're very trusting, Mariam."

He sat back in his chair and checked his cellphone for messages.

"Do you have to do that now?"

Ali ignored her. Among the postings in his inbox, there was an announcement about an upcoming lecture on Islam in the Modern World, a note from the imam, something about continued medical training. Ah, and something else. A brief message from...a friend. "Drinks?" she wrote. "Or pinks." What did that mean? He tried to figure out whether there was a hidden subtext to the note. After all, she liked to play games sometimes. He took off his glasses and read the message again, but nothing had changed. Then he realized—it was a typo or an auto-correction. The word was *kinks*, not *pinks*. Then he understood.

His wife was saying something. The doctor looked up. Yasmin had appeared in the doorway, and his first impression was not good. Her dress was too short, her shoulders too bare, and her makeup too thick. Coral lipstick, red streaks on the cheeks, something purple around the eyes.

"This is not acceptable," he said. "Go upstairs and change."

Yasmin turned to her mother. "What is wrong with him?" she squealed.

"Upstairs!" he thundered.

Yasmin started crying and ran out of the room. Her mother followed.

Dr. Ali just sighed. He didn't want to fight with his daughter, but he was, to put it simply, worried.

\* \* \*

"So what happened?" Farid asked his friend in the half-dark of the restaurant.

"When I was a kid, I couldn't sit still. In school I was, like, bouncing off the walls. The teachers sent me to the principal's office or tried to shove me into special needs classes, but nothing worked, so my mom—her and my stepdad—got some quack to write me a prescription."

"For OxyContin?"

"No, brother. I told you it was a long story. For Ritalin. I stopped bouncing off the walls, but that wasn't necessarily a good thing. I stayed still long enough to tell Earl—that was my stepdad's name—to go fuck himself. He threw me outta the house."

"That sucks, man." The alcohol was loosening his tongue.

"Right. So I dropped out of school, got a job carrying two-by-fours at a construction site, thought about joining the Marines. But on the way to the recruiting office I met Megan."

Farid pushed his chair back and headed for the bar. "I think I will have that beer," he said.

When he came back, Tariq was eyeing more photos on his phone. "She's the greatest thing that ever happened to me. Beautiful, smart, sweet. I have no idea what she saw in me." He laughed.

"How long were you together?"

"A year, almost two. I moved into her apartment. We got a dog. I got a better job."

"And then?"

"Then, one day, I couldn't breathe. It was, like, ten o'clock at night and I had taken the dog out for a walk. It was cold and raining and dark, and I couldn't see three feet ahead of me. A car careened around a corner, blinded me with its lights, came so close it almost hit me."

"Really?"

"No, not really. Probably not. But that's what it felt like."

Farid took a long drink. He was thirsty, and the cold beer felt good.

"So Butch—our English bulldog—was standing there shivering in the cold and the wet, and I was like half-blind with the lights and shaking because I thought the asshole was going to run me over and, all of a sudden, I couldn't breathe. I gasped for air, I choked, Butch looked at me like he wanted to help but couldn't figure out how. I thought I was going to black out and die."

"Damn, that sounds scary."

"So after I managed to stagger home, Megan drove me to the emergency room, where they did lots of tests and decided there was nothing the fuck wrong with me."

"Not much help."

"Hell no. And they came back, those panic attacks. Not as bad as the first time, but bad enough. I figured I had to do something."

"So you took painkillers?"

Tariq drank the last drop of his beer. "Well, me and this dude Freddie Khan had become friendly playing pickup basketball. Everyone knew that Freddie was a reliable source of prescription meds, so we got to talking and he gave me some OxyContin—free, no strings attached—and from that day forward my moods improved and the panic attacks went away."

"But you kept taking the pills."

Tariq nodded. "For a while, I did. I started working two jobs to pay for them, until I got fired. I stole some money from ol' Earl, then I lifted a necklace of my mom's and sold that."

"Whoa."

Tariq nodded. "I know, I know. But remember, I was in bad shape. I couldn't breathe. I needed meds, and the docs didn't give a shit."

"But the pill pusher did."

"Don't blame Freddie. He was just trying to help. In fact, about this time, he was trying to get out of the business. His parents were Pakistani, he grew up a Muslim, and now he started praying five times a day, going to the *masjid* for prayers and study sessions, wearing a *kufi* like this one." He touched the cap on his head, lovingly. "And guess what, brother. I started praying with him!"

"Wow."

"I started studying the Qur'an. I started doing the prayers five times a day. It made a lot more sense than the Bible shit I'd heard in Sunday School growing up."

"We all pray to the same God, Tariq. We all come from Ibrahim, our father."

"You don't know my Sunday School."

"So you found Allah and tossed the OxyContin?"

"Pretty much, yeah. I mean, it was a long process. Periods of remission, relapses, stints in rehab. Megan paid for the rehab, she stuck by me, but the more I prayed the more nervous she got."

"Too bad she wasn't more supportive."

"Well, she freaked out after the last relapse. I don't blame her. I miss her, but I don't blame her."

Farid was silent. Finally, he said, "What happened with Freddie?"

Tariq frowned. "He moved away. Last I heard he died of an overdose."

\* \* \*

Dressed in washed-out jeans and a red-and-black cotton-polyester shirt, Jonathan brushed his hair and told his father not to wait up for him. Kaufmann clenched his teeth; they had had this conversation before.

"How late are you going to be?"

His son shrugged. "I don't know. Two. Three."

"That's when all the drunk drivers are out. Not to mention the meth addicts and the gangbangers."

"Zach's a good driver, and if I had my own car—"

"I'm not talking about Zach. I'm talking about the other drivers."

Jonathan was halfway out the door. "I'll be sure to watch out for them."

"If it's really late, maybe you should just sleep over. That would be safer."

"At Allison's house? I can't ask Allison if I can sleep at her house."

"Why not?"

"I don't even know her."

"Ask her parents. I'm sure they wouldn't mind."

"Maybe I should just get a police escort. You think you could arrange that?" Now he really was out the door.

"Jonathan—" his dad called after him.

"What?" he called back.

"Be safe."

\* \* \*

The combination of fog and moonlight cast a garish glow over Allison's house, an elegant Tudor mini-mansion with gabled roofs and narrow windows.

"Hey," said the girl who answered the door. She was wearing a low-cut blouse, big dangling earrings, and shiny pink lipstick. Jonathan had never seen her before.

"Hey," said Zach.

Jonathan mumbled something and stepped inside. Despite his fancy shirt, he was feeling under-dressed in his faded jeans and ratty sneakers. Zach looked cool in some kind of fake designer threads.

The girl asked them if she could get them something to drink and led them into the kitchen, where a gleaming espresso machine competed for counter space with several bottles of hard liquor. A couple of other teenagers were standing around chatting.

Zach asked her where Allison was.

"Probably in the basement. The party's happening downstairs. I"—she pursed her lips like a rock star crooning—"I just came up for air."

"Yeah," said Zach. "I get it."

"So what would you like? Gin, vodka, scotch, Kahlua?"

Zach said he would like a vodka martini.

"One vodka martini coming up."

Jonathan poked his friend in the ribs.

"I like martinis," Zach insisted.

Jonathan grabbed a beer and nodded to the others. There were two guys from his football team and a girl from his biology class. Some kind of electronic trance music was blasting out of hidden speakers. He bumped into a guy with thick glasses who said his name was Youssef.

"But you can call me Joe," said Youssef.

They shook hands. Jonathan asked him if he went to Noire.

He shook his head. "Rouge."

"So how do you know Allison?"

Joe shrugged. "Friend of a friend."

Zach seemed to have vanished. Jonathan tried to make small talk with the girl in the pink lipstick, but she seemed more interested in a guy with long, stringy hair hanging down over his eyes. After a while, chasing his beer with a fruity gin and tonic, he headed downstairs to the basement.

* * *

The comedians on "Saturday Night Live" were doing mildly amusing impersonations of the candidates, but when a commercial came on, Kaufmann hit the mute button and checked the messages on his phone. A notice of a new credit card bill. A sales pitch for a better handgun. An urgent text from Captain Schroeder. What could be so important that it couldn't wait till Sunday? The detective clicked on the link. It seemed that Jeff Hampton, the leader of the Christian picketers, had been arrested for assaulting his wife. He was being held in the county jail, a hundred miles away in Day Shoots.

* * *

The light was dim except for a naked bulb dangling over a billiard table where a couple of guys who wielded their pool cues like hockey sticks were showing off with behind-the-back trick shots while three pretty girls cheered them on. The rest of the basement was filled with castoff couches and semi-broken chairs turned toward the wall or facing each other in cozy groupings. Jonathan could hear a number of hushed conversations, if not the actual words, and he could smell the weed that some of the basement crowd was smoking.

In fact, someone came up to him and offered him a joint. It was Cody Rasmussen, a tall, pimply-faced kid he knew from AP American History. Intelligent but eccentric, Cody was always raising his hand and offering alternative opinions on key issues in American history, like the causes of the American Revolution or the relative merits of rebel spy Nathan Hale and turncoat Benedict Arnold (the real patriot, according to Cody). Even in the first few weeks of school, he had managed to make himself almost universally disliked.

"Thanks," said Jonathan before taking the joint between his fingertips and inhaling the acrid smoke.

Cody was wearing a tweed jacket and a tie that seemed to be choking off his air supply. If he had been smoking a pipe instead of a joint, he might have looked like a child prodigy college professor.

His classmate asked him if he had started the paper on the Federalist controversy yet.

Jonathan shook his head, blew out the smoke that had been trapped in his lungs, and handed back the roach. "No, but I've got an idea for it."

"What's that, man?"

"I'm going do the whole thing as a rap, like 'Hamilton.'"

Cody smiled. "Not bad, Kaufmann. I'm sure Mr. Chang will go for that, as long as you cite your sources."

"I plan to, Cody," Jonathan replied, then drank some of his gin and tonic to quench his thirst.

"Maybe you could perform some of it in class."

Each one was trying to top the other's clever comments, but Jonathan was getting tired of the game. "That's an idea, but I'm already busy with 'Merchant.'"

"Oh, right. The 'quality of mercy' and all that crap."

As his classmate drifted away, Jonathan sat down on an ottoman in a dark corner of the room and sipped his drink. The hypnotic drone-music was giving him a headache. Where the hell did Zach go? He heard the sound of one billiard ball striking another, followed by goofy laughter.

Suddenly a gentle hand slid up his leg. He flinched, spilling some of his drink. A young girl, dark-haired, olive-skinned, was looking up at him with large hazel eyes. It was Yasmin, the girl from the high school parking lot. Instead of an oversized sweatshirt, she was wearing a skimpy, dark green dress that was barely held up by skinny straps tied back over her slight shoulders.

"Hey," he said.

She put her finger over her lips and began to stroke his thigh. Was she even fourteen?

"What are you doing?"

Every time Yasmin slid her hand up, it went higher. Jonathan bent down to kiss her, but she turned her head away. The trance music continued to throb.

The girl pulled his zipper down and fished around in his underwear. His prick sprang out of its hiding place and got hard quickly. She nuzzled it with delicate fingers.

"What the fuck?" he said.

"Relax."

After stroking his penis a few times, she took a deep breath, leaned down, and caressed it with her mouth.

The steady beat of the music, the hushed whispers from the dark corners of the room, the chatter of the pool players, and the carom of the billiard balls off the sides of the table commingled in his mind like the sweet sound of a stream flowing over rocks in paradise. He thought he heard a muted click, then another, and another, but he couldn't separate that odd sound from the background noises and his fantasy of the heavenly river.

The rhythmic sucking of the post-middle-school water nymph with the deep, beautiful eyes made him want to melt or explode or cry out. He rocked back and forth on the old ottoman, and the nymph's head bobbed up and down to the same rhythm. The strange word *ottoman* brought to mind harem fantasies from the History Channel or old issues of *National Geographic*. Up and down. Up and down. It was like a dance. He didn't know the steps, but it didn't matter because he didn't need to use his feet. A yell went up from the billiard table. One ball had hit another, he guessed, and the second ball had scooted down the rabbit hole. He gasped for air. The water nymph lifted her head, smiled at him, and ran away, leaving him splayed and exposed on the ottoman, wondering what the hell had just happened.

"Yasmin!" he called after her, but she was gone.

# Sunday: Missing

*He was lying on a brush-covered hill looking up at the clear blue sky—the hill had a name, an odd name, Turkey—when he realized that his arms and legs were tied and a whole bunch of little people—tiny people like leprechauns or (what were they called?) Lilliputians—were scurrying back and forth over the hill and crawling all over his body. The little people felt like annoying ants or spiders except that one of them was actually a girl, a pretty young girl, apparently Turkish, who was fiddling with his zipper while saying something unintelligible in Turkish or some other Middle Eastern language. Soon enough she succeeded in pulling out his penis, putting it in her mouth, and sucking on it. The insistent sucking of the Turkish girl seemed to coincide with the melodic piping of a reed-like instrument and then with the steady beating of a drum. Although the sucking felt good, he felt naked and helpless among all the little people and he worried that he might hurt the girl, even though he was the one who was tied down and she seemed to want to do what she was doing.*

But now he turned over on his side and opened one eye to the faint, predawn light and realized that he wasn't tied down after all. The melodic piping faded away, but the drumming continued.

\* \* \*

"Do you want me to wake her up?" Farid had asked his mother.

The rest of the family was ready for predawn prayers.

"Let her sleep," said Mariam. "She was out late last night."

"That's the problem," her husband said as he brushed his unshaven cheek with his hand. "Better to pray than to sleep, but she stays up partying."

Farid had already taken off and Ahmed was just about to leave for Sunday hours at the clinic when, almost two hours later, Mariam knocked on her daughter's door.

"Wake up, sleepyhead."

She knocked again.

"It's late, Yasmin. You've missed breakfast."

She knocked more loudly, then gently pushed the door open. The bed was undisturbed, the pillow as fluffed as it was the night before. Yasmin's favorite stuffed animal was propped up on the pillow as if waiting for its owner to come to bed. Mariam glanced quickly around the room. Schoolbooks were scattered on the tiny wood-laminate desk, and notebooks spilled out of a mauve-colored backpack lying half-open on the floor. The computer had gone to sleep. The shades were open, letting in a flood of morning light. Yasmin's purse was sitting motionless in a corner like a wind-up toy that needed to be rewound.

Mariam ran out into the hallway and shouted to her husband. "Ahmed! Ahmed! Yasmin's not here!"

"What?" he called back, lazily.

"Yasmin's gone! Her bed hasn't been slept in."

Ahmed appeared in the hallway. "Maybe she went home with one of her friends. That girl has a mind of her own, you know."

"Her purse is here."

Ahmed dismissed her concerns with a wave of the hand. "Is there anything in it? Maybe she took another purse."

Mariam opened the purse and found a comb, some kleenex, a tube of lipstick, and a wallet containing a ten-dollar-bill and three singles.

"Let's not get excited," said her husband, though his eyes said something different. "We can call her cell."

He found his own phone and clicked on his daughter's number. But the call went straight to voice mail.

"I'm going to try Haniya," said Mariam.

Yasmin and her friend Haniya had gone to middle school together, but they now went to separate high schools. When Mariam called the number, the girl said she had not spoken to Yasmin in months.

* * *

72

The insistent drumbeat awakened Aisha in the early hours like a steady rain. She would get up soon, make some breakfast for herself, and say the day's first prayers. As a ten-year-old, Hanan—or Anna, as the kids at school called her—could eat later, after daybreak, though she had been starting to fast part of the time. Similarly, she had been starting to wear a scarf over her hair though Aisha didn't encourage or discourage her.

She and her daughter lived in a no-frills apartment with an old refrigerator that rumbled and shook and an even more antique radiator that made her sweat or freeze, depending upon its mood. From the third-floor window, one could see laundry flapping on clotheslines, the back walls of stores covered with graffiti, and a concrete playground where kids kicked a soccer ball and old men played chess.

Hanan pushed open the door to her mother's room and stood by the side of her bed.

"What is it?" mumbled Aisha, drowsily.

"Something woke me up. Can I get into bed with you?"

"It's just the drum man, sweetie. Go back to bed."

Hanan stood there, a doubtful expression on her face.

Aisha sighed. "Are you excited about seeing Daddy? Is that why you can't sleep?"

Sunday was the day she saw her father, but Hanan shook her head.

"What is it then?"

Hanan didn't say anything.

"Oh, all right. Get in." She lifted the covers and her daughter scooted into the bed. "But we can't stay in bed too long. The sun will be up soon."

Hanan snuggled up next to her mother and closed her eyes. Aisha lay awake, thinking.

For a long time, she had paid more attention to her career than her personal life, attending semi-political lectures, writing articles for a local Palestinian newspaper, rarely going out on dates except for a few carefully-arranged meetings that didn't go much further. A two-year relationship with a distant cousin ended with him telling her it wasn't working out. Funny, she hadn't even noticed.

She was already living in the States when she met her future husband. They were casual friends who frequented the same cafés, poetry readings, and cheap restaurants. He was not like the other men, less volatile though harder to pin down. He wrote poems for her; she fed his cat. He needed a green card. In a burst of generosity that caught them both by surprise, she married him. At first it was just a marriage of convenience, in which they memorized each other's backgrounds, birthmarks, and food preferences in order to fool the immigration agents. But soon he began to notice her flimsy nightgowns; she studied his strong arms and bristly face. They had coffee in the morning, tea in the afternoon. One night they had sex. She got pregnant. They fell in love. Was that how it went? Like blocks that could be arranged in random order.

"Mom?" said her daughter in a sleepy voice.

"Yes, dear?"

"Somebody pulled my scarf off in PE."

"A boy?" Apparently boys and girls did sports and exercises together.

Hanan's head shifted slightly on the pillow. "No, a girl."

"But why?"

"I don't know, but she called me a raghead."

Aisha held her daughter closer and said, "Don't worry, sweetheart. Sometimes children say bad things to each other. It doesn't mean anything."

"I started crying and everyone looked at me."

"Don't cry. I'm sure the other girl feels bad about what she said."

\* \* \*

Brodsky didn't hear the drummer, but that was because there was always an orchestra's worth of sounds to jolt him awake in the mornings, even on Sundays: the clanging of garbage can covers, the banging of car doors, the slamming of windows, the barking of dogs. When the dogs barked, Anton raised his head and looked around, then closed his eyes and went back to sleep. When the windows slammed, Brodsky turned over, felt the crick in his neck and the stiffness in the rest of his joints, patted Anton, and tried to remember what he was doing sleeping in his car. Then he remembered. One thought led to another, and he felt like saying something to somebody, but instead he shut his eyes again and tried to forget everything.

\* \* \*

Kaufmann turned on the radio and tried to find a news station, but all he got was pop music, Christian preaching from a high-powered station somewhere in the Bible Belt, Garrison Keillor reading a fake commercial for the Ketchup Advisory Board, a local Arabic program which he didn't understand, and previews of the afternoon's pro football games.

The highway was nearly deserted on Sunday morning, and he knew he would have no trouble making it to Day Shoots—the name a corruption of some French phrase referring to the falls of a nearby river—by a little after ten. After being shunted the wrong way on a one-way street by his car's GPS system, he consulted a tattered map that seemed to omit several key thoroughfares. The map led him to a neighborhood of simple cottages as tattered as the map, with grass growing as high as corn, laundry flapping in the breeze, and nonfunctioning automobiles arranged willy-nilly in the front yards. One of them belonged to Hampton and his wife. The detective knew that this used to be farm country 150 years ago, cornfields in fact, but the family plots had given way to giant factory farms, the cheap houses built originally for farm workers now housing the farmers' displaced descendants.

Kaufmann cruised the quiet streets for a while and then circled back to the town's main street. The squat, concrete county jail with the American flag flying in front seemed like a throwback to a simpler time when everybody knew everybody else and local drunks would ask the sheriff to lock them up for the night so that they could sleep off their inebriation in peace and safety. The detective knew that Day Shoots had been an important stop on the Underground Railroad funneling escaped slaves from the South to Canada, but evidently nothing had happened there since. Well, nothing except a notorious lynching in 1923 and a devastating flood in 1937 or -8.

Kaufmann had called ahead, and the sergeant on duty ushered him into the cell where Jeff Hampton was confined. He was lying on a cot, reading a book.

"Light reading?" asked the detective.

"It's about the last days of Jesus," said Hampton, not bothering to look up.

"I thought the Gospels pretty much told that story."

"Not everything. You can never learn enough about our Lord."

"Mind if I talk to you?" said Kaufmann.

Grudgingly, the prisoner put his book aside and sat up. "I already told you everything."

"Why did you hit your wife?"

Hampton scowled. "I didn't hit her. She threw a knife at me."

"Is that the story you're selling?"

"What business is it of yours? Aren't you a little far from home?"

"Just curious," said the detective. "So why did your wife throw a knife at you?"

The man shrugged. "You'll have to ask her."

"Did you strike her before or after she threw the knife?"

Hampton laughed. "I told you, I didn't hit her."

"So you're a model of self-restraint?"

"I might have pointed my gun at her. Just kidding around. She took offense, grabbed a kitchen knife, and chucked it. She's a good woman, but she can get a little out of control sometimes."

The detective took a notebook out of his pocket and jotted this down. *Pointed gun. Just kidding. Took offense.*

"And why did you point a gun at her?"

The prisoner shrugged again. "You can ask my lawyer." He glanced down at his left wrist as if there were a watch there and said, "He's supposed to be here soon."

Kaufmann wrote the word *lawyer* in his notebook, though he wasn't sure why. "Mr. Hampton, I understand that your wife accompanied you when you were picketing at the summer fair last month."

"That's right. She's always out there with me."

"Does she also carry a gun?"

Hampton sighed. "No, why would she need a gun? It's *my* job to protect *her.*"

"Is that what you were doing on the picket line? Protecting your wife?" He and Hampton had had this conversation before.

"In case you haven't noticed, Detective, there's a lot of crazies out there."

\* \* \*

Kaufmann opened the screen door and knocked. The front porch was sagging, but the yard was well-maintained and a pickup truck, recently washed, was parked neatly in the dirt driveway.

"Ms. Hampton?" he asked the woman who answered the door.

"Yes?"

About thirty years old, she had soft, pudding-like features and a swelling bosom. Somehow the old-fashioned word seemed appropriate.

"Ms. Hampton, I'm Detective Kaufmann of the Terre Nouveau Police." He flashed his badge.

"I told them, I'm not pressing charges. It's all a big mistake."

A baby was crying somewhere inside.

"Do you mind if I come in?"

Shielding her eyes from the sun, she said, "I need to change my baby's diaper."

Kaufmann nodded. "I can wait."

She let him in, then retreated to a back room. The over-upholstered parlor was dark, the shades drawn against the morning sun. After a few minutes, she came back with the baby in her arms—a beautiful, wispy-haired infant with big eyes and an anxious expression on its big round face—and a glass of iced tea for the detective.

After thanking her for the tea, he said, "So it was just a mistake? A misunderstanding?"

She nodded. "We were watching television—one of those cop shows—and Jeff says, 'That's not how you shoot a gun,' like he can do it better. Then he gets up and fetches the gun from the drawer and starts demonstrating how you hold a gun, how you aim it, how you—"

"Shoot it?"

"Well, he didn't actually shoot it."

"Was it loaded?"

She shifted the baby from one arm to the other. "It's always loaded. Except when he's cleaning it. But I was worried because he'd had a few beers and was getting riled up by the TV show."

Kaufmann took out his notebook, jotted down the wife's name, and started taking more notes. "So…"

"So I asked him to put the gun away, and he said something he probably regrets. I know he didn't mean it."

"What did he say?"

"I'd rather not repeat it."

"He says you threw a knife at him."

She opened her eyes wide. In that moment, she looked a lot like her baby, who was eerily quiet. "Is that what he says? I think Mr. Heinrich told him to say that."

"Who's Mr. Heinrich?"

"A friend. And a lawyer."

Kaufmann wrote down Heinrich's name.

"Ms. Hampton, what do you have against Muslims?"

The woman seemed surprised by the question. "Muslims?"

"The summer fair? You and your husband were carrying signs, marching around, calling people names?"

"You mean, apart from the fact that they want to kill us and are stealing our jobs and taking over our cities?"

The detective jotted this down. "You think the Muslims who live in Terre Nouveau want to kill you?"

Again she seemed surprised by the question. "Not all of them. But how can we tell the bad apples from the good ones?"

Kaufmann wrote *bad apples* and underlined it. "And you don't think that law enforcement—the police, the Sheriff's Department, the FBI—can protect you?"

She laughed. "No, not hardly. They're protecting the Moslems. But my husband will protect me. Me and my baby. That's why he has a gun."

Kaufmann sighed and wrote *back to square one* in the notebook.

"Detective, you'll have to excuse me. I need to get ready for church."

\* \* \*

Dropping in at the central office to check his schedule for the week, Jamal found that he didn't have enough hours and the hours he did have came at awkward times, like twelve-hour shifts that ended at dawn. Muttering to himself, he ran into two other drivers playing penny-ante poker in the break room. He nodded a greeting and made himself a cup of tea. The other drivers started talking about the upcoming election, so he took his tea and went back to the main room where the dispatcher worked and the schedules were posted. He complained to the dispatcher on duty— a fifty-something woman with an oddly husky voice—about his schedule, but she said it was out of her hands.

Afterwards, he returned to the break room and washed out his cup. One of the poker players asked him if he wanted to join the game. He said no, but he sat down and watched them play. Although it seemed silly to play two-handed poker, the two players seemed serious, shuffling, dealing the cards, bluffing, betting. Pretty soon another driver showed up, and he agreed to join the other two. The betting lasted longer now, the pot got bigger, and the winning hand was a little more impressive, like a straight or three of a kind.

After one hand, the new player turned over one of the cards, examined the design, and said, in something like a Russian accent, "Bicycle. Why bicycle?"

"It's a brand," said one of the other guys. "Bicycle playing cards."

"My son," said the Russian while the other shuffled, "my son want bicycle for his birthday."

The other player finished shuffling and started dealing.

"But," the Russian continued, shrugging, "we have no money for bike."

The dealer announced the game: five-card draw. After examining his hand, the Russian bet a nickel and went on with his story.

"Not just bicycle. We have no money for buy television or fix brakes on taxi. My wife, Nadia, she want me to go refugee agency for help."

No one seemed to be paying much attention, but Jamal was curious.

The Russian continued, "Agency help us leave Russia. Agency help me get job driving taxi. We have money for to put food on table and shoes on feet. Is enough. We don't need charity."

"How many cards?" said the dealer.

The Russian put two cards face down on the table, and the dealer gave him two more.

"What about the bicycle?" said Jamal. "Did your son ever get his bike?" The Russian shrugged and bet another nickel.

* * *

Aisha had dressed Hanan in a pretty blue dress with matching sky-blue ribbons in her hair. When she answered the knock at the door, she found her ex-husband standing there with a scraggly three-day beard, a shirt that hadn't been ironed in months, and sneakers with holes so big you could see the socks underneath.

"Hi, Daddy," said Hanan, giving her father a hug.

"That's the best you could do?" muttered Aisha in Arabic, glaring.

"What?"

She bit her tongue and shook her head.

He continued in Arabic, which their daughter didn't understand. "Why are you always criticizing me? Why is everything I do wrong?"

"Maybe you should ask yourself that."

"You're always stabbing me in the back, Aisha. What did you tell Henry?"

"Henry? What does this have to do with Henry?"

"We were very happy, Henry and me. Why did you have to ruin it?"

"What are you talking about?" She didn't know why he was getting so worked up.

"Poison. You were poison from the start."

"Me!? You know what happened." How could he blame her for the inevitable breakup?

Hanan was staring at them. Although she didn't know the exact meaning of their conversation, she could figure out the gist of it. Suddenly Aisha felt gloomy and depressed.

"Okay, sweetie," she said in English, as brightly as she could manage. "Time to go. Have a good time with your father." When they reached the door, she added, "Hanan is fasting today. No falafel or ice cream cones for her."

* * *

Mariam sat on her daughter's unruffled bed and almost tore her hair out. She had called several parents, but none of them knew anything about Yasmin's whereabouts. Ahmed said that she would show up soon, that she was probably just watching an old movie with one of her friends. He would ground her when she got home. But she knew he was worried too. He was merely trying to reassure her.

Until recently Yasmin had been a sweet, good-natured child, doing her homework diligently, observing the traditions, and playing with her stuffed animals. But sometime toward the end of middle school, she had started developing an interest in boys. She would listen to naughty music, wear revealing clothes, and talk back to her father. She used to cover her hair with a scarf when she went out of the house, but her mother knew that she took it off as soon as she was halfway down the street. Now she didn't even pretend.

Mariam propped a chestnut-colored toy horse against the pillow and sighed.

She remembered how Yasmin used to talk on the phone with Haniya for hours. Now that she attended a different school, she had lost touch with her old friends. Everything had changed.

It had been simpler with Farid, she decided. He prayed five times a day, observed the fasts, fulfilled the duties of a son, and had never strayed from the right path. A management trainee at Toys 'R' Us, he was trying to better himself by taking classes at the community college. True, he rode around on his friend Timothy or Tariq's motorcycle and played video games for hours on end in the room Tariq rented from a young couple with three children, but he also attended study sessions at the *masjid* and surfed religious websites on the internet. He was a good boy.

Yasmin was a good girl too, just a little out of control, and now she was missing. She picked up her cellphone and called her son. He answered after four rings.

"Mom," he said, peevishly, "I told you not to call me when I'm at work."

"It's an emergency, Farid. Yasmin is missing."

"What do you mean *missing*?"

"She didn't come home last night. Her bed hasn't been slept in."

"You're kidding."

Mariam sighed. "Listen, Farid, do you know the name of the girl who gave the party? The one Yasmin went to last night?"

Farid said something to one of his coworkers, then came back on the line. "No. I don't even know the names of her old friends, so how should I know the names of her new ones?"

"Okay, Farid. Thank you. If you hear anything—anything at all—let me or your father know immediately."

\* \* \*

With his dad out of town on something related to a case, Jonathan stayed in his room working on his history paper. Federalists, Anti-Federalists. Big government, small government. Personal freedoms, states' rights, effective democracy. The issues were complicated, and they hadn't gone away. Maybe he really should turn the paper into a rap musical. It would certainly be more fun that way. But then he got a text from Zach.

**Hold on 2 yr hat, dude,** said the message. **Check out these pix.**

The photos were dark, too dark to see clearly. Most of them seemed to show young men and women standing around talking, drinking, or playing pool, but it was impossible to identify any of the people. The last photo, poorly lit and out of focus, appeared to show the side of a girl's head as she was bending over…somebody's arm or leg. He looked at it more closely. The girl looked familiar. Wait a minute. Jesus! It was Yasmin, the girl from the party, and the guy was…him!

**Holy shit,** Jonathan texted back. **Where u get these?**

**Allison,** wrote Zach, **posted them on her FB page.**

What was going on? Why the hell had someone taken those pictures? Why had Allison posted them? And why in God's name had Yasmin come on to him like that?

To Zach he wrote back, simply, **?**

A few minutes later, a reply zipped in over the airwaves.

**Smthg else Allison sez on her page. Congrats 2 everyone on the list.**

List? What list?

An A-list, as opposed to a B-list? The list of people she had invited to the party? A list of folks whose photos she wanted to put in the class yearbook? Whatever it was, he sure as hell hoped he wasn't on it.

# Monday: Pound of Flesh

The self-appointed community drummer woke up Jamal before dawn once again. He closed his eyes, opened them, wondered whether he should be feeling happy or sad, then remembered that Henry had broken up with him. He was tempted to roll over, bury his head in the pillow, and go back to sleep, but he knew that was unlikely.

Instead, he dragged himself out of bed and petted Muhammad, who meowed until he was fed. Then Jamal made himself a cup of tea and walked over to the front door to collect the morning paper. The headlines reflected the usual mix of natural disasters, economic crises, political scandals, and random and not-so-random outbreaks of violence that he saw every morning. The world was in bad shape, the country was confused, the city was struggling.

Muhammad finished his breakfast and nuzzled his master's legs.

"Good boy, peace be upon you," he said to the cat as he scratched his ears.

On the first page of the local features section, he noticed a piece by his ex-wife about a foreclosure. A family that lived here in Little Mecca was being evicted. The combination of Aisha's byline, the story of the family's hard times, and the photo of their possessions sitting on the street triggered in him a long series of memories that unfolded like faded snapshots in his brain: the dusty streets, full of stray cats and dogs, of the refugee camp where he had grown up; the nondescript courthouse where, in the company of a few friends, he and Aisha had gotten married; the delivery room, with its bright lights and pistachio-green gowns, where his daughter had been born; the dark bar where he had first met Henry; the spartan bedroom—sometimes too cold, sometimes hot, depending on the season—where they had slept.

He turned the page.

\* \* \*

When Jonathan spotted Allison in front of her locker, he went up to her and said, "Why did you post those pictures?"

Allison screwed up her face and looked at him as if he were crazy. "Do I know you?"

"Jonathan Kaufmann. I was at your party."

"Oh, well, I hope you had a good time."

"Why did you plaster those photos over your Facebook page?"

Allison shrugged. "I've got to get to class."

She started to close her locker, but Jonathan put his hand on the door and stopped her. "Have you seen Yasmin?"

"Yasmin?"

"The girl at your party. The one who—"

She cut him off. "Listen, John or Jeff or whoever you are, are you sure I invited you?"

"I just want to talk to her," he said, but when his fingers slipped she slammed the locker door and hustled off to class.

\* \* \*

"Have you heard anything?" Mariam asked her husband on the phone.

"No, nothing," said Ali, sounding somber.

They had woken up before another dismal dawn. The Ramadan drummer—a long-time member of the mosque who managed produce at a local grocery store and played percussion in the city's part-time symphony orchestra—had made his presence known as usual, but Yasmin's bed was untouched, her ragged stuffed animals silently awaiting her return. With Farid, they went through the motions of the *suhoor* meal, but it wasn't the same without their daughter's sweet face.

"You said you were going to get the boys from the mosque to look for her."

"I did. They're looking. I told them to leave no stone unturned."

Mariam made a dismissive sound. She was standing in the beautiful, modern kitchen of their new house, with its gleaming, stainless steel surfaces and its cherrywood cabinets. She stared at the expensive toaster they had bought when they moved in.

She told him she was calling the police.

84

"The police?" he snorted. "The police are not interested in us or our daughter. All they care about is spying on our activities and pretending to investigate problems. It's been over a month, and they still haven't figured out the shooting of that child."

"If they're spying on us, why don't they know where Yasmin is?"

"Why don't you ask them?"

"That's the first good idea you've had," she said.

Her husband grunted noisily. She was about to hang up when he added, with a catch in his voice, "Listen, Mariam. I know you're upset. I'm upset too. But Yasmin isn't like this. If she didn't come home, I'm sure there's a reason for it."

"That's what I'm afraid of, Ahmed! That's what I'm afraid of."

\* \* \*

Aisha was sitting at her desk in the noisy and crowded newsroom when she got a call from Ibrahim Ghazal, the civil engineer whose family had just been evicted. He had seen her article in the paper and wanted to give her the latest news.

"We are lucky. Very lucky."

"Lucky? Foreclosure. Eviction. Losing your house. What do you mean?"

She could hear Sameh and the other kids running around in the background.

"We don't have to move after all."

"Really? What happened?"

"The bank says okay. They changed their mind and let us move back into our house."

"But why? How?"

Ibrahim laughed. "I still don't know. If I was religious, I'd say it was a miracle. A Ramadan miracle."

The clack-clack of computer keyboards and the jangle of a dozen conversations were making it hard for her to hear, so she pressed the phone into one ear and put her hand over the other.

"Was it, uh, your friend on the City Council?"

"No, no. Not that one."

She could hear Ibrahim's wife saying something to him.

"Then—"

"Mrs. Ali. She's on the council too. They had some kind of meeting about the foreclosures, the rise in real estate prices, the lack of affordable housing, God knows what. I thought it was all hot air. Just for show. The next thing I know, Dr. Ali steps in."

"Steps in?"

"Takes over the mortgage. Takes it off our hands."

Aisha switched the phone from her right ear to her left. "Wow. That's very generous of him."

Ibrahim laughed again. "Nadia, my wife, loves him better than she loves me. But it's not just charity. We have to pay it back."

"Oh, I see."

"Still, we don't have to pay interest. It's the Islamic way. No interest, lower payments, we pay what we can afford. It's a good deal, right?"

"Certainly sounds like it." She wanted to ask more questions, but for the moment she simply wished him and his family a happy Ramadan.

"*Ramadan Mubarak*, Mrs. Hassan."

* * *

Having spent the night at a bare-bones motel that the interstate had rendered obsolete, Kaufmann drank a cup of coffee at a nearby Starbucks. Even the small town of Day Shoots had at least one Starbucks, which evidently had not yet been rendered obsolete. It was just like the coffee giant's outposts in Terre Nouveau, except that there were fewer laptops among the patrons and the sound system was playing twangy country music instead of coffee-house pop. The detective was there to meet with Ernest Heinrich, the "Christian" activist's lawyer, who was late for their appointment.

He was about to check the time again when a short, stocky man in a rumpled suit pushed open the door, blinked a few times, and scanned the room. Kaufmann stood up. They shook hands.

"You'll have to excuse me," said Heinrich. "I was in court on behalf of my client."

"Hampton?"

The attorney nodded. "Bail was reduced. I'm, uh, friends with the judge."

Heinrich excused himself again to join the line at the counter. He ordered a latte while Kaufmann fidgeted.

"So he's out?" the detective asked him when he returned.

Heinrich checked his watch. "Being released as we speak."

"Back home to his wife?"

The lawyer took a long sip of his latte. "I advised my client to spend the night somewhere else."

"How long have you known Jeff Hampton, Mr. Heinrich?"

"Please, call me Ernie. We've been friends since high school. Attended the same church. Belonged to the same youth group."

"And what church is that?"

"Church of the Holy Redeemer. Out on Route 9, among the corn fields. Founded a hundred and fifty-three years ago by German immigrants. Lutherans, Mennonites, and even some Catholics who broke off on their own."

"Why?"

"Why did they break away?" The detective nodded. "I don't know. I think they just wanted something they could all be comfortable with. Nowadays, we believe strictly in the Gospel of Jesus Christ and the need to accept Him as our personal savior."

"What about the Muslim-bashing?"

Heinrich frowned. "Jeff was always a little rough around the edges. He was president of the student council but got into lots of fights. Loyal to his friends but a bulldog if you crossed him."

"Did you ever cross him?"

The lawyer laughed. "Me? No. I was his best friend. Still am."

"So how did he develop this thing about Muslims?"

Heinrich slurped up the last of his latte with a satisfied smack of his lips. "You have to understand, Detective, that the recession was pretty hard on folks out here and most people haven't recovered. The workers on the auto assembly lines lost their jobs, the farmers lost their farms, and the rest of us pretty near lost our homes. It's not the American dream. The American dream's gone to China."

"So you blame Muslims for that?"

"Are you asking me to speak for Jeff?"

The detective didn't say anything.

"No, I blame the Jewish bankers on Wall Street for selling us out—and the illegal Mexican immigrants for taking what was left."

"What about the Muslims?"

"Look, I've got nothing against the good Muslims. Just the ones that are stabbing us in the back."

"What exactly are you referring to?"

Heinrich laughed. "Maybe that was a little harsh. Besides, I can't speak for Jeff, so I won't even try."

"Wouldn't fairer economic policies make things better for everyone?"

The lawyer leaned forward. "If you mean policies that benefit Americans, sure. But I'm talking about Americans, not Jews or Mexicans or Muslims. Or blacks."

Kaufmann raised his eyebrows. "African Americans aren't Americans?"

"Don't get me started."

\* \* \*

"Ron, I need your help," said Mariam.

She had the chief's personal number, and he had answered on the first ring.

"What's the problem?"

Somehow his gravelly voice seemed reassuring.

"My daughter is missing."

"Missing? How long?"

"Since yesterday morning. Or Saturday night, actually. She never came home."

"What was she doing on Saturday night?"

Mariam sighed. "Attending a party. But we don't—I mean, it's a new high school, new friends."

"So you don't know what happened at the party?"

She shook her head even though she knew the chief couldn't see her. "No. Of course we should have talked to the parents, made sure it was a good family, but—I don't know—we were busy with Ramadan. It slipped our minds. We never expected something like this."

"No, of course not," said the police chief. "I'll get my boys right on it."

"Thank you, Ron. Ahmed and I—we really appreciate it."

"Don't worry, Mariam. We'll find her."

\* \* \*

There was a break in rehearsal. Jonathan and the other cast members were standing around the stage or checking their phones for messages when Mr. Blankenship started telling them about the "blood libel" myth. He didn't like to waste an opportunity to teach, and some of the crew members listened in too. The notion of a Jewish moneylender demanding a "pound of flesh" penalty for nonpayment appears in Shakespeare's main source, an Italian story, their teacher explained, but the idea may have had a broader basis. In the Middle Ages, the belief spread throughout Europe that Jews used the blood of Christian children in the making of matzos for Passover. The idea was both so absurd and so horrific that some of the students laughed nervously. In the English city of Lincoln, a child's body was discovered in a well belonging to a Jewish man. Under torture, the man supposedly confessed that Jews had collaborated to crucify the child, and he and eighteen other Jews were executed. All Jews were soon expelled from the country, and the child was celebrated in popular folksongs as a Christian martyr. The story became well-known, and presumably (their teacher said) Shakespeare was familiar with it—and others like it.

"What if Shylock were a Muslim?" shouted someone in the back row.

It was Cody Rasmussen, the outspoken young man from American History class, wearing his trademark tweed sports coat. Classes were over for the day, and along with a few other students, he was evidently doing his homework in the auditorium.

"Sorry?" said Mr. Blankenship.

Jonathan glanced over at Zach, who played the part of Shylock, but he just shrugged. Olivia, the Terre Rouge student who had the role of Shylock's daughter, spoke up.

"Muslims don't charge interest. It's more like a shared investment."

"I'm talking about the pound of flesh," replied Cody. "If Shylock was a Muslim, he could threaten to cut off Antonio's head if he didn't pay up. You know, like ISIS. How much does a head weigh anyway?"

Nadim, the other Terre Rouge cast member, walked to the front of the stage. "Those people aren't real Muslims. They're fanatics."

There were a few whispers onstage.

Mr. Blankenship tried to intervene. "Okay, folks, break is over. Let's get back to rehearsal."

Cody pressed his point. "According to them, you're not a real Muslim. They may be fanatics, but they're fanatic Muslims."

Nadim came down from the stage and took a few steps toward Cody. "What kind of bullshit are you spouting?"

"It's not bullshit, and it's a fact that they like to cut off people's heads. They seem to get a kick out of it."

"Hey, man," Nadim said as he walked up the aisle, "I don't like you, but I don't want to chop off your head."

Cody snickered. "I appreciate that."

The cast, the crew, and the random students who had been catching up on their homework were buzzing. Shylock a Muslim? A Muslim moneylender? Well, thought Jonathan, one thing wouldn't change. The ill will of the merchants and traders in Venice.

"Okay, that's enough," said Mr. Blankenship. "We have a play to put on, and I'm going to ask everyone who's not part of the cast or the crew to leave."

There was some grumbling, but most of the extras lazily began to gather up their belongings.

"Now!" said Blankenship.

\* \* \*

Mariam was sitting across from a police sergeant named Khoury in the large, elegant living room of their house.

"You sure you don't want a cup of tea?"

"No, thank you," said the sergeant.

The sofa and loveseat were shrouded in white slipcovers. Together with the white curtains, polar-bear-white rug, and pale lighting, the shrouded furniture lent an arctic chill to the room. Even Mariam could feel it. She pulled her sweater closer around her shoulders.

"I'm sure something has happened to her. This is not like her."

Khoury nodded. "How old is your daughter?"

"Thirteen. I mean fourteen. She just turned fourteen."

"Is this the first time she's stayed out all night?"

"What? What are you talking about?"

"We have to cover all our bases, Ms. Ali. Teenagers don't always play by the rules."

"This is the first time," said Mariam, her voice shaking slightly. "The first time my daughter has not slept in her own bed."

"She's never slept over at a girlfriend's house? Gone to a slumber party?"

Mariam shook her head. "We are a close-knit family. The children have always stayed close to home."

"I see," said Khoury, taking notes. "Have you tried calling her friends?"

"Yes, of course. But...she has new friends now."

"Have you tried the hospitals?"

"Hospitals?"

"In case she was in an accident."

A sudden jolt of fear hit Mariam in the pit of her stomach. "Umm, no, we haven't checked any hospitals."

"Don't worry. We'll look into it."

Mariam felt that she and the police officer were straining to talk to each other across the great expanse of the coffee table.

"So she doesn't answer her phone?" the sergeant was saying.

"No. Her voicemail is full."

"Do you mind if we look at her computer?"

"No, of course not. Whatever will help."

"And she hasn't seemed depressed lately?"

Mariam shook her head again. The strain of her daughter's disappearance, the relentlessness of the sergeant's questions, and the emptiness of her stomach were giving her a headache.

"Anxious, upset, out of sorts?"

She sighed. "Sergeant Khoury, do you have children?"

Now the sergeant shook his head.

"Teenagers are moody," she explained. "You say yes, they say no. You say heads, they say tails. It's impossible to keep up with them."

Khoury wrote down something in his notebook. Then he looked up.

"What about boys? Does your daughter have a boyfriend?"

"Sergeant, this is impossible. Excuse me for being so personal, but are you...a Muslim?"

"My parents are Christian. Lebanese."

"Well, we are a Muslim family. Yasmin is only fourteen."

Khoury nodded. "Didn't mean to offend you, Ms. Ali, but I want to help you find your daughter."

"I understand."

"So what was she doing at this party?"

Mariam started to answer, but a sudden spasm of helplessness came over her and she fought to hold back tears. Sergeant Khoury waited while she struggled to regain her composure.

\* \* \*

"I'm a friend from the *masjid*," Aisha was telling the receptionist at Dr. Ali's clinic, where people paid what they could and no one was turned away. Located in an asphalt-and-concrete strip mall next to a heavily trafficked street, the clinic was just a small rented office with skewed Venetian blinds on the windows and peeling linoleum on the floors.

"The doctor is busy," said the affable receptionist, "but I'll see if he has a moment. Would you like to have a seat while you wait?"

Aisha sat down in the crowded waiting room and picked up a copy of a health-and-wellness magazine that featured articles on losing weight, protecting one's skin from the sun, and getting regular exercise. Fasting during daylight hours for a month, wearing a scarf over her head, and going places without a car couldn't hurt, she figured. Around her, old people with hidden ailments leafed through golf and Oprah magazines, and mothers in *hijab* comforted young children with nasty colds.

When she got bored, she gazed at striped and multicolored fish swimming endless loops in their tiny aquarium. Her watch said four o'clock. She had been waiting for more than half an hour, but of course she didn't have an appointment and she wasn't sick.

When Dr. Ali finally appeared, a black-and-silver stethoscope hanging over his white lab coat, there were bags under his large, sympathetic eyes and he looked more harried than usual.

"Mrs. Hassan," he greeted her, smiling broadly, "what can I do for you?"

She apologized for bothering him while he was at work but added, "Is there somewhere where we can talk?"

"Of course."

He led her to a closet-sized though neatly organized office, and she sat down on a metal folding chair on the opposite side of his desk.

"I'm doing a series on the different dimensions of our community, the different sorts of people who are part of it, and I just did a story on the Ghazal family, who were recently evicted from their home."

The doctor nodded, absently.

"Well, it seems that somebody bailed them out. Took over their mortgage, gave them a no-interest loan they could pay back over a long period of time."

Ali shrugged. "It's wrong to make money off of one's fellow Muslims."

"Still, many do it."

"During the Holy Month of Ramadan, we are called upon to give alms, to do what we can to aid the poor."

With the low-cost medical clinic that was not likely to generate much of a profit, the unpaid position at the *masjid*, the underpaid City Council job, and the expensive house in the hills, Aisha wondered how Dr. and Mrs. Ali made their money. But the good doctor also had private patients and was rumored to have made a killing in real estate investments.

"So I heard what you did—the wonderful thing that you did—and I thought I should write a profile of you for the paper. It would be a great addition to our series."

Dr. Ali frowned, his graying moustache turning down at the corners. "Mrs. Hassan, I'm a private man. I don't crave publicity."

Really? He was president of the mosque, the face of the Islamic community at many public functions, the husband of a prominent city official.

He stood up. She started to speak, but he cut her off. "Look, I have patients to see. Please find someone else to write about." Seeing her expression, he softened. "I—I'm sorry. The thing is—my daughter—we don't know where she is."

"What do you mean?"

"She's gone, disappeared. Mariam and I"—he threw his hands up—"we're very worried."

"Have you called the police?"

He nodded.

Aisha reached out and put a hand on his arm. "Don't worry. I'm sure she'll turn up soon."

\* \* \*

"Nice of you to join us," the coach told Jonathan as he raced onto the field.

He had sprinted over to the gym after rehearsal, hurriedly put on his cleats and pads, and left one of his shoes untied. In the next hour, he practiced taking handoffs, did backwards running drills, and participated in five or six plays from scrimmage.

Afterwards, while he and the other guys were showering, a large linebacker known as Big Ben Kosinski said, "I've got an idea."

"Uh-oh," yelled somebody above the sound of water pounding on the tiles. "Ben's got an idea."

"No, seriously," said Ben. "Let's go over to Rouge and do some scouting."

The big game with their crosstown rivals was on Friday, though Jonathan would have to miss the game because it was also the opening night of the play.

"They won't be there," Jonathan shouted over the noise. "They're practicing at night."

"Why the hell would they do that?" said a skinny wide receiver named Jason.

"Ramadan," Jonathan explained, relaying what his father had told him. "They can't eat or drink till after sundown. No Gatorade in the afternoon."

"That's weird," muttered Ben.

Jonathan shrugged.

A few minutes later, as they were standing by their lockers getting dressed, Ben said, "I think we should check it out for ourselves. Who's in?"

"No, really," said Jonathan. "They won't be there."

"Who's in?" the big linebacker repeated.

Jason raised his hand. Seeking more recruits, Ben looked over at Carlton Edwards, the only African American member of the team.

"Okay," said Carlton. "Why not?"

Jonathan finished dressing and left the locker room ahead of the others. Hoping to catch a ride, he poked around the halls for a few minutes to see if Zach was still around. But the corridors were empty, and he dragged his backpack out to the parking lot. Most of the cars were already gone, but suddenly a luxury silver SUV careened around the aisle and squealed to a stop two feet from him. A door opened, and Big Ben's long arm reached out and reeled him in.

"What the fuck?"

"C'mon, man," said the linebacker. "You got nothing better to do."

Jason was behind the wheel. They rolled out of the parking lot and drove the five miles to the other school amid jokes and chatter. Jonathan tried to tell them it was a wild goose chase, but they weren't convinced.

Stray blades of grass peeked through the asphalt parking lot of Terre Rouge High School, a two-story brick shoebox that looked nothing like Terre Noire's polished pavilions. It was almost seven o'clock, the sun was sinking rapidly, and the school looked gloomy. The football field—bare in spots, yellowing in others—was deserted, though a single runner was doggedly circling the track.

Carlton, a first-string running back, picked up a pebble and flung it down the field.

"I told you," said Jonathan.

"Hey!" Ben yelled to the young man on the running track. "Where's the football team?"

Either the kid didn't hear him or he didn't want to answer.

Disappointed, the four of them turned around and shuffled back toward the car, but the linebacker stopped to draw a stick-figure version of a camel on the outside wall of the gym. Jason laughed. "Jesus," Jonathan said to himself.

They were driving out of the parking lot when they spotted two cute girls in headscarves—one pink scarf, one purple—walking across the parking lot. Ben lowered his window and whistled. The girls giggled but turned away. Jason made a wide turn and followed them, slowly.

"Hey, guys," said Jonathan. "I need to get home."

Jason asked the girls if they were free that weekend. The girls picked up their pace.

"C'mon, fellas. It's getting late."

Ben told him to lighten up.

"Hey, girls," the big guy called out the window. "Wanna go for a ride?"

The girl in the purple headscarf said something under her breath to her friend.

"We'll have you back in time for evening prayers."

Jason and Carlton laughed.

The young woman in the pink scarf turned around and shouted, "This isn't your school! Why don't you go after the girls at your own school?"

"'Cause they're too easy," Ben shouted back.

Jason raced the engine and peeled out of the lot. Jonathan slid down in the back seat and hoped no one could see him.

\* \* \*

Returning home after his visit to Day Shoots, Kaufmann opened the mailbox, collected the usual assortment of bills and junk mail, and brought it inside.

Somewhere amid the electric bill, a clothes catalog, and a personal message from Robert Redford about environmental problems was a familiar-looking, lightly perfumed envelope. He ripped it open and discovered, sure enough, that it was another letter from the anonymous "ftirl" who had stood him up the previous weekend. Or maybe he had stood her up.

"Sorry we missed each other," the letter began.

It went on to suggest getting a bite to eat at Jake's on Friday night. "I would really like to see you," the letter-writer assured him. Jake's? It was a hangout frequented by off-duty cops and beat reporters from the *Register-Guardian*. "But if you don't like Jake's, we can try someplace else. Maybe that new Mediterranean place. Levant."

Levant? Mediterranean? Wasn't that the kind of restaurant Aisha would pick?

"Just give me a signal," the letter concluded.

A signal? What kind of signal? As usual, there was no signature or contact information. And if it was Aisha, why was she playing these cat and mouse games with him? All she had to do was call him.

\* \* \*

95

When Jamal pushed open the door to his apartment, Muhammad opened his eyes without meowing and gazed sleepily from his perch on the threadbare sofa. As the cab driver deposited his keys on the mail table and emptied his pockets of forgotten grocery lists, stray notes, and copies of the credit card receipts he had prepared for his customers, the cat slowly raised himself on his scrawny legs and stretched his limber body.

Finally, Muhammad sidled over to what the cat probably took to be the large friendly creature that always seemed to be there when he woke up from his naps, meowed three times, and rubbed his fur against his ankles. Jamal scratched him between the ears, murmuring, "Good boy, Muhammad. Good boy."

The cat had never cared much for Henry. He used to hide under a chair and pounce on the intruder. When Jamal and Henry lay together semi-naked on the hard bed with the lumpy mattress, Muhammad would jump between them and try to keep them apart, scratching Henry in the process. But Henry didn't mind. He just laughed off the cat's antics and stroked Jamal's bare skin.

"God is great," Jamal declared now while rubbing the cat's belly, "but life is hard, so it doesn't really matter."

He opened a can of cat food and spooned it into a dish. Muhammad sniffed it warily and then started eating, his tongue making noisy smacking sounds. Jamal sat down at the kitchen table and sifted through the day's mail. A phone bill, a notice of a neighborhood meeting, a flyer from a local grocery store, something from his landlord. Nothing from Henry.

He opened the refrigerator and peered inside. It was past sundown, so he didn't have to feel guilty about eating dinner. But except for a few slices of bread, a small jar of tahini, an old hard piece of cheese, and an eggplant which he didn't feel like dealing with, the refrigerator was empty. He got some crackers out of the cupboard, spread some tahini on it, and sat down again at the table.

As it turned out, the landlord was raising his rent. Jamal was willing to pay more to stay in the tiny apartment with the cockroaches that were polite enough to come out only at night and the view of the stunted lemon tree in the back yard that, along with the empty bottles and forgotten trash cans, reminded him of the back alleys of the refugee camp of his youth. But the rent increase was a whopping three hundred dollars, and the landlord—pleading financial uncertainties, investment losses, the rising cost of repairs, and so on and so forth, as if he were worse off than Jamal—threatened to evict him if he didn't comply. What he didn't mention was the prospect that he could sell the building for a handsome profit if he could just get rid of pesky tenants like Jamal.

Licking his chops, the cat waltzed over to the table and hopped into the taxi driver's lap. Jamal scratched the top of his head. Muhammad started purring.

Too bad he couldn't move in with Henry. Under the circumstances, he didn't know whether to try to find another place or jump out of a window. Maybe he should write a poem about the situation. It wouldn't bring in any money, but it might make him feel better.

He took out his notebook and cleared a place at the table. The first lines that popped into his head were...

*When they come to evict me*
*I will steal one last glance at the lemon tree*
*arrange my furniture on the sidewalk*
*prop the bed frame against the kitchen table*
*a matchbook under one of its feet*
*the poetry table I call it*
*where my best writing gets done*
*and the nightstand with the books of poetry on it*
*more poetry to warm the soul and ward off doubt*
*not to mention the mattress sticky with love*

# Tuesday: The List

Kaufmann was standing in the kitchen with a cup of black coffee in his hand when his son shuffled in sleepily and grabbed a box of cereal from a cabinet.

"Morning," said the detective.

"Mrng," Jonathan grunted.

"Hey, how was that party Saturday night?"

Jonathan opened the refrigerator and took out a carton of milk. "'Kay."

"You went with Zach?"

Jonathan nodded. He poured the cereal and the milk into a bowl and sat down to eat.

"Meet anyone else there?"

Jonathan shrugged.

Kaufmann finished the coffee in his cup and said, "Practice today?"

With his mouth full of cereal, Jonathan more or less nodded.

"Well, see you tonight."

\* \* \*

Khoury didn't want to attract attention to himself. Wearing an ironed blue shirt and broken-in jeans, he could pass for a hip young teacher or an older brother of one of the students. The principal had let him use a small, spartan conference room off the gym to interview some of the missing girl's friends, but either they weren't close friends with the girl or they weren't revealing much.

The next one to enter the room was a heavyset ninth grader named Andrea Banacek. He introduced himself and said he wanted to ask her a few questions about Yasmin Ali.

"Why? Is there anything wrong?" She fiddled with her books.

"Have you heard that there is?"

Andrea's eyes opened wide. "No, but she wasn't in class today."

"She hasn't checked in with her parents lately, and we want to make sure she's all right."

The young woman nodded.

"How long have you known Yasmin?"

"Just since the start of school. A month."

"And you two became friends?"

"Yeah, kind of. We're both in beginning Spanish, and we hang out together in the cafeteria sometimes."

"Were you at the big party last Saturday night?"

Andrea blinked a couple of times. "No." The sergeant waited, and the young woman continued, "I wasn't invited, and anyway I don't go to parties much."

Khoury jotted down the information.

"Yasmin seems to be well-liked."

Andrea nodded.

"Does she have any, uh, enemies? Mean girls who decided to pick on her? Boys she might have rejected?"

The young woman shook her head. "She's just fun to be around. I can't see why people wouldn't like her."

"Hmm," said Khoury. "What about the fact that she's Muslim? There aren't many Muslims here at Terre Noire, are there?"

"Muslim? Is she Muslim? I never thought about it."

* * *

Brodsky found a parking spot near Lincoln Park, a quiet place where he often ate lunch. He attached a leash to Anton's collar, grabbed his brown bag lunch and a cold thermos from the glove compartment, and shut the door of the taxi. He trudged along the path with the dog at his heels and sat down on a vacant green bench, Anton nestling beside him.

The park wasn't crowded. A few toddlers were being pushed on swings by young mothers wearing headscarves. Two boys were shooting baskets. An older man and a younger were playing some kind of board game, maybe checkers. The sky was clouding over.

The bag contained a lunch of herring, onions, and crackers, the same lunch that his wife Elena used to prepare for him every day for years. He gave some of the herring to Anton, who wolfed it down in a couple of quick bites.

Just then a young woman in a long dress glided by on a simple, no-gear bicycle with upright handlebars and a basket in the front. He wondered how she managed to avoid getting her clothes caught in the chain. The sight of the woman on the bike reminded him of the bicycle that Sasha wanted for his birthday. Elena knew they couldn't afford it, but she spoiled Sasha and kept prodding him to make it happen.

One day, an overcast day just like this one, he had been eating his lunch in a park very similar to the one he found himself in now, when he spotted a bicycle— a ten-speed with shiny red metal parts—resting in a bike rack under a tree whose leaves were gently swaying in the wind. Nearby, children were playing on the playground equipment. Their mothers (and one father) were keeping an eye on them, sending them flying on the swings or catching them at the bottom of the slides. No one was looking at the bike. Brodsky walked over to it, with Anton trotting after him, and examined it more closely. It didn't have a lock. He walked back to his bench and went back to eating his lunch. No one came to claim the bike.

Dark clouds were massing overhead that day. Perhaps worried that it was going to rain, a couple of the mothers left, taking their children with them.

Brodsky had gotten up and returned to the bike rack. He looked around. His hands were sweating and his heart was pounding, but no one was paying any attention. He climbed onto the bike. No one took notice even though it was a child's bike and he was much too big for it. Anton started growling, but he signaled for the dog to stop. After a dizzying moment of indecision, he rode off with his legs scraping the ground and the bicycle's wheels wobbling. Anton followed at a steady pace. Later, like a criminal returning to the scene of the crime, he went back to reclaim his taxi.

Now Anton was nuzzling his leg, asking to be petted. He reached down and stroked his furry head. The dog sighed contentedly.

Brodsky dug an old tennis ball out of his pocket and tossed it onto the grass. Anton quickly loped after it, picked it up with his mouth, and brought it back to his master, his tongue hanging out, his eyes looking up at him adoringly.

"You think life is good, hah, Anton?"

He threw the ball further, and the dog retrieved it again.

"What you know, old friend? What you know?"

* * *

Jonathan and Becky were jogging around the track along with thirty other sweaty high school students in their coed PE class. Black clouds had appeared in the sky. Despite the hills that rose up behind the school and offered some protection, the wind was beginning to whip across the grassy football field.

Jonathan wore an oversized sweatshirt, a pair of baggy sweatpants, and the same beat-up sneakers he had worn to school that day, while Becky seemed comfortable in a loose T-shirt and snug shorts.

"You ready for opening night?" she panted.

He was listening to music while he ran, but now he pulled out the earbuds.

"Uh, I guess. I'm trying not to think about it." Her part—the clever and resourceful Portia, who outwits Shylock and hoodwinks her future husband for the fun of it—was far bigger and more important than his. "How about you?"

"Well, I'm trying to channel my character. She wouldn't be scared. She'd be cool no matter what you threw at her."

Jonathan took off his sweatshirt. Despite the wind, he was starting to sweat.

"Hey," he said, a little out of breath, "did you ever hear Allison talk about a list?"

Becky angled her head to look at him. "A list?"

"Yeah. Does it have something to do with those photos on her Facebook page?"

Becky took a few more strides before replying. "What photos?"

He glanced over at her, questioningly.

"Okay," said Becky, taking a deep breath, "I'll tell you what I've heard. There *is* a list. It's a slut list."

"What?"

"A slut list. It's a list of girls who tart themselves up, get high on E or opioids, and, well—"

Jonathan didn't say anything.

"It's not what it sounds like. I mean, girls kill to get on it."

Jonathan felt he was in over his head. "Uh, why?"

"It's a way to get in with the popular crowd."

"Popular?"

"Not with guys. With girls."

Now Jonathan felt as if his head were spinning. He slowed his pace.

"I don't get it."

"Well, here's how it works. The senior girls—the popular ones—get together and decide which first-years they want in their clique. They put those girls on the list."

Jonathan's legs were getting tired. A few cold raindrops fell on his face. "So what happens when you make the list?"

"You have to go through this, like, initiation or whatever. To prove you're a slut."

Other runners jostled them as they straggled toward the finish. The rain was starting to come down.

"And how do you do that?"

Becky looked at him. "I think you can guess."

"Tell me."

"Well, they have to perform, like, sexual acts on guys. That's their initiation."

It was like those gang initiations where boys barely into their teens had to attack people—maybe even kill them—just to prove they could. This was a gang initiation for girls. A clique initiation.

The early autumn sky was black. As the rain poured down, the runners staggered through the finish line. Most just kept on running toward the locker rooms, but a few collapsed onto the track and lay sprawled out in the rain.

Jonathan and Becky stood still, their hands on their knees, trying to catch their breath. He thought he understood the idea of the slut list, but *why me?*, he wondered. *Was he on some other list? Or was it just his lucky day?*

Her T-shirt, getting soaked, was clinging to her well-proportioned breasts. A single, prolonged shiver ran through her from head to toe, and she sprinted inside.

\* \* \*

Farid and the plainclothes policeman walked along the street as the cop, wearing a baggy gray-green sports jacket and a loose tie, munched on a Big Mac. A brief squall had threatened to flood the area, but now the sun was peeking out and a patch of blue sky was visible.

"Everything okay at home?"

Farid shrugged. "I already told you. My sister—she's a brat. My dad threatened to send her back home. To, like, straighten her out."

"What did she do?"

"Shrieked like a baby and ran into her room."

The policeman ate another bite of his hamburger. "Sorry to eat in front of you, kid. I know you're fasting."

Farid waved off the apology. "No worries."

"What about the word on the street? Have you heard anything?"

It wasn't just his sister's disappearance he was asking about. Farid was a mosque crawler, an irregularly paid informant who had been recruited when he got into trouble over a drug bust. He had been smoking pot for a few foolish months in high school, selling a little to finance his own purchases, and he had made the mistake of selling to an undercover policeman near the children's slides in Lincoln Park. It was his second offense, after he had shoplifted some sneakers when he was still in middle school and old enough to know better.

"No, nothing. People are tired from fasting, from waking up early, going to prayers, and making big family meals. They're not interested in causing trouble."

Down at the station the cops had given him a choice—plead guilty, pay a fine, maybe spend a year in juvy, or go scot-free and become a mosque crawler. The year in juvy didn't scare him; telling his father did. He chose to work for the cops.

"Mnn," said the cop. "What about Friday prayers? The weekly sermon?"

"The imam talked about doing your own thing, joining a convent if you have to. I mean, it wasn't *jihadi* or anything."

The plainclothes police officer finished his Big Mac and threw the empty wrapper onto the steet. "A convent? What did he mean?"

"I don't know, but some people might have taken it the wrong way."

* * *

The cafeteria of Terre Rouge High School was virtually empty on that Tuesday in Ramadan, but Aisha had received permission from the principal to meet there with a few kids who had known Yasmin in the old days, when they all attended the same middle school. She didn't want to pry into the Ali family's affairs, but her editor told her it was her obligation as a reporter to investigate.

"Everybody says you're her oldest friend," Aisha began.

A small, shy girl, Haniya kept glancing at the gleaming but unattended cafeteria tables as if wondering where everybody was.

"So how did you two meet?"

Aisha was trying to keep her tone light and friendly, but the glare of the low-hanging fluorescent lights made the interview seem like an interrogation.

"My mom took me to the park to play when I was little. Her mom did the same. We started playing together, and our moms kept an eye on us and talked."

As usual, Aisha took notes. "So your parents are friends too?"

Haniya shook her head. "The only thing they had in common was us. Her parents had more money than we did. Her dad's a doctor, mine works for the post office. Her mom's on the City Council. Mine stays home and keeps track of me and my brother and my sisters. There's five of us overall."

"But you two hit it off."

Haniya adjusted her pale blue headscarf and nodded. "We, like, text each other all the time. I mean, we did, until this past summer."

"What happened this past summer?"

A cloud seemed to pass between the sun and the nearest window. "I don't know. Yasmin went to a couple of get-acquainted sessions for new students at Terre Noire, and she sort of forgot about us."

"So you haven't heard from her in a while?"

"No. Is she all right?"

"I'm not sure," said Aisha. "Is she?"

Haniya seemed confused by the question. "I told you, I haven't talked to her in, like, ages."

"Well," the reporter explained, "her parents haven't heard from her in a few days, so they're getting worried."

The young woman fiddled with her scarf. "That sounds scary."

Aisha tried to reassure her, then asked for the names of some of Yasmin's other friends.

\* \* \*

The young man was shooting hoops at a backboard in the driveway of his family's house. The ball bounced off the rim and rolled through a puddle toward Kaufmann, who was walking up the drive. He picked it up, dried it off on his brown corduroy pants, took a few dribbles, and tried a shot of his own. By some chance it went in.

"Do you have a minute to talk, Haroun?"

"Uh, who are you?"

"Ezra Kaufmann of the Terre Nouveau Police. We're talking to people in the community."

The young man, tall and thin like a giraffe on stilts, hit a twenty-foot jumper. "About what?"

"Nothing in particular. Just trying to get to know folks. And trying to show them the face behind the badge."

"Yeah, well, okay."

"I understand you're pretty religious."

Haroun took another jump shot and said, "I follow the five pillars of Islam." He was wearing a sweaty T-shirt and long shiny basketball shorts that reached down almost to his knees.

"So you're fasting right now?"

"Of course."

He passed the ball to the detective, who shot again and missed badly.

"But you're not praying."

"I pray five times a day. It's not time for prayer." He spoke with what sounded like a hint of a French accent.

"You're on the basketball team?"

Haroun nodded, then tossed the ball to Kaufmann. "Wanna play a game of HORSE?"

"Okay. You first."

The young man set up on an imaginary free throw line, took a few preliminary dribbles, and swished it. He handed the ball to Kaufmann, who stepped to the line, took a deep breath, and let fly. The ball bounced off the backboard and fell in.

Haroun found a spot at the edge of his stepmother's flower garden, jumped a little off the muddy ground, and sent the ball soaring toward the hoop in a perfect parabola. It rattled around for a few seconds but dropped in. Kaufmann tried to duplicate the shot, heaving instead of jumping, and missed.

"You win," said the detective.

"We won't keep score," said the gangly youth. "Square up next time. You're off balance."

Kaufmann laughed. "I know I'm off balance. I need to work on that."

Haroun took a few dribbles toward the hole and dunked the ball.

"Is that your shot?" asked Kaufmann.

"You can do a layup if you want."

"Okay." He dribbled toward the basket and let the ball kiss the backboard. Panting slightly, he said, "I gather you're more religious than a lot of Muslims."

Haroun stopped shooting. "There is no more religious or less religious. Either you follow the dictates of Islam or you don't."

"But some people are, let's say, more strict and some people less so."

The young man held the ball at his side and didn't say anything.

"So how did you become one of the stricter ones?"

Haroun shrugged. "My father was a fishmonger in Morocco. The fish was always fresh, and the price was always fair. In France, he became a dishwasher. The money they paid him was not enough to feed him or his family. When we came here, he got a job as a fry cook at McDonalds. The pay was worse. Even though it was *halal*, he never ate the food at the McDonalds, and he never took us to eat the food at the McDonalds. He always pointed to the Qur'an and said there is more nourishment in the Holy Qur'an than there is in a Big Mac. Or a thousand Big Macs."

"But aren't there many interpretations of the Qur'an and of Muhammad's *hadith*?"

The youth shook his head. "There is only one Qur'an, and many who say they are following the teachings of the Holy Book have not read it in the original Arabic. Not all of it."

"You have?"

"No, but I listen to those who have."

"So," said the detective, "what does the Qur'an say about basketball? Is it permissible to play basketball during the Holy Month of Ramadan?"

Haroun responded without hesitation. "Of course. As long as it doesn't interfere with the commands to fast, to read as much of the Qur'an as possible, to give alms, and so on."

The detective nodded. "If you don't mind my asking, do you have a picture of your father?"

The young man shifted the ball from his left hand to his right. "My father died five years ago."

"I know. I'm sorry."

Haroun raised his eyebrows.

"I just wondered whether you kept any photos of him. To remember him by."

"Of course. I love my father and honor his memory."

"But doesn't the Qur'an say it is wrong to make representations of human beings—or other animals—since only Allah can do that?"

Haroun bounced the basketball a couple of times. It was wet and dirty. "That doesn't mean photographs. It means paintings and drawings."

"Really? Why?"

"Because a camera only records what Allah has created. It doesn't attempt to create new things."

"And a painting does?"

Haroun muttered something under his breath. "Detective, you need to go now. I have to pray."

"What about a Rorschach test?" He knew he was going out on a limb, but he wanted to see how the kid would react. "A few lines and squiggles that might or might not look like…something. Does that violate the commandment?"

The young man started walking toward the house. The sun had disappeared behind the clouds again.

"Or a child's drawing of a face, a few circles and slashes that sort of make us think of a face?"

Haroun had reached the back door.

107

"You wouldn't blame a child for making something like that, would you, Haroun? And you wouldn't blame him if somebody painted a face on his face, would you?"

The door slammed, and the rain started falling.

\* \* \*

Jamal had fed Muhammad and was just sitting down to a dinner of ground lamb, tomatoes, and onions, sautéed in a skillet and stuffed into a warm pita, when he heard a vigorous knock on the door. The only people he was used to seeing were his lover, now ex-lover, and his wife, also ex-, and he was not expecting either of them.

He pushed his chair back from the kitchen table, crossed the living area of his small apartment, and opened the door.

Standing there in a jacket and tie, smoking a cigar, was his landlord, Dr. Ali.

"*As-salamu alaikum*," said Ali.

"*Wa alaikum as-salaam*."

"*Ramadan Mubarak*."

Jamal mumbled something in reply.

"Did you get the notice about the rent?" Ali continued between puffs on his cigar.

"You want another three hundred a month for this dump?"

"I'm prepared to make some improvements."

"Good to know, but I don't have the money."

Ali filled the hallway like a guest who didn't know when to leave, but Jamal didn't invite him into the apartment.

"You'll just have to find it," said the doctor.

Jamal could feel his blood pressure rising. Maybe the doctor could help him with that. Muhammad came up behind him and rubbed against his legs.

"Look, I've lived here for almost two years. I've always paid my rent on time, even though you raised it just after I moved in. But this is too much. I can't afford it. My fares are down. No one rides a real cab anymore. What do you want me to do?"

"You have friends, relatives? Parents? A wife?"

"I don't have anybody," said Jamal. "It's just me and the cat."

"Can I come in?" asked Ali.

"No."

"I insist. It's my apartment."

Jamal felt like putting his hands around the man's neck and choking him until the cigar popped out of his mouth like a cork from a bottle of champagne. Instead he picked up Muhammad, stroked his soft fur, and returned to the kitchen.

The two men sat down at the table. Jamal's dinner was getting cold. He knew he should offer the landlord something to eat, but he wasn't in a hospitable mood.

"Let's work something out," said Ali.

Jamal snorted. "Like what? You're going to loan me the money I need to pay the rent, and I will spend the rest of my life trying to pay it back?"

"That's a possibility. Or"—Ali puffed on his cigar, which was beginning to make Jamal sick—"we could make a deal."

"What kind of deal? You already own everything." He took a bite of his pita sandwich.

"Taxi driver deal. I freeze the rent, and you become my eyes and ears. An extra set, for when I'm not around."

"What are you talking about?"

Dr. Ali took the cigar out of his mouth and coughed hoarsely. "A child is shot. Who did it? Another child disappears. Where did she go? Who is responsible? How can this happen?"

The sweet, beautiful face of his own daughter flashed before his eyes. "Listen, I just drive a taxi. I don't listen to what my customers say. I don't follow them once they get out of the cab."

"You could start."

Jamal laughed. "Why not hire one of those unemployed religious fanatics who prowl the streets looking for trouble?"

Ali stubbed his cigar on one of Jamal's dishes. "Half of them work for the police. I need other people to watch over them."

"You mean spying?"

"Intelligence. Counter-intelligence. Call it what you want. Besides the usual lowlifes and petty crooks, the neighborhood is swarming with people who aren't what they seem—police informants, undercover cops, plainclothes whatevers. We need good, honest Muslims to spy on the spies."

Jamal sighed. "That's crazy. No one cares what goes on in Little Mecca because, despite some people's best efforts, nothing ever does. It's a dull place."

The doctor shrugged. "Enough talking. You agree to the deal, or you leave the apartment by the end of the month."

"It's the Holy Month of Ramadan," Jamal pointed out. "Not a good time to throw someone out on the street."

Ali nodded. "I meant the Western month. September."

Jamal frowned and took another bite of his now-cold food.

The doctor let himself out. "*Ramadan Mubarak,*" he said again.

\* \* \*

Kaufmann was driving home in a steady drizzle when he received a call from his partner on his Bluetooth-enabled phone.

"I just got a text from Schroeder," said Sergeant Khoury.

"Yeah?"

"It seems the kid is back in the hospital."

The windshield wipers were making a holy racket, and he could hardly hear what the sergeant was saying.

"The kid? The one who was shot?"

"That's right, boss."

"But he went home several weeks ago. I thought he was out of the woods."

"You know how these things are. Internal bleeding, damage to inner organs, pressure on the brain."

The detective spit out an epithet which he hoped his partner couldn't hear. "Do you have a medical degree, Sergeant Khoury?"

"No, sir. I just know what can happen."

"Fucking Christ."

"What did you say, boss?"

"I said, I hope the kid is all right."

"Me too," said Khoury.

# Wednesday: Photos

*He could hear his mom retching in the bathroom. He had stayed away from her because she was listless and depressed and no longer fun to be around. He had played video games and texted his friends and made plans for the weekend as if things would go on like they always had. Why didn't his dad tell him she was dying? Of course he had, but somehow he had tuned it out, refused to accept it. This time, in the dream, he knew what was happening.*

Jonathan flipped over in bed like a clumsy cat chasing its tail. Trying to shake his head free from the terrible memories, he suddenly opened his eyes and found himself awake in the middle of the night. A noise like a hammer was coming from far away. He wondered who would be hammering at that hour. The room was pitch black, his head felt like a bowling ball, and he knew there was no point in looking at the clock.

\* \* \*

Hours later, unshaven and sleepy-eyed, Kaufmann walked outside to get the morning paper. Wet leaves were strewn over the driveway, but the storm had passed and the sun warmed his face. He could hear birds singing in the nearby trees. It was almost enough to lift his spirits.

But not really. The little boy was back in the hospital, and they had done little to solve the case. Rachel had died. She couldn't hear songbirds or anything else. He and his son, the survivors, were barely speaking to each other.

He remembered a road trip, years ago, to a summer Shakespeare festival hundreds of miles away. Preoccupied with another tough case, he didn't want to go, but Rachel, who loved good books and live theater, insisted that it would be good for them to get away. Trying to save money, they had camped out in a wooded, hilly area several twisty miles outside of town. By the time they put up their tent, ate their rations, washed their metal dishes the old-fashioned way, with grass and dirt, and returned to town to watch the play, they were so exhausted that they slept through half of it. Which play was it, again? In any case, the show went off without a hitch. At this summer festival, no one picketed, no one was shot. After climbing back into the hills, finding their campsite, and crawling into their tent, they made love. Nine months later, their son was born. Maybe that was how Jonathan had acquired his interest in Shakespeare.

"Morning," said Kaufmann.

Jonathan, having shuffled into the kitchen on bare feet, mumbled some kind of sleepy response.

"How's the play going?"

"Good."

"What part do you play again?"

Jonathan rubbed his eyes and said, "Lorenzo."

Kaufmann drank some of the strong black coffee he had made.

His son added, "The guy who runs off with Shylock's daughter. It's a small part."

"No small parts, right?"

"If you say so."

He checked the messages on his phone. Khoury had lined up a meeting with Dr. Ali at his clinic. The doctor's daughter had gone missing, and Captain Schroeder had asked them to investigate. As if they didn't have enough on their plate already… Maybe the captain was taking them off the other case, and this was her way of easing them out.

Jonathan shut the refrigerator and said, "Hey, Dad—"

"Yeah?"

"I'll be home late tonight. Rehearsal."

* * *

The clinic was crowded with wizened old men, fresh-faced young mothers, and sniffling, red-eyed young children. The bright lights and gleaming white walls gave the office a reassuringly professional appearance, more or less like the police department headquarters downtown. The two policemen, trying not to look as out of place as they felt, leafed through *National Geographic* and *American Muslim* magazines. Kaufmann read an article about Ramadan in the latter. Just as one was not supposed to eat during the day, one was supposed to refrain from sexual relations. It was permissible to embrace one's spouse, however, as long as one was able to control oneself. He wondered what orthodox Jews, with their own elaborate rules and prohibitions, including wigs for married women to cover their hair and trips to the ritual baths to purify themselves after menstruation, would think of that.

The smiling receptionist stood over them. "The doctor will see you now," she said.

She ushered them into a back room where a shelf was lined with medical books and journals.

"So what have you found?" said Dr. Ali, whose thick eyebrows and fleshy face did not completely hide his wary eyes.

Sergeant Khoury said, "I've been talking to your daughter's friends, sir."

"And?"

"They're really concerned about her."

Ali sighed. "But they don't know what happened."

"We were hoping you could help with that."

"Me? How?" He looked to Kaufmann for help, but the detective let his partner take the lead.

"Tell us about your daughter's state of mind over the last few weeks."

"State of mind?"

"Happy, sad. Anxious, calm. Open, guarded."

Dr. Ali touched his stethoscope as if for good luck. "Yasmin has always been a happy girl."

"How did she feel about attending a new school?"

"Eager, excited."

"How was she handling the homework? The transition from middle school to high school can be daunting."

Kaufmann looked at his partner. As far as he knew, Khoury did not have any children.

"Yasmin doesn't have problems with schoolwork. She's a smart girl."

"What about social life? High school can be intense."

Ali frowned. "She seems to have made a lot of friends in a short time."

"And how do you feel about that?"

"Of course I am happy for her."

"Your wife suggested that you might have been a bit worried about her new friends." He added, "The drinking, the late hours, the greater intimacy with boys."

The doctor slammed his fist on the desk. "Drinking? Intimacy? Boys? Sergeant, we are Muslims! These words do not apply to our daughters."

While waiting for Ali to calm down, Kaufmann and Khoury exchanged glances.

The sergeant resumed, "Dr. Ali, we know you're worried about your daughter. We're just trying to help."

The doctor took a deep breath. "Yasmin is an intelligent young woman. I know she will make the right decisions in the end."

Kaufmann, trying to connect dots, said, "If you don't mind me asking, sir, what was your daughter doing when the shots were fired at the summer fair?"

The doctor's eyes narrowed. "The fair? She was off with her friends."

"Her friends?"

"Yes, they were listening to music."

"And you're sure about that?"

There was a knock at the door. The receptionist opened it a crack and told the doctor that his patients were waiting.

"You'll have to excuse me," said Ali, standing up.

"One more thing," said the detective. "What were you doing—when the shots were fired?"

The doctor frowned again. "Me? I was having a good time, enjoying the fact that other members of our community—Muslims and non-Muslims—were having a good time. Why did anyone want to spoil it?"

"That's what we'd like to know," said Kaufmann.

Halfway out the door, Ali turned back. "If you find out anything, whatever it is, call me immediately. Day or night."

* * *

"What do you think?" the detective asked his partner on the ride back to headquarters.

"Well, he's upset."

Khoury was driving the hulking, black-and-silver squad car, but so sedately he could have been a grandmother out for a Sunday drive.

Kaufmann watched the trees glide by, their pale green leaves just beginning to turn gold and brown. The doctor's missing daughter reminded him of the eerie experience of seeing his wife walking along the street, then vanishing. Missing, forever. It was a warm, sunny fall day, and he wished he could just contemplate the leaves turning color without thinking of the past or the future.

He turned back to Khoury. "Do you think he's hiding anything?"

The sergeant nodded. "Father and daughter aren't getting along. He's threatening to send her back home to get her under control."

"How do you know that?"

"The brother is working with us."

"What do you mean?"

"Mosque crawler. Informant. I heard the bit about the family from his handler."

Kaufmann whistled through his teeth. "You're kidding."

Khoury shook his head.

A light went off in the detective's brain. "Could someone be trying to get back at the brother through the sister?"

Khoury made a left turn. "He's undercover. No one knows."

"In theory."

"In theory."

"What about Dr. Ali? Maybe he already has shipped her back to Pakistan."

Khoury shook his head. "I already thought of that. Checked the airline passenger lists. Not to mention hospital admissions logs and police accident reports."

"Call me day or night? Do you think he meant it?"

The sergeant stopped at a red light, then turned right. "Either he's genuinely concerned—"

"Or he wants us to think he is."

Khoury nodded. They were almost at the station.

"The good doctor blows hot and cold," mused Kaufmann. "I'm not sure I trust him. He wants us to find his daughter, but he doesn't want to tell us he's been threatening her. Not physically, I suppose, but still." He switched gears. "Do you think he could have anything to do with the incident in the park?"

Khoury pulled into the parking garage. "Dr. Ali? He's a Muslim. Active in the community. President of the mosque."

"Maybe it was some personal dispute, something about money or power."

They sat in the car with the engine cooling down. The sun was out there somewhere, but the garage was dark.

"So," said Khoury, "a three-year-old child was shot because of a financial dispute?"

The detective shrugged. He knew he was grasping at straws. "Maybe there was a power struggle in the mosque, and Dr. Ali hired someone to scare someone…"

"And the kid just got in the way."

"Exactly."

\* \* \*

Chief Ron Bukowski was holding a press briefing in one of the conference rooms at City Hall. The audience consisted of curious city employees, several police officers, and a few reporters, including Aisha Hassan. The detective and his partner were standing in the back, sipping weak coffee out of styrofoam cups.

"I want to correct a serious misapprehension," said the chief, a lifelong cop with a sturdily upright posture and an impeccably neat uniform that he never seemed to take off. "Pankaj Mehta, the young boy who was shot a month ago in Lincoln Park, is doing fine. He's not back in the hospital." Kaufmann and Khoury looked at each other. "His mother, however, is. This has been a very stressful period for her, and she has taken her doctor's advice to enter the hospital to be treated for nervous exhaustion."

Richter, the beefy rookie, was also in the room. Kaufmann wondered what he was doing there. The rookie whispered something to a buddy, and the journalists started taking notes.

"We believe she is in good hands and just needs some rest. The family asks you to respect their privacy. At the same time, we're actively pursuing several leads in the case and are hoping to have something definite to tell you as soon as possible." The detective and his partner exchanged another glance.

Chief Bukowski made some further comments about the importance of bringing diverse segments of the community together. He mentioned the upcoming Eid celebrations, the Police Athletic League baseball playoffs, next month's Halloween Harvest Festival, and Friday's big game between the city's rival high school football teams. When he was finished, a few hands shot up.

"Chief," said a man whom Kaufmann believed to be a reporter from a local radio station, "how long is Mrs. Mehta expected to stay in the hospital?"

"A few days, a week. As long as it takes."

Aisha Hassan followed up. "Who's taking care of Pankaj?"

Bukowski checked with one of his aides before replying. "We believe Mr. Mehta is taking his son to work with him at the food cart site."

"You said you have several leads," said another reporter, perhaps from out of town. "Can you be more specific?"

"I'm afraid I can't give you details at this time. We don't want to compromise the delicate nature of our investigations."

Aisha jumped in. "Mr. Hampton, the leader of the group that was picketing the summer fair, was arrested for assaulting his wife. Are you continuing to investigate him and his group?"

"I can't comment on that directly. But we're not closing off any avenues."

"Doesn't this arrest indicate a propensity for violence? Isn't that an obvious red flag?"

The chief snorted. "Yes, it's a red flag. Any further questions?"

The man from the radio station said, "Are you convinced the shooting was an Islamophobic attack? Or are you looking into the possibility that it came from within the Muslim community?"

"As I said, we're not closing off any avenues. Everything's on the table."

There didn't seem to be any other questions. The clerks and other employees started to drift away, and the journalists folded up their notebooks.

But Aisha spoke again. "The observance of Eid, the end of Ramadan, is next week. It would bring some peace of mind to our community if you could announce some actual progress by then."

"Is that a statement or a question, Ms. Hassan?"

"Do you have any comment?"

"We're doing our best," said the chief. "And we appreciate the cooperation of all concerned."

* * *

On their way out of the building, the detective and his partner shook their heads over the chief's false assurances.

"He's just trying to cover his ass," said Kaufmann.

"He's going to get more flak if he doesn't produce results."

"So will we."

"So what now, boss?"

The detective took a deep breath. "I'm going back to the park. Try to see it with fresh eyes. Maybe find something that Forensics missed. You can come if you want."

Khoury shook his head. "I better work on the girl's disappearance."

"Any leads?"

"No, not really, but I'm tracking the brother, Farid. Maybe he'll lead us to the missing girl."

The sergeant headed off to the parking garage. The detective proceeded to the front entrance, where he crossed paths with Aisha.

"Chief Bukowski is pretty good at blowing smoke," she said, "isn't he?"

Kaufmann barely suppressed a smile. "Is that a statement or a question, Ms. Hassan?"

She smiled too, then asked him if he wanted to get a cup of coffee.

"Uh, sure." The park could wait.

It was past noon, and with the sun bearing down on them from overhead, the detective took off his rumpled sports jacket and carried it over his shoulder.

"You doing all right?" she asked, as if tension was visible on his face.

"Yeah, I'm fine. How about you?"

In the sunlight, her pale pink headscarf looked almost white. The pale color contrasted nicely with her brown hair, her olive skin, and her soft, brownish-green eyes. Was it permissible to notice an observant Muslim woman's beauty, or did that violate the spirit of the headscarf?

"I'm doing well, thank you. My daughter has started her last year of elementary school, so I'm bracing for big changes in the years ahead."

They had reached the door of the café. Wait, Kaufmann thought. Coffee? Starbucks? The woman who wrote those anonymous letters? Who had asked him out on another "date"? He sneaked a long sideways look at his companion and tried to guess what was going on inside her head.

"Can I get you something to drink?"

She shook her head. "Not for me, thanks. I'm fasting."

Kaufmann stopped in his tracks. "Of course. I forgot. But then—"

"You get something. I'll just grab a table."

"Why don't we go to Lincoln Park instead? It's a beautiful day, and I was going there anyway."

The reporter agreed, and they started walking.

* * *

"So," said the detective, "do you have any other kids?"

"No, just the one. My parents had six children and I don't have any family here, so it's a different experience for me. How about you?"

"Just one son. A junior in high school. Plays football, does drama, likes history."

"How is it—having a teenager?"

The detective sighed. "Jonathan was always a happy child. Could play by himself for hours. He did become more moody when he turned twelve or thirteen, but what really hurt—" They were passing through a neighborhood of shady, tree-lined streets. "We need to turn here," he said.

After about ten more paces, she said, "What?"

"Hmm?"

"What really hurt?"

Kaufmann shook his head. "It's too nice day. I don't need to talk about it."

"No, please. I'd like to hear about your family."

He smiled, ruefully. "What about you? What does your husband do?"

118

Now she shook her head. "He drives a taxi. But we're divorced. It happened a few years ago."

"Oh. I'm sorry."

"Don't be. He's a good father, but we turned out to be not very…compatible."

They had reached the entrance to the park. The Ferris wheel had been dismantled, but in the grassy meadow where it had stood, a number of boys were kicking around a soccer ball. Why weren't they in school?

The two of them sat down on a sea-green bench partly shaded by some old trees that still retained most of their leaves.

Kaufmann spoke first. "How well do you know Dr. Ali?"

Aisha turned toward him. "Pretty well. He's a fixture in the community. Much admired. He's active in the mosque, treats people at his clinic even when they can't afford to pay. I wrote a story recently about a family that was getting evicted from their house. Couldn't pay their mortgage. Evidently he heard about it and bailed them out."

"Sounds like a knight in shining armor."

"It was a loan, not a gift, but still…"

"Are there any, uh, politics in the mosque? Conflicts? How well do he and the imam get along?"

"Fine, as far as I know." The detective nodded. "Wait—I do remember some discussion when some of the women started talking to Ousmane about a separate prayer space."

A light breeze stirred the leaves above them.

"What kind of discussion?"

"The more conservative elders in the *masjid* were opposed to it. They thought the current arrangement was fine."

"You mean, keeping the women at the back of the bus?"

She gave him a quizzical look.

"Sorry," he said. "Not my place to criticize."

"It's okay. I'm grateful we have such an open-minded imam."

"And Dr. Ali? Is he grateful?"

Aisha paused for a moment. "He was one of those elders."

\* \* \*

The two of them sat quietly in the warmth of the dappled sun and the refreshing coolness of the late-summer breeze.

"There's something I wanted to ask you," said Aisha. "It's about the missing Ali girl."

News travels fast, thought the detective.

"There's a rumor going around about the party she attended."

"A rumor?" He thought reporters didn't put much stock in rumors.

"People say it was, you know, a wild party. Drinking, drugs, sex—what have you."

"Wait. She's only fourteen, isn't she?"

"I'm just telling you what people are saying."

"Who are these people? Were they there?"

"I don't know how the rumor started, but it's going around the neighborhood."

"Are you're planning to put this in a story?"

She shook her head. "Not until I can verify it. But wait, there's more. People are saying that photos were taken."

"Photos? You mean selfies?"

"Suggestive photos. Photos in which Yasmin appears."

Kaufmann mulled this latest bit of gossip. "So what did you want to ask me?"

"Whether it's true."

The detective took a deep breath. "To be honest, my partner's taking the lead on this case, and this is the first I've heard about any photos."

The soccer players shouted, and a chess player whose intense-looking face Kaufmann caught out of the corner of his eye made a move.

He picked up the thread. "Wild party. Suggestive pictures. Rumor. Maybe it's just a figment of nervous parents' imaginations."

She turned to him. "You mean traditional parents who might be especially nervous about wild parties?"

"Yes."

"Yes, of course. It's possible. It's just that—I'm worried. About the girl. As you say, she's only fourteen years old. My daughter is ten, and she'll be there soon enough."

The detective nodded. "I understand. My son just turned seventeen, but it's different for girls. Double standard and all that."

The reporter adjusted her long skirt. "Your wife—what does she think about bringing up a teenager?"

"She was a social worker, so she was always more patient and understanding than I was. Worked with children from very troubled homes. You know, drugs, domestic violence, all kinds of abuse."

"Was?"

"She died."

"Oh, I'm sorry."

"Yes, well…" His voice trailed off. "That was what really hurt Jonathan. Having his mother die when he was barely old enough to figure out what was happening."

"I'm sorry."

* * *

As rehearsal was about to begin that afternoon, Jonathan noticed Zach chatting with Olivia, one of the guest performers from Rouge. Flirting, more like it, since they were standing a couple of inches apart, laughing, she touching his arm to punctuate a point. But his attention was diverted when Nadim, the other Rouge student, ran into him.

"Hey, man," said Nadim, "how you doing?"

"Fine," said Jonathan. "Hey, Nadim, do you know Yasmin Ali?"

"Uh, sort of."

"Do you have any idea where she is?"

"Me? No. I haven't seen her the last few days."

"You went to the same middle school, right?"

"Yeah, but she's a freshman, isn't she? We didn't overlap." He was about to drift away when Nadim continued, "But my brother used to hang out with her brother. You want me to ask him?"

Jonathan nodded. "Sure. That'd be great."

Mr. Blankenship called the cast together, and the conversation broke up.

The students seemed more nervous this time around, maybe because opening night was only a couple of days away. In terms of their progress, it seemed like one step forward, two steps back. But Becky, in her role as Portia, appeared to be nailing her performance. She was haughty when she needed to be, clever when she had to use her wits, always regal. If he were in her suitor Bassanio's shoes, he might be falling in love with her.

In the play, things got ugly when—the merchant being unable to pay back the loan—Shylock insisted on claiming his pound of flesh, and Portia, disguised as a legal scholar, gave a beautiful speech on mercy, appeared to side with the moneylender, then came up with the angels-on-the-head-of-a-pin argument that Shylock would be liable if he shed a drop of "Christian" blood or cut out anything more or less than an exact pound of flesh. The "Jew"—an uncomfortable-looking

Zach—quickly backs off, and in the end the Duke spares his life but takes all his money and forces him to convert to Christianity. In fact, some of the money goes to his own character Lorenzo, the Christian guy who has run off with Shylock's daughter. All's well that ends well?

* * *

After quizzing several of Yasmin's classmates, Sergeant Khoury learned the name of the girl who had hosted the party on Saturday night. He caught up with her as she was playing field hockey on one of the athletic fields outside the high school.

They leaned against a fence during a break in the game.

"Yasmin. Yasmin Ali," said the sergeant, naming the girl who had gone missing.

"No, that doesn't ring a bell," said Allison, breathily, still panting from the exertion of running around the field. She was wearing a white shirt and navy-blue shorts.

"Other kids have said you two are friends."

"Friends? Why would I be friends with a freshman?"

"How did you know she was a freshman?"

Allison's eyes flicked open more widely. "You said she was new to the school."

Khoury wrote something in his notebook, more to intimidate the young woman in front of him than to record information. "So you're not sure who was or wasn't at your party?"

Allison shrugged. "It was a big party. People brought their friends."

"And your parents were cool with that?"

"Sure. Why not?"

"And they didn't mind alcohol being served? Marijuana being smoked?"

Allison frowned, then embarked on an answer. "I don't know anything about that, Sergeant. If somebody brought weed or sneaked in a bottle of booze, it's news to me."

"So, as far as you know, kids just drank lemonade and danced to golden oldies?"

Allison smiled. "Yeah, something like that. It was a fun party."

* * *

After Aisha left, Kaufmann started looking around the park—examining the area near the swings where the face-painters had set up shop, staking out the spot where the Ferris wheel had spun, poking holes in the dirt where the anti-Islamic activists had picketed.

But what was he looking for? Spent shells, discarded weapons, handwritten notes, incriminating fingerprints? Or just some trick of sound and sight, some accidental configuration of cloud and sunlight and children's cries that would jumpstart the sluggish thought processes of his tired brain.

If the shooter hadn't intended to hit either the food cart vendor or his three-year-old son, then who or what was the real target? Was Haroun Malouf or some other ultraorthodox Muslim aiming at one of the face-painters instead? Was some rabid Islamophobe firing at random into the crowd, hoping to send some sort of blunt message? In that case, the picketers, sealed off by a cordon of uniformed police, would have been a brilliant diversion. Or maybe it was a personal matter after all, but with Mehta or his son as the intended target. Maybe he had an enemy or a rival, someone who wanted to kill him or warn him or send a message to him by harming his most precious and most personal "possession." The child.

The detective found a long stick and stuck it in the ground at the point where the boy had been shot. Then he returned to the location of the phantom Ferris wheel and tried to re-imagine the sight line from the top of the wheel to the spot above Mehta's shoulders where the child might have been sitting. Had Forensics really examined every nook and cranny of every car? Wouldn't other riders have heard the shot or shots? Or was the noise drowned out by the chatter of the crowd, the sound of the musical performance, the creaking of the Ferris wheel itself? Maybe the riders heard the shots but thought they were fireworks. After all, no one had come forward. Another dead end.

A child squealed with joy as she slipped down a slide, and—wait! The idea sounded crazy, but what if Mehta's enemy was none other than his long-suffering wife? What if they were having marital troubles, financial difficulties, problems adjusting to a new culture—and the nervous exhaustion she was suffering from was really a nervous breakdown? A breakdown that made her blame her husband for everything that had gone wrong. What if she had hired someone to go after her husband and the child had gotten in the way? What if she was so angry at him that she would risk—or even consider—attacking her own child? Crazy, yes, but he had read about such things, and in his many years on the force he had come across stranger stuff.

He took a deep breath. At least he knew what to do next. Visit Padma Mehta in the hospital.

* * *

Jamal's taxi was empty. He was cruising through the streets of Little Mecca in search of a fare when the cars ahead of him slowed to a crawl. On the sidewalk, pedestrians were walking home or popping in and out of stores to purchase food for the evening meal or pick up a prescription at the drugstore, but there was no reason for heavy traffic on a Wednesday evening in September, even during Ramadan.

As he crept closer, he saw that two young women in pants and sneakers had stepped out of their car and were arguing with a young man who was himself wearing a sweatshirt, faded jeans, and incongruous burnt-orange tennis shoes. What were they arguing about? The precise time when it was permitted to break the day's fast? The length of the women's pants? The color of his shoes or theirs?

The young women got back into their car and drove off.

Inching forward, Jamal slowly brought his car to the crossing point.

"License," said the young man, not much older than a boy, in a bored monotone. His unlined face was adorned with a wispy beard and moustache.

"Who are you?" said Jamal.

"I need to see your driver's license."

"Is this some kind of joke?"

The boy took a deep breath and asked if he lived in the area.

Jamal muttered a mild curse and said, "A few blocks from here."

"This is your taxi?"

"Well, it belongs to the company."

"Step out of the car."

"Listen, *habibi*, I'm a taxi driver. You're costing me money. Do you need a ride somewhere?"

The young man waved his hand. "Step out of the car."

"I told you, I live here. I'm a Muslim, more or less. Nothing to worry about."

The lone sentry reminded him of militia checkpoints on the streets of Beirut during the civil war. The only thing missing was the Kalashnikovs. Whitman wouldn't have recognized it. But Whitman had lived through a Civil War of his own. He had tended sick and wounded soldiers as a hospital nurse. He wrote *Drum Taps* about his experiences. He might have witnessed draft riots, gang wars, and slave auctions. Sadly, the more things changed, the more they remained the same.

"Step out of the car, sir. Please."

"Well, since you asked so nicely…" Jamal opened the door and got out of the car. He glanced back at the row of vehicles lining up behind him and shrugged.

Meanwhile, the young man was rummaging around in the glove compartment. He emerged holding a magazine.

"What's this?"

"A magazine," said Jamal. "An art magazine."

It was a remnant of his life with Henry. The front cover displayed a bright, shiny painting of suburban tract houses that looked as real as a photograph. Of course it was a photograph—a photograph of a painting that looked like a photograph. Art, according to Henry.

The young man flipped through the pages.

"And this?"

He opened the magazine to a set of abstract paintings.

"Art," said Jamal. "It's an art magazine."

The young man continued to flip through the magazine, stopping at a section containing photos of nude men. His eyes opened wide.

"What is this?" he said.

"Art. Those are art photos."

The young man ducked back inside the car, removed the key from the ignition, and slipped it into his pocket. "Wait here," he said and ran off in his orange shoes to find someone who could tell him what to do.

\* \* \*

There was a break in rehearsal, and somebody said, "Let's call out for pizza." But Mr. Blankenship nixed that idea. He said it would spoil everyone's concentration and, anyway, they needed only an hour more to smooth out a couple of rough patches.

Jonathan was standing next to Becky, and it dawned on him that he could ask her to go out for pizza with him—just the two of them—afterwards. She was still dressed in the shapeless gray outfit that was supposed to denote a Renaissance legal scholar's robes. He cleared his throat and was starting to speak when Nadim approached.

"I talked to my brother."

"Yeah?"

"He said he hasn't run into Farid in years, but he still has his old number. You want it?"

Jonathan took the number and stepped outside the back door of the auditorium, which opened onto a corner of the parking lot. The sun had just gone down, but the asphalt, the trees, and the nearby football field were still bathed in soft light.

After four or five rings, someone answered.

"Farid Ali?"

"Who is this?" said Farid, gruffly.

"A friend of Yasmin's. From school."

"What do you want?"

"She hasn't been in class the last few days."

"So?"

"So," said Jonathan, "her friends are worried about her. She's not in any trouble, is she?"

There was a pause while the brother said something to someone and looked for a quieter place to talk. "Look, I'm at work. Do you have something you want to tell me?"

Jonathan watched a lone figure running around the track in the fading light. "No. I just want to know if she's okay."

"Okay? Yeah, I want to know that too."

\* \* \*

A nurse led the detective into the dark hospital room where Padma Mehta was sleeping. Her husband wasn't there—he was no doubt home with the child—and the room's other bed was empty. Kaufmann sat down on a white plastic chair and waited.

With her eyes closed, the young woman's smooth, round face seemed pretty and somehow sweet. Her breathing was light and even. In, out. In, out. Could she really have wanted to harm her husband or her son? Could the shock of having been transplanted to an alien culture have been so traumatic?

Her pale brown eyelids fluttered like twin butterflies. Perhaps she was dreaming. Was she dreaming of a park in late summer? Of revenge and retribution?

As twenty minutes slowly passed, the detective himself almost fell asleep, but the woman's eyelids gently began to open. After a couple of seconds of trying to orient herself, she suddenly raised her head.

"Who are you?" she said.

Kaufmann introduced himself, said he'd like to ask her a few questions.

She waved him away like an annoying mosquito. "No more questions. I came here to rest."

"Ms. Mehta, what were you doing when your son and husband were at the park?"

"I told you—"

"I promise you I'll leave you alone in a few minutes. We just want to find out who shot Pankaj."

The young woman slumped back down in the bed.

"Can you tell me what you were doing that day?"

She spoke in fits and starts, as if agitated. "I took a nap. I woke up. I started to make dinner." She sighed. "I had a headache. I lay down again to rest." She stopped, exhausted, then started up again. "Things were hard at work. I just needed"—she searched for the word—"a break."

"Does your husband help you with the housework and the care of the child?"

She nodded. "Yes, but—"

"But what?"

"But since I am the woman, the lion's share—"

The nurse came back into the room, switched on the harsh lights, and gave her some pills and a paper cup of water to wash them down with. In the light, Kaufmann could see delicate lines around the young woman's eyes and mouth.

"The lion's share?"

She shook her head as if trying to shake out the wrinkles in her brain. "Can you leave me alone now, Detective? I'm tired."

"Did you study nursing in India?"

She nodded. "I, um, dropped out of university, got a job in a call center. My parents weren't happy, but…"

"What?"

"They thought I would marry a doctor or an engineer, so it wouldn't really matter." He waited for her to continue. "It didn't work out that way. When we came here, we needed money, and the options were, um, limited."

"Do you and your husband argue?"

"Argue? Sometimes."

"About what?"

Parma closed her eyes. The detective worried that she might fall asleep again.

Flicking her eyes open, she replied, "Little things. Money. Time. News stories."

"You argue about news stories?"

"I talk back to the television set. He says we can't change things, so why complain?"

Kaufmann scratched his chin. He felt as if he were plunging down one blind alley after another. "You mentioned time. Do you and your husband spend much time away from each other?"

She frowned, and the creases around her eyes and mouth became more pronounced. "What do you mean?"

Kaufmann didn't answer.

"We work long hours. Even when we are together, we—"

"Yes?"

"Our time is taken up with Pankaj."

"Ms. Mehta, does your husband have any friends? People he spends time with when he's not home with you?"

A hard-to-read expression came over the young woman's face. "When he's not with me?" She closed her eyes, then opened them again, but they didn't seem to focus. "Just the other food cart vendors."

The nurse returned to the hospital room and told the detective that it was time to leave.

Kaufmann stood up. "Thank you, Ms. Mehta. I hope you feel better soon."

* * *

His taxi was stuck in the middle of the street, and the other cars were lining up behind him. But it did not take long for the boy with the wispy beard to return, accompanied by a tall, thin young man with a raspberry-red *kufi* on his head.

The tall man carried the magazine under his arm.

"Come with us," he said, and before he knew it Jamal was blindfolded and hustled away in someone else's car.

Soon he was sitting in a dank, stuffy room, maybe someone's basement or attic, with a hood over his face and his hands tied behind his back, trying to make sense of the questions his interrogator was throwing at him. *What's your name? Where do you come from? Why do you have disgusting magazines in your car? Are you sure you're a taxi driver? Are you a faggot? Are you a Muslim?* When he offered some answers, the man came back with more questions. *Did you leave Lebanon because you wanted to practice your disgusting homosexuality? You say you used to be married? Did you get divorced in order to sleep with men? Do you know what Islam says about homosexuality? Do you know what the fucking punishment is?*

"Can I have some water?" Jamal asked through the hood. The room was hot, and he was feeling faint.

"It's Ramadan," said the interrogator's voice. "Nothing can pass your lips until nightfall."

"I can't breathe," said Jamal.

"Answer the damn questions," said the man.

"I told you," said Jamal, "it's just an art magazine. The photos are artistic, not sexual. I drive a taxi, I write some poetry, I live in the neighborhood. I left Lebanon because I was treated like a second-class citizen."

"And you're treated better here?"

"This is America. You're not the police, and I haven't broken any laws."

"Why did you leave your wife and child?"

"I didn't leave them. She left me."

"Why?"

Jamal shrugged, though it was hard to shrug with his hands tied. He was sweating.

"I don't know. Ask her."

"Did she divorce you because she found you in bed with a man?"

"No."

"No, she didn't find you in bed, or, no, you aren't a faggot?"

Jamal didn't answer. The sweat was running down his back, under his bound hands.

"When are you going to let me go?"

The questions must have continued for another hour, but Jamal had lost track of time.

"Can I have water now?" he whispered through his parched throat.

No one answered. The hood was still draped over his face, and he had no idea whether he was alone in the room.

"Water, damn it."

\* \* \*

*Trying to get used to new surroundings,* she wrote on the scrap of paper that constituted her makeshift diary. *Boxes crammed with broken toys and old photos. Bare wooden floor. I don't mind the ceiling so cramped I can hardly stand or the thin mattress on the hard floor, but I wake up with a stiff neck. I think cracks in the walls let in air from outside. It's hot during the day, cold at night. Dark, but a small window lets in a little light.* She had gotten the idea for the diary from that book they had read in middle school, the one by Anne Frank. Along with her parents and another family, the girl had also lived in an attic. For years. *Anne was full of hope,* she wrote now, *but look what happened to her.*

# Thursday: Rumor

The mood around the breakfast table that morning was grim. The windows were still dark, and after a short and miserable sleep, the electric lights were giving Farid a headache. His parents hadn't heard from Yasmin. The police claimed to have uncovered some leads, but they weren't very forthcoming.

His father looked at him. "Don't you know anything about this party she went to, Farid?"

"Sorry, no," he replied. "I don't have much to do with high school freshmen."

His mom took a sip of juice and turned to his father. "I knew we shouldn't have moved," she said. "The values are different. Too many temptations. No respect for elders."

"But you wanted this. A nice kitchen, a bigger bath. A better school for our daughter."

Farid looked down at his plate and munched on a piece of toast.

"I was wrong. Rouge High School was good enough for our son, and it would have been good enough—better—for Yasmin. Thanks be to Allah for Farid."

His father muttered something and took a sip of his coffee.

"Ahmed," his mother continued, "do you—do you really think she's all right? Maybe she's been in an accident."

Farid detected a flicker of doubt on his father's face before he replied, "If she was in an accident, the police would know about it. It's just teenage craziness. Stubbornness and hormones. When we find her, we'll take her away from these temptations and send her to her cousins for a few months."

"You keep threatening, but you do nothing. You're like a dog that barks but doesn't know how to bite."

His father flinched, but then he cursed under his breath and turned to his son.

"Farid, what about your friend Tariq? Maybe he knows something."

Farid frowned. "I don't think so. He doesn't hang out with high school kids either."

"Who does he, mnn, hang out with?"

"Me. But I haven't seen him lately. He wasn't in class the last few days."

His mother spoke up. "So he's missing too?"

Farid shook his head. "It's normal for him. He disappears for a few days, then shows up like nothing's happened. But the prof doesn't like it."

She stood up and started clearing the dishes.

But his father wasn't finished. "How did you meet him, Farid? He never comes to the mosque."

"He likes to pray by himself. I met him at the Islamic bookstore. He wanted to educate himself about Islam."

"But why did he want to become a Muslim? It's not often that an average, apple-pie American decides to change his name to Tariq and embrace the five pillars of Islam."

Farid shrugged. "It's a long story." He stood up and started to put away the food.

"I have a bad feeling about that Tariq."

His mother placed a freshly washed dish in the strainer and said, "You don't even know the boy."

"Timothy, Tariq. Christian, Muslim. I think he's a police informant. A mosque crawler."

Now Farid flinched. "How can he be a mosque crawler? He doesn't hang out in the mosque."

"That doesn't matter. He hangs out with you, and you tell him everything that goes on."

Yes, it was true, but his father had gotten things backwards. "C'mon, Dad. You've got a wild imagination."

His dad still wasn't finished. "And if he can spy for the police, he can kidnap my daughter."

Farid laughed, nervously. Hadn't his father blamed Yasmin's disappearance on hormones? "Dad! Why would he do that?"

Dr. Ali shrugged. "Your mother and I—we have many friends. People who respect us. People who know how much we do for the community. But some people don't like us. People who resent our position."

His mother interjected, "What does this have to do with Tariq?"

"Maybe you offended some constituent about something."

"What something?"

Dr. Ali exhaled. "I don't know. Maybe the constituent had a drink with his friend on the police force, who got a loose cannon like Timothy or Tariq to do something stupid."

It was still only five o'clock in the morning, but Farid said he had to go to work.

His mother sighed. "Some people blame Muslims for everything. You blame the police."

"Not for everything," his father countered. "But I don't trust them."

* * *

It was hard enough to sleep sitting up on a plain wooden chair with your head smothered under a hood and your hands tied behind your back, but it was worse to be awakened before dawn by the pounding of a drum. Even the stiff, awkward sleep he had fallen into was too sweet to give up.

Jamal muttered a brief curse and sighed.

It seemed that a couple of people were moving around and talking to each other in the stuffy room.

"Hey, faggot! Time for morning prayers!" said last night's interrogator.

"I need to go to the bathroom," said Jamal.

"So many demands," said the man.

"Untie my hands. I need to pee."

The man continued to rummage around the room. "Can't do that," he said. "Hands stay tied."

"But I need to go to the bathroom."

Jamal heard some whispering, like the rustling of leaves.

"Okay, Kadiye will take you."

Someone, presumably Kadiye, crossed the room and helped him to stand up. Jamal's joints ached, his mouth felt dry and unclean, and his bladder told him he really needed to empty it. Kadiye led him across the room. It must have been a large room since they took twenty steps before reaching anything. Then the guard opened a door and switched on a light. The floor was hard and unyielding, probably tile.

"Wait," said Kadiye, who by the sound of it lifted the toilet seat. "Okay, now."

"I can't. My hands are tied."

"I'm not supposed to untie hands."

"But I have to pee. Can you unzip my pants?"

There was no answer. Just breathing. Eventually a hand found his zipper and pulled it down.

"Uhh, can you take it out for me? I don't want to pee all over my pants."

133

Again, there was no answer. Of course Kadiye was embarrassed. Jamal was embarrassed too, but he needed to go to the bathroom.

"Look, if you don't want to do it, just untie my hands. Nobody will know."

Instead, Kadiye fished around in Jamal's underwear and pulled out his penis.

"There. Go ahead. Just aim toward toilet."

Aim? How could you aim with your eyes covered? Under the circumstances, it was hard to relax enough to release the stream, but soon Jamal was peeing into the bowl. At least he hoped it was into the bowl.

He sighed again. "Thank you," he said.

Kadiye didn't reply.

\* \* \*

Taking the bus to work, watching the sun climb in the eastern sky, Farid remembered once when he was three or four years old and was supposed to go to the mosque with his parents. Not yet able to appreciate the value of his religion, he hid under the bed. His father threatened to beat him. He thundered at him like an angry god, if another god besides Allah, the Compassionate, the Merciful, were possible. Yes, his father was volatile, quick to anger, but he had many sides. He was impossible to pin down. At the mosque, people hung on his every word. His patients, too, treated him like a god, distant but benevolent. He was known for driving a hard bargain, but he spent generously, provided free medical care, supported many charities, and sent monthly checks to poor relatives overseas (or maybe, for all he knew, they were *jihadis*). He was a good husband and father—at least everyone said so—but Farid had heard the rumor that he had a mistress in another part of the city. That only added to his mystique. Even Tariq had clapped him on the back and said, chip off the old block, right?

\* \* \*

There was no sign of Yasmin in the cafeteria, but Jonathan ran into Becky. They carried their trays—grilled cheese sandwiches, baked beans, fruit salad—to a Formica table that smelled of industrial-strength cleaning solution and sat down opposite each other.

"I'm pretty nervous," he said, referring to the play.

"It's just a rehearsal."

He took a bite out of his sandwich, which tasted like cheese-flavored cardboard.

"So what do I do on opening night?"

"Take three deep breaths," she advised, "and pretend it's still a rehearsal."

He laughed.

"Easy for you. You've got Portia down pat. Cool, clever, elegant—beautiful."

Was he blushing?

"Um, thanks. Everything I'm not in real life."

Now they both laughed.

"Listen," he continued, taking a bite of fruit salad, "do you know Yasmin? Yasmin Ali? She's a first-year."

Becky shook her head. "No. Why?"

"Well, I met her at the game last Friday. Then—well, she hasn't been in school this week, and I'm kind of worried about her."

All around them, the other students were talking noisily. Trays clattered, and chairs scraped on the floor.

Becky asked him why he was worried.

"You know how people sometimes get a little wild at parties. I think she might have gotten a little wild at Allison's party, and she might be embarrassed about it. Or worse."

"Worse?"

"Not just embarrassed. Ashamed. I'm worried she might be so ashamed that she might do something to herself."

"Jesus."

Jonathan nodded, grimly.

Of course he didn't know how Yasmin felt. Maybe she wasn't ashamed at all. Maybe someone else was ashamed for her. Or by her. Someone who wanted to punish her for not feeling what she was supposed to feel.

What would happen then?

\* \* \*

Jamal's guard, the one called Kadiye, removed his hood and untied his hands. There was no one else in the room. A naked bulb dangled over his head, and only a small amount of natural light slipped through a few cracked, grimy windows.

It wasn't someone's basement. More like a disused warehouse, half-filled with old boxes, rusty tools, semi-permanent cobwebs, and a puke-green sofa whose stuffing was emerging like the guts of a recently killed fish.

Kadiye—he recognized him as the young man with the orange shoes who had discovered the magazine in his glove box—handed him a copy of the Qur'an.

"I'm supposed to eat this?" said Jamal. It was lunchtime, and he was feeling hungry.

"Ramadan," explained the other, a slightly built young man with an unshaven face and green eyes a deeper shade than the puke green of the sofa. "One is not supposed to eat."

"One is not supposed to," said Jamal, "but the body has a mind of its own."

Jamal opened the holy book at random and read a few pages about the prophet Ibrahim.

"Where do you come from?" asked Kadiye, breaking his train of thought.

"A few blocks from here. Or a few miles. Where am I? My cat is starving by now and I have to feed him."

A railroad whistle sounded nearby.

"No, I mean where do you *come* from?" Kadiye blinked several times. It was almost a nervous tic.

"Palestine."

"And they allow that in Palestine?"

"Allow what?" said Jamal.

Kadiye didn't reply. The young man seemed to be looking at him with genuine curiosity.

"Actually, Lebanon," Jamal explained. "My father was born in Palestine, a few years before the *naqba*." The catastrophe, an Arabic word that denoted the creation of Israel, the first Arab-Israeli war, and the exile of many Palestinians. "I grew up in a refugee camp."

"And they allow that there? In Lebanon?"

"Lebanon is a tolerant place, but the tolerance level goes up and down depending on who's in charge and whether there's a war going on."

Kadiye scratched his beard. "Mnn. I know about this so-called tolerance. Pornography, prostitution, perversion."

"Big words, my friend. So where do you come from?"

The young man hesitated, then said, "Enough talk. It is time for prayer."

Kadiye laid a prayer mat on the dirty floor, prostrated himself, and began to repeat the familiar phrases.

Jamal shrugged and returned to his reading of the Qur'an. He found something about the Jews of Medina, where Muhammad and his followers had gone after leaving Mecca. Even then different tribes, different peoples, were jockeying for position.

136

After his captor finished praying, Jamal raised his head and continued, "But the tolerance never extended to Palestinians. They were not allowed to hold certain jobs, to live where they wanted to, to join political parties. They—we—were second-class citizens."

"So you've never been to Palestine?"

"No. My grandfather lived there, in the old days. He liked to say that the Jews and the Arabs got along well in those days."

"Really?"

"Well, sometimes anyway. They were all Palestinians. Palestinian Jews and Palestinian Arabs."

The young man nodded. "So what happened?"

Jamal shrugged. "Push came to shove."

He looked at the dust motes floating in the stuffy air and started coughing.

"Listen," he said, "I need to feed my cat. Let me go to my apartment so I can see how he's doing. I promise I'll come back after I make sure he's all right."

The young man blinked three times. Finally, he said, "Sorry. Is not possible." Kadiye took back the copy of the Qur'an and began to tie Jamal's hands behind his back once again. "Sorry."

"Damn it," Jamal said. "Who's behind this bullshit? What's going on?"

The guard said nothing.

\* \* \*

Working on the story of Yasmin Ali's disappearance, Aisha ran into her friend Zainab Awad in the mosque preparing for her afterschool class later that day. Zainab worked as a bank teller but volunteered to teach young girls to read the Qur'an and to understand the basic elements of their religion.

Aisha asked her if she had heard anything.

"Let me close the door," Zainab said.

The walls of the small, sunlit classroom were covered with pictures of smiling children, posters highlighting key Islamic concepts, and colorful drawings made by the students themselves.

"The girl is going to be punished," said the teacher, breathlessly. She covered her hair but wore lipstick and eye shadow.

"What do you mean?"

"In the park. Saturday. Ninety-nine lashes."

"What? That's crazy."

"Of course it's crazy," said Zainab, "but somebody must have been crazy to kidnap the poor girl."

"Where did you hear this?"

"At the grocery store. Last night. Two women were talking in the produce area. About my age, maybe younger. They were wearing the *hijab*. I couldn't help but overhear."

"Are you sure you heard right?"

"Yes. Absolutely. I was picking out ripe tomatoes, and I heard them talking about modesty, shocking behavior, the need for punishment."

"Is this a rumor, or do they have firsthand information?"

Zainab shook her head. "I don't know. I'd never seen them before and didn't want to seem nosy."

Aisha had been friends with Zainab for several years. Married with a two-year-old child of her own, she was known to be a responsible and hard-working teacher. In fact, Aisha's own daughter had attended the class. Hanan loved her.

"You said Saturday. What time?"

"Noon. I think they said noon."

Aisha wrote down the details in her notebook. She knew she couldn't put unconfirmed rumors and gossip in the paper, but it wasn't something she could ignore.

* * *

Sergeant Khoury was holed up in a quiet corner of the public library, a few blocks from the school. He was interviewing yet another student, who wore an old-fashioned tweed jacket and a red bow tie.

"So you attended Allison Yorke's party?"

Rasmussen nodded.

"Did you have fun?"

"Depends what you mean by fun."

Khoury waited for him to continue.

"It was okay, I guess. Not a lot of stimulating conversation."

"Is that what you go to parties for—conversation?"

The young man shrugged.

"I assume the liquor was flowing, so what went wrong?"

Rasmussen scrunched up his face. "A general lack of intelligence. No amount of alcohol can make up for that."

At study tables nearby, a few earnest teenagers were poring over books, taking notes. Retirees reclined in padded chairs, reading the daily newspaper. Young mothers trooped by with little kids on the way to the children's section.

The sergeant continued, "Did anything unusual happen? Anything unexpected?"

"No. What do you mean?"

"Did you notice anyone taking pictures?"

Another frown. "Pictures? Of what?"

"Apparently someone took photos of sexual activity"—his partner had relayed the rumor to him—"and posted them to the internet."

The young man's eyes opened wide, but he didn't say anything.

"So you didn't see that?"

"No. I guess I missed all the fun."

\* \* \*

Aisha's exchange with Zainab triggered memories of growing up in East Jerusalem, when her mother's small stabs at independence—selling her homemade pastries to the proprietors of cafés and market stalls, meeting with other women in one or another's kitchen, attending public lectures in the Arab part of the city—alternated with her father's belated attempts to rein her in. He demanded that she stay home and make his dinner or turn over the proceeds of her pastry sales so that he could spend the money on a new television set to watch even more soccer after he ate the dinner she made. Sometimes the push-pull of their relationship ended with shouts and tears. When that happened, she and her sisters ran into the bedroom they shared and hid, but their brothers crouched in a doorway and watched.

With her older brother out of the house, looking for work, and she herself taking classes with Jews and other Arabs at Hebrew University, her father directed his anger at her younger sister. She had provoked gossip in the neighborhood by walking with a young boy in the narrow streets behind the market. The word got around that they were holding hands and kissing though they were still in secondary school. Their father told her to be careful, to make sure she acted like a good Muslim girl. Her sister and her mother held whispered conferences while their father was off selling fresh pomegranate juice to Christian tourists and Israeli soldiers in his Old City café.

One day a bunch of rowdy boys spotted the young lovers in a back alley. According to what her sister told her later, they started making obscene noises and chased the pair through the streets. When the young man ran off, the gang pelted her sister with stones. As she kneeled in the dusty street, her face bleeding, they called her names. Her tears mixed with blood, she called them worse names, and they finally left her alone.

When their father heard about the incident, instead of comforting her, he threw her out of the house. She stayed at a cousin's for a month, then moved to Jaffa, next to Tel Aviv. Two years later her young lover was accidentally killed by a stray Israeli shell, but that was another story.

Now the rumors swirling around the missing girl made her shudder. It could have been her sister. Or her daughter.

\* \* \*

Kaufmann walked around the food cart pod trying to figure out which one of the vendors might know Arvind Mehta better than the others. Finally, he picked out a young Indian man who made French crêpes—sweet or savory, wheat or buckwheat—on a hot greased griddle. It was one of the more popular food carts in the area.

But the crêpe-maker said he hardly knew Mehta and referred him to a young woman named Ingrid, whose cart offered an eclectic assortment of wraps. The detective got in line.

"What would you like?" she asked him when he reached the front.

He chose chicken with a spicy peanut sauce, flashed his badge, and asked her if they could chat for a few minutes.

"About what?" she asked nervously.

"Nothing serious," he lied. "Just checking some things out."

Some time later, when she was finally able to get away, they sat down at an empty table twenty or thirty yards from Mehta's samosa cart, where he probably couldn't see them.

"So how well do you get along with your fellow food cart workers?" he asked the young woman. He knew that some of the vendors owned their carts, others rented them, while still others just worked for the people who owned the carts and made the food.

"Good," she said, beginning to relax. She wore jeans, a T-shirt, and pink tennis shoes. Her blonde hair was pulled back, and there was a tiny stud on the side of her nose. "We're all in the same business. Most of us are young. We eat each other's food, learn about each other's cultures. It's like a mini-United Nations here."

He nodded. "My chicken wrap was great. Thai peanut."

"Thanks. Lots of people ask for it."

"So how well do you know the other vendors?"

She shrugged. "I don't hang out with them if that's what you mean. I talk to them, eat their food, but at the end of the day I'm too tired to do anything but go home and collapse on my bed."

"You know the young Indian guy over there?" He indicated Mehta's cart.

"Sure. It's crazy what happened at the park."

"Do you know any reason why someone would want to harm him—or his son?"

"No, of course not. He's a laid-back guy. Everybody likes him. And his son is just a little kid."

"Have you ever, say, gone out with him for a bite to eat? Somewhere away from the pod?"

She hesitated. The detective waited.

"I might have. Once or twice."

"You just said you're exhausted after work. And Mr. Mehta is married with a young child, so I assume he's also eager to go home."

"It was just a beer. We were hot, and there's a nice brewpub around the corner."

"Once? Or was it twice?"

The young woman shook her head. "Something like that. I don't remember."

"And have you gone out for beers with other vendors?"

She smiled, nervously. "What is this, the inquisition?"

"Is it possible that someone—someone like Mr. Mehta's wife—might have gotten the wrong impression?"

She cleared her throat. "No, I don't see how that could happen, Detective. Besides, I have a boyfriend."

"Oh? What's his name?"

She looked around before answering, like a small animal checking the landscape for predators. "I don't see why we have to drag him into this."

"Into what?"

"I told you, I just had a couple of beers with the guy." She stood up. "Now I gotta get back to work."

The detective handed her his card. "Thank you, Ingrid. If you think of anything else, please give me a call."

* * *

Aisha's text came in to Kaufmann's phone while he was still at the food cart pod. It asked him to call her as soon as possible, which he did.

"I'm so glad you called. It's about Yasmin Ali."

He could hear schoolchildren shouting and laughing in the background. "What's up? Do you know where she is?"

"No, but I heard that her kidnappers—"

"Kidnappers?"

"If they have her, I presume they kidnapped her. I heard that they may be bringing her to the park on Saturday in order to punish her."

"They? Who are you talking about?"

"I don't know."

"Punish her for what?"

"Misbehaving. Violating Islamic rules of modesty and decency."

"Where did you hear that?"

"A friend of mine—a teacher at the *masjid*—overheard some young women talking about it at the supermarket."

"And where did they hear it?"

The detective could hear the reporter talking to someone at the other end.

"Sorry," she said finally. "I'm just picking my daughter up from school. What did you say?"

"I said, what's the source of the information? How do you know it's reliable?"

"I—I don't. But I trust Zainab. She wouldn't make up something like that."

Kaufmann headed for his car. "So what do you want me to do?"

"Detective Kaufmann—Ezra—I'm a reporter. I keep my eyes and ears open. I report what I find out. It's not my job to get involved."

"Right. I understand."

He could hear her sigh. "But this is different. I can't stand by while a poor girl is abused. And I—I can't let these fanatics decide what's right for everybody else."

"No, of course not. So…"

There was a long pause as Kaufmann reached his car and the shouts of the schoolchildren faded in the background.

"I'm a reporter; you're a policeman. Surely you can do something."

He sat behind the wheel without turning on the ignition. "All right. I'll talk to my boss. Maybe she can get the chief to send in a couple of officers."

He heard her emit a small sigh of relief. "Thank you, Ezra. That makes me feel better."

\* \* \*

Farid caught up with Tariq before class that evening. The sun was setting a little earlier each day, and the light was already fading. They were hanging out in the designated smoking area at the edge of the parking lot, and Tariq was sucking on yet another cigarette.

"So where you been, brother?" said Farid.

"Busy."

"With what?"

"You know. Whatever."

"You heard about my sister?"

"No, what?" He took a long drag on his cigarette, held the smoke in his lungs a moment, then blew it out.

"She's missing."

"Missing? She's like thirteen, right?"

"Fourteen."

"So where did she go?"

It was time to for class. The other smokers started crushing their cigarette butts under their feet and traipsing off across campus.

"She just disappeared after this party she went to. I thought maybe you could help me find her."

"Me? How would I know?"

"You got friends. They might know something."

"Friends? Not really."

"You're patrolling the neighborhood, checking who's coming and going."

"Yeah, well, I didn't see no fourteen-year-old girl."

Farid sighed. "Listen, Tariq, you gotta help me. I'm starting to get worried."

His friend finished his cigarette and tossed it into the bushes. "Didn't you say she was at a party?"

Farid nodded.

"What kind of party? Boys and girls mixing? Drinking liquor? Taking drugs?"

"It's not her fault. She's just hanging out with the wrong crowd."

"A fourteen-year-old Muslim girl shouldn't be doing those things. She made her bed, now she can lie in it."

"Thanks a lot," said Farid, then followed the other students to class.

\* \* \*

Discovering that Farid worked at Toys 'R' Us, Jonathan managed to speak with one of his co-workers, who told him that he would probably be at the community college that evening. Now, before the final *Merchant* rehearsal, he was peering out the back window of Zach's car while Zach and Becky watched from the front. The narrow aisles of the college parking lot were crowded with automobiles jockeying for spaces, and many hapless students seemed to be circling endlessly in a vain search for an empty spot.

Becky had spied a tall, skinny young man in a religious-looking red hat talking to another guy shorter and rounder than he was. Maybe one of them was Farid. Maybe Farid would lead them to Yasmin.

"Should we talk to them?" said Zach.

"They're not going to tell us anything," said Jonathan, "and that would only blow our cover. Let's just keep an eye on them and see what they do."

So they kept watch while the red-hatted guy smoked and the two talked back and forth. The other smokers finished their cigarettes and went off to class, and eventually Red and his friend did too.

"Let's follow them," said Jonathan.

"I can't just leave my car here," said Zach. "It's not a legal spot."

"Okay, you stay here. Circle around if you have to. Becky and I will tail them."

\* \* \*

Kaufmann had stood awkwardly in Captain Schroeder's paper-strewn office as she explained why she wasn't going to do anything about the reported punishment in the park. She didn't trust an uncorroborated rumor and wasn't going to stick her neck out by asking the chief to send in the troops.

"What if the rumor is true?" he had asked.

"We can't be prepared for every 'what if,'" she had replied, though Kaufmann figured that was exactly what they needed to prepare for.

"The girl is still missing," he pointed out.

"And a little boy was almost killed. You need to get back to work."

Why was one case more important than the other? Hadn't Schroeder assigned them to the missing persons case as well?

The detective knew he hadn't prevented the boy from being shot or the girl from being kidnapped, but at least he could try to save her from being beaten—and publicly humiliated. Besides, he realized, he didn't want to let Aisha down.

He'd just have to go by himself.

Later, back home, he was texting Aisha with an update when he heard Jonathan fumbling with his key in the front door.

She thanked him for his help and asked him if he'd like to return to Friday prayers the next day at the mosque. **Nearing end of Ramadan**, she wrote, **and imam always has something interesting to say**.

Jonathan opened the door and lumbered—books, jacket, heavy shoes, and all—into the living room. He deposited his book bag on the mail table and threw his jacket over a chair.

**Sure**, the detective wrote back.

**Wonderful. See you then.**

It was already past eleven, but his son started foraging in the kitchen for something to eat.

"Hey, Jonathan…" he called out to him.

"Yeah?" His son sounded as if his head was stuck inside the refrigerator.

"Do you know a girl named Yasmin Ali?"

Jonathan, still in the kitchen, didn't answer. He repeated the question.

"Uh, not really," his son yelled back.

"What does that mean?"

Jonathan stood in the doorway with a white takeout container in his hand. "It means I've heard the name. I think."

"So you didn't see her at that party last weekend?"

"No, I don't think so."

The detective nodded. His son retreated, and Kaufmann followed him into the kitchen.

"So how was rehearsal?"

"Great. It's really coming together."

"You got your lines down?"

Jonathan took a forkful of the leftover food and nodded.

"So how was the party anyway? You never really told me."

"Good, good," he said while chewing. "I had a great time."

\* \* \*

Kadiye, his youthful captor, was praying quietly and Jamal—his eyes uncovered—was staring at a wall when, suddenly, the door opened and the tall man with the red *kufi* shoved a scared-looking young boy into the room. *What now?* Jamal said to himself.

# Friday: Villainy

The man with the *kufi* left as soon as he had come, and the boy, about ten years old, with big brown eyes, short hair, and a round face, said little. Kadiye gave him something to eat. When it came time for them to go to sleep, he produced a leaky air mattress for the boy to lie on and let Jamal sleep on the lumpy, puke-green sofa. He wished them good night, but the boy, exhausted from his ordeal, was no longer awake.

Jamal endured a night of vivid, disturbing dreams. He dreamed of long-forgotten humiliations and horrors from his childhood in Lebanon—the time he had asked for a loaf of bread but didn't have enough money to pay the baker; the day he was beaten by a policeman because he didn't know he was supposed to bribe him; the night the militias invaded the refugee camp and massacred hundreds of people while he and his parents cowered in a closet—and each time he felt as if he couldn't move or even speak. Was he asleep or awake? The dreams seemed so real.

Somehow, he was back in Lebanon, still a child, not the man who had made his way to America, started earning money, married, had a child, acquired his taxi driver's license, taken a lover, come to terms with his own secret feelings, and lost first his wife, then his lover, and now maybe his apartment and maybe even his taxi. At least he still had his sweet, beautiful daughter, though he saw her only once a week and she was growing up as fast as a *jinni* that had been let out of a bottle and was never going back in.

But those dreams paled beside the one that finally woke him up.

He dreamt that *he and Henry were making love in the bedroom of his spartan apartment. They were becoming more and more excited when Aisha suddenly appeared in the room. Two things were strange about Aisha in the dream. She was wearing a niqab that hid all of her face except her eyes, and she was brandishing a stick, which she used to beat the two of them. She insisted that they continue their lovemaking, but the more they went at it the harder she beat them.*

*Meanwhile a whole crowd of onlookers in religious garb materialized in the tiny bedroom and watched the sexual activity and the beating, laughing and jeering the whole time.* Tossing and turning in his sleep, he tried to escape, but he felt glued to the bed. "Help! Help!" he yelled, but no one heard him.

Suddenly he was awake. He gritted his teeth and turned over on the narrow couch. The warehouse was pitch black and the only sounds he could make out were the light breathing of the boy, the rasping and snoring of the guard, and the occasional squeal of a car going by on the street outside. His head felt like a watermelon, and his back and legs felt as if they really had been beaten. He tossed and turned for another hour, but eventually he fell asleep again.

Ten minutes or an hour later—it was impossible to tell—he began to be aware of an insistent drumming sound like the beating of rain on a roof. The drumming continued, until gradually the steady beat of the rain was transformed into the hand-slaps or stick-taps of the Ramadan drummer. He wondered where the drummer was and whether he and his drums were getting soaked by the rain. But no, it wasn't raining. It was just the sound of the drumming.

It was still dark out, but Jamal could make out the boy sleeping soundly on the mattress, his skinny chest gently rising and falling. Kadiye was already preparing some food.

* * *

Jonathan's sprawling limbs rearranged themselves in the bed.

*Up, down. Up, down. The girl's head moved up and down, as if she were bobbing for apples, and every time she bobbed he felt himself getting harder and stiffer, like a balloon about to pop.*

*The girl looked familiar. But it wasn't Yasmin, the girl from the party. Instead of her thick, darkly beautiful curls he found himself staring at the soft, fine, reddish-blonde strands of Becky's hair. There was raw, pulsating music in the background, heavy on percussion. Drums, spoons on tabletops, fingernails on chalkboards. Gunfire. He was lying in his own bed, and he saw Becky's naked body—her red toenails, her pink breasts, her arched back—stretched out in front of him.*

*Up, down. Up, down. Apples. Balloon. Becky. The thin, taut skin of the balloon about to ex...PLODE!*

The alarm had not yet gone off, but a hint of pale light was already filtering through the blinds. He heard birds beginning to sing, early commuters driving off to work, sanitation workers dragging garbage cans over sidewalks.

148

He reached down and felt his pajamas. *Fuck*, he thought. *Laundry.*

\* \* \*

The prisoners and their guard sat around a rickety card table like unlikely guests at a séance. The cracked and filthy windows were still dark, the darkness relieved only slightly by the dim glow of streetlights and the light emanating from the pinpricks of distant stars. Jamal thought about making a break for it but decided to bide his time until the moment was right.

Kadiye had prepared a small meal of dates and yogurt. The dates were wrinkled and dry, but the yogurt was refreshing. Afterwards, the guard tied their hands behind their backs and cleaned up the remains of the meal. But soon he left them alone in the locked warehouse.

"So what did you do?" Jamal asked the kid.

The boy looked at him nervously.

"N—nothing," he said, shaking his head.

"Nothing at all? Come on, you call tell me."

The boy looked at him but said nothing.

"Did you break the fast during the day? Forget to say your prayers? Fail to do your chores?"

The boy gave a slight shake of his head.

"Disrespect your parents?"

At the mention of the last transgression, the boy's eyes widened slightly.

"Aha. You must have talked back to your parents."

The boy shook his head.

"So what did you do?"

The boy didn't answer. Jamal sighed and closed his eyes. He was worried about Muhammad. It must have been thirty-six hours since the poor cat had eaten. If only he could get Aisha or even Henry to go over and feed him.

"I—I stole a comic book from my uncle's grocery store," said the boy.

"Oh, comic books," replied Jamal, opening his eyes again. "You like comic books?"

The boy nodded.

"When I was young, I used to read Donald Duck and Superman. I couldn't understand the words, but the pictures told the stories."

"Do you think they'll—" The boy didn't finish his thought, but he seemed about to cry.

"What?"

"Do you think they'll cut off my hand?"

"Cut off your hand? Why?"

"Because I stole something. The Qur'an says that thieves should be punished by having their hands cut off."

Jamal thought about the boy's precocious knowledge of the Qur'an. He wanted to put his arms around the kid's shoulders and comfort him, but his hands were tied.

"No," said Jamal, "they won't cut off your hand. They just want to scare you. If you stay strong, I'm sure everything will work out. Your uncle will forgive you, your parents will welcome you back, and you will all sit down to a delicious *iftar* meal. Okay?"

"My father is dead," the boy said.

Jamal shook his head. "I'm sorry."

"My uncle will beat me. And if he doesn't, my mother will."

At that moment, Kadiye returned.

\* \* \*

Aisha was getting worried. She hadn't heard from Jamal since the previous weekend, and she needed someone to watch Hanan on Saturday. Her ex-husband's apartment was located in a nondescript but respectable stretch of stores, houses, and apartment buildings. Some buildings were run-down, while others were being fixed up with a fresh coat of paint or new signs.

Having taken a bus to his neighborhood, she walked the last few blocks and went inside. An old woman with a shopping bag and a cane was hobbling down the stairs. On the landing between the first and second floors, she noticed some graffiti in different languages.

Jamal's apartment was at the end of a dimly lit corridor. She rang the bell and held her breath, but no one answered. She tried again. Someone walked by, a man. He glanced at the scarf on her head and wished her a Happy Ramadan. She replied in kind. After he left, she looked under the mat and found a key.

Inside, everything was quiet. Books and magazines were in their place. She walked through the living area into the kitchen. The dishes had been put away and the sink was clean, but she noticed an unpleasant odor.

The cat emerged from the bedroom and walked slowly, cautiously, into the kitchen. He looked thin.

"Muhammad! What happened?"

150

She disapproved of the name, but he was Jamal's cat. When they separated, she took their daughter and he took the cat.

She petted Muhammad, and he started to purr.

The cat dish was empty. Aisha found some dry food and poured it into the bowl. Muhammad ran to the food and started to devour it. She filled another bowl with water.

While the cat was eating, she looked around. The bed was made, but the litter box in the bathroom needed cleaning and the cat had had several accidents in various places throughout the apartment. She took care of the box and cleaned up the accidents as well as she could.

The cat was following her.

"Poor Muhammad," she said, stroking his fur.

When she was done cleaning, she put more food in the bowl and wrote a note for Jamal.

*Where are you?* it said. *You didn't answer your phone, so I came over to see what was going on. Muhammad was starving. Call me when you get this. Aisha.* She thought for a second and added, *P.S. Will you see Hanan on Sunday as usual?*

She left the apartment and placed the key back under the mat.

\* \* \*

"Can you give me a pencil?" Jamal asked the guard.

"What you need a pencil for?"

"I have an idea for a poem."

A puzzled expression crossed Kadiye's face. The boy, who was fidgeting on his chair, glanced at Jamal.

"Poem? What kind of poem?"

"About the things that are happening to me. I want to write something about being kidnapped by religious fanatics who aren't yet old enough to grow a decent beard."

"Your hands are tied. You can't write poem with hands tied."

"Look," argued Jamal, "I won't run away. I just want to write in my notebook."

Kadiye snorted.

"I swear in the name of Allah, the All-Merciful."

Kadiye checked the door, then looked back at him. "Okay, but don't tell…" Presumably he meant the man in the red *kufi*. "He is very strict."

151

The guard untied Jamal's hands, found a chewed-up pencil stub in his pocket, and handed it to the taxi driver. Jamal asked him if he could use the card table. Kadiye muttered something but helped his captive set it up again.

"What about him?" Jamal said, nodding in the direction of the boy.

"Him? The thief? He needs to be tied up. He might steal something."

Jamal laughed. "Like what?"

Kadiye looked around the room. "Alarm clock. Shoes. Qur'an."

"Isn't it a virtuous act to steal a copy of the holy book?"

The boy continued to fidget.

"What do you know about these things?" said Kadiye. "Have you studied the *hadiths*? Are you a *shaykh*?"

"No. Are you?"

The guard had no reply, and when they had finished setting up the table, he asked him if he needed paper.

"My notebook. You took it from me."

"Notebook? What notebook?"

"My poetry notebook. The one you confiscated."

Kadiye shook his head, scratched the stubble on his young face, and began to rummage in boxes and drawers. Jamal sat down at the table and started thinking of the lines he wanted to write. Meanwhile, the boy tried to stretch his arms, which were still tied behind his back, and groaned.

"Here. Is this what you mean?" said the guard.

He took the notebook, found a blank page, and began writing.

*Forgive me, Muhammad*
*I have broken*
*my vow to feed you and take care of you*
*My hands were tied*
*The zealots locked me up*

He raised his head and looked around the desolate room. Recalling a poem by Allen Ginsberg, he bent over his notebook and wrote some more.

*America, I don't recognize you anymore*
*America, you remind me of Lebanon*
*America, what's gotten into you*
*Ramadan Mubarak, America*
*Better to pray than to eat*
*But Muhammad is starving*
*If something happens to him I'm blaming*
*You America*

*And you Muhammad*
*Not the cat but the Prophet*
*Peace be upon you*
*And upon you too, Muhammad*

Jamal looked up from his notebook. Kadiye, who had settled down on the couch to read from the Qur'an, appeared to have fallen asleep. After he untied the boy's wrists, the two of them tiptoed cautiously to the ugly old sofa and made sure. Jamal pointed to the door of the warehouse, and the boy tiptoed after him. He fiddled with the locks, trying not to wake the guard. When he managed to get the door open, he pushed the boy outside into the gray light of a cloudy day. The boy looked back at him and Jamal whispered, "Go!"

"What about you?"

"Don't worry about me," said Jamal. He had given his word, and, besides, he felt a bit of sympathy for the young guard and didn't want to cause trouble for him. "Tell your mother to give you a big hug."

As the boy ran off, Jamal shut the door and double-locked it once more. Kadiye was still sleeping.

\* \* \*

"So," said his handler, puffing on a cigarette, "you haven't heard the rumor about the ninety-nine lashes?"

Farid, neatly dressed in gray slacks and a pinstriped shirt, was standing on the loading dock behind Toys 'R' Us. It was a gray but muggy day, and the day wasn't improved by the view from the back of the hulking commercial building.

"No," he said. "And you think this has something to do with Yasmin?"

"That's what I'm asking you."

Farid glanced at the picture of a shiny red toy on the box in front of him. There were many hours to go in his shift. "I can't imagine who would do that. I mean, this isn't Saudi Arabia."

"So you don't know any, well, strict believers? Folks who might want to take religious law into their own hands?"

Farid thought for a moment. "Maybe whoever started this rumor doesn't even have Yasmin. Maybe they just want to send a message."

"What kind of message?" said the cop, tossing his cigarette away.

"Don't stray from the right and true path."

\* \* \*

It was just another nondescript concrete building on a busy street, but the mosque was attracting numerous visitors in the middle of the Friday workday. The sky was overcast, but that didn't seem to dampen anyone's mood. The detective joined the flow of worshipers, nodding occasionally to others who smiled at him.

Once again, the men and women separated, the women proceeding to a back entrance and the men removing their shoes—their flip-flops and wingtips and Nikes—before entering the hall and kneeling on the floor. As before, the detective did not take his place among the worshipers but leaned against a wall and watched. The imposing Senegalese imam, arrayed in colorful robes and a white prayer cap, was already standing at the front, and after everyone was settled he greeted them in Arabic and launched into his weekly sermon.

"Brothers and sisters, as we approach the Eid al-Fitr holiday, the end of Ramadan, we should recall the practices we are called upon to follow during the holy month. One, of course, is to fast during the day, to refrain from eating and drinking and other pleasurable activities. Another is to perform the nightly *Tarawih* prayers, reading the entire Qur'an if possible over the course of the month. Still another is to give alms. We are commanded to give, according to our means, to the poor and needy."

The assembled worshipers listened and nodded. Kaufmann glanced at the women's section, and this time he caught a glimpse of Aisha.

"This practice," the imam continued, "called *zakat,* stands in contrast to the Western principle of making money and spending as much as possible on oneself." The guy has a point, thought the detective, though Christians and others did give each other gifts on Christmas. "In fact, we are encouraged to give even more, over and above what we are expected to provide; this is called *sadaqah.* Performing *zakat* and *sadaqah* during Ramadan is even more worthy than at any other time." More nodding of heads. "But these practices are not just about money."

A few eyes opened. Ears perked up.

"They also mean that we should treat others with kindness and compassion, especially during this holy month. You may have heard that the young daughter of our esteemed president, Dr. Ahmed Ali"—whom Kaufmann spotted near the front of the hall—"and his gracious wife Mariam, a highly respected member of our City Council, is missing. This is a terrible and disturbing event, and we pray for Yasmin's safe return." Murmurs of assent. The detective wondered where the imam was going with his sermon. "But now comes word that some person or persons are planning to punish Yasmin for un-Islamic behavior tomorrow, in Lincoln Park." The murmurs changed to agitated whispers as people turned to their neighbors.

"Punish?, you may ask. Why? What did the young girl do?"

The doctor seemed to squirm, and Kaufmann wondered if his wife was trying to hide in the back.

"It appears," the imam continued, "that their daughter may have attended a party. She may have danced with members of the opposite sex. She may even have consumed some alcohol. Good people, if you are honest with yourselves, you know that young Yasmin is not alone in doing these things. Our sons and daughters are tempted every day, every night—surely every Saturday night. They cannot always resist these temptations"—the whispering continued—"but we, their elders, cannot always resist the temptation to punish their transgressions." The whispers grew louder. Accompanied by a few shouts and whistles. "And in some cases, this temptation is just as evil, if not more so, than the others."

The imam waited for the murmuring to die down.

"Brothers and sisters, only Allah knows what was in Yasmin's heart. Only He, the compassionate, the merciful, can judge her. It is not the place of self-proclaimed guardians of virtue to punish those who may have made a mistake. The poor girl has suffered enough. What she did or didn't do is a matter for her and her parents to consider. Whoever is responsible for, it seems, kidnapping her and threatening to punish her are making a grave mistake. That is not the way of Islam. Ramadan is a time for compassion, for forgiveness, and for self-reflection, and we must call upon the kidnappers to practice all three. May Allah guide them in finding and following the true path."

The detective caught Aisha's eye, or maybe it was the other way around. She gave a slight tilt of her head, as if to underscore what the imam was saying. *That* was not the way of Islam, and *this* was.

* * *

"Son of a whore!" said Kadiye when he woke up and realized the boy was gone.

He jumped up from the green sofa with the stuffing coming out, undid the locks, and ran outside. The Qur'an was still lying open where he had left it. Jamal tore a scrap of paper from his notebook, walked over to the sofa, and bookmarked the page Kadiye had been reading.

In a few minutes the guard returned, breathing hard. He shouted something unintelligible at Jamal and threw up his hands. Then he pushed him across the room to a hard wooden chair, tied his hands roughly behind his back, and shoved the hood back over his head.

"But—" Jamal started to say.

"Shut up!" said the guard. "No more poetry. No more chitter-chatter. You just sit there in the dark and think about all the bad things you've done."

\* \* \*

Sergeant Khoury had arranged another meeting with Allison Yorke by the playing field next to the school. She was dressed in her field hockey uniform of white shirt, navy-blue shorts, and knee-high navy-blue socks, but her face looked bored. The other girls were running around the field, dribbling and passing the solid plastic ball.

"What do you want from me?" Allison asked.

"I want to know what happened—what really happened—at your party."

"I told you, nothing happened. It was a party. People had a good time."

"You said you didn't know anything about drugs or alcohol. What about sex? Were people making out in corners, going at it in spare bedrooms?"

Allison just laughed.

"Did someone take advantage of Yasmin Ali when she was drunk?"

Her eyes opened slightly. "Yasmin? She doesn't drink."

"I thought you didn't know her."

Allison shrugged and turned to watch the game.

"What about the pictures?"

"Pictures?" She still wasn't looking at him.

"Photos of Yasmin. Why did you take them?"

Another shrug.

"Were you trying to embarrass her? Or her parents? Are you blackmailing Dr. and Mrs. Ali?"

A puzzled expression came over her face. "Blackmail? What are you talking about?"

Khoury didn't say anything. He felt the warm breeze and watched the young women run around the field until one of them scored a goal.

Allison took a deep breath and turned to face him. "Okay," she said, "I'll tell you. It was an initiation."

"Initiation?" He started taking notes.

"Right. There's a list, a slut list, and Yasmin was on it."

"Slut list?"

"Making the list is kind of like winning a popularity contest. But then they have to go through the initiation."

Khoury wrote down the information. "Meaning?"

"They have to sleep with a guy or take their clothes off in public or suck some guy's dick."

"Jesus," said the sergeant and took a long look into Allison's eyes. "And that's what you took pictures of?"

Allison nodded.

"So who—who was the guy?"

She fixed some strands of hair that had blown across her face. "Does it matter?"

"It might."

She frowned. "Jason—no, Jonathan—Kaufmann. I don't really know him."

The sergeant stopped writing. "Kaufmann?"

"Right. Listen, Officer, can I go now?"

"One more thing."

A big sigh. "What?"

"Show me the pictures."

* * *

Becky didn't have a car, so the two of them took the bus to Rouge High School. Again, Jonathan was struck by the contrast between the old-fashioned brick building and the swooping glass-and-steel design of their own school, built a hundred years later at the foot of the nearby hills. Grass was still poking through the cracked black asphalt of the parking lot, and the cars remaining in the lot after school seemed to be at least ten years old, with bashed-in fenders and broken windows.

Nadim was meeting them. Standing next to him on the front steps was a tall and gangly young woman, her head covered with a plain white scarf.

"This is Fatima," said Nadim. They nodded at each other. "She knew the Ali girl in middle school."

"We used to hang out together after school," said Fatima in a firm, quiet voice. "Homework at the library, Starbucks for lattes."

They went inside. A locker slammed somewhere down the dark hallway.

"But you don't know what might have happened to her?" asked Jonathan.

"No, I don't."

"She didn't have, like, enemies?"

Fatima shook her head. "I don't know what it's like at your school. Here we've got, you know, cliques. Popular kids, jocks, nerds. But there wasn't much of that in middle school. Me, Yasmin, Haniya, Diana—we all got along."

"Haniya and Diana," said Becky. "They were also friends of Yasmin?"

"Right."

"And now they go to Rouge?"

The other young woman nodded. "I think Diana's at band practice. You want to talk to her?"

Nadim excused himself. They would meet again in a few hours, at the play's opening performance.

He went one way, and they went the other. After a minute, they took a right turn, and as they got closer, they could hear horns and strings performing a silky rendition of the Beatles' song "Yesterday." When they reached the music room, Fatima turned the doorknob very quietly and tiptoed in.

She emerged a short time later and told them Diana would be busy practicing for at least another thirty or forty minutes.

"What about Haniya?"

"I think she went home right after school."

Fatima gave Jonathan her number, then left them alone.

"At least it's something," he said.

Now the band was rehearsing "Penny Lane."

"Hey," said Becky, "you're not, like, in love with her, are you?"

For a second he didn't know what she was talking about. "Yasmin? Of course not."

"Then why are you trying so hard to find her?"

"'Cause I'm worried about her and—and I feel like I'm partly to blame for getting her into this mess."

"You? Why?"

* * *

When Kaufmann arrived at Jake's Tavern in a linen shirt with fancy buttons, the bar was crowded and he could barely find a seat. It was Friday night. He exchanged greetings with two or three cops he knew and nodded in the direction of someone he half-recognized as a sports reporter for the local daily. He scanned the bar and the rest of the restaurant for Aisha or anyone else who might be there on a blind date, but there was no sign of Aisha and no one else approached him.

The bartender—a twenty-something woman dressed like a matador in a white tuxedo shirt and tight black pants, with stylish black glasses and short black hair to match—asked him what he wanted. He ordered a whiskey and soda.

"Anything to eat?"

"Not yet," he shouted over the din. "I might be waiting for someone." Might be? That hadn't come out right.

She handed him a bar menu that featured sliders, a cheese plate, buffalo wings, grilled asparagus, and something with bacon, shrimp, and avocado.

The guy to the left of him was drinking a beer, chatting with the woman on his left and glancing up from time to time at a European soccer match playing on the TV. The expanse of the field was enormous, the players scurrying back and forth and back again without seeming to get anywhere, and the grass appeared to be an unnaturally bright green. On his own right, a blonde woman in a low-cut blouse was nursing a glass of white wine.

"Is that a Spanish wine?" he asked the woman, just to say something.

"Californian. A bit fruity but crisp. Do you want to try it?"

"No, that's okay."

After ten minutes, his opposite number still hadn't arrived.

Taking another sip of his whiskey, he let his eyes drift over the room. A couple about his own age were sharing a bottle of red wine, talking and laughing. The man, though more animated and probably better looking than he was, looked a little like him, with a long neck, bushy eyebrows, and a slightly crooked smile. The woman looked exactly like Rachel. A time warp? Some kind of alternate universe? But if he was there at that table having dinner with his wife, who was sitting at the bar at this very moment, waiting for another woman?

Maybe Rachel was trying to tell him something.

A sudden pang of doubt hit him in the stomach, and he wondered again whether Aisha was the anonymous woman who had written the flirtatious letters. Who else could it be? The blonde woman drinking the California wine? No, impossible. She hadn't said anything about looking for someone. But every other woman in the bar, except for the sexy bartender in the androgynous bullfighter's outfit, seemed to be with someone else.

Wait! What if the woman who wrote the letter, the one who wanted to *flirt* with him, wasn't a woman at all? That might explain the secrecy, the anonymity. Jesus! He began to sweat under the arms of his linen shirt. Not that he had anything against gay people, but he didn't want to date one. Not that it was a date.

He checked his watch. Whoever it was was twenty minutes late.

He took out some bills and laid them on the bar.

Maybe the whole thing was some kind of practical joke. Maybe Sergeant Khoury had written the letter. Maybe Khoury and the other guys were having a few beers at another bar right now, laughing at his gullibility and having a lot of fun at his expense. Maybe they were going to hold a surprise party for him in which they would read the stupid anonymous letters out loud to the assembled guests. That would bring a laugh. They would show photos of him perched on this very barstool in his expensive sweat-stained shirt like some out-of-place, drab-looking bird who had migrated from somewhere else and didn't know how to get home. He was like a goose that had lost its mate, lonely and aimless.

He stood up, flapped his fucking wings, and prepared to stumble out of the bar when he noticed a woman sitting by herself at a small table in the back of the restaurant. She looked vaguely familiar. Medium height, more plump than not, salt and pepper hair. She was reading a book. But no, he didn't know her.

\* \* \*

It was after dark, and Farid and Tariq were eating Big Macs and fries at the *halal* McDonalds. Even seated on a low plastic bench, the rangy Tariq towered over him.

"I told you," his friend said, "I'm not going to go on a wild goose chase looking for a girl that wears revealing clothes and rubs her body against boys. A girl who doesn't even want to be found."

"Doesn't want to be found? Why the hell would you say that?"

Tariq took a large bite out of his hamburger and shrugged.

Farid drank some warm, sickly-sweet Diet Coke. "Hey, man, you sure you don't know anything about her disappearance?" Maybe his father was right. Maybe Tariq was somehow involved in all this.

"Me? What are you talking about?"

"You get into an argument about religion with a face-painter. You patrol the neighborhood, keep out the infidels, check the length of women's skirts. Maybe you're mixed up with the guys who want to punish my sister. Maybe you think that's what being a good Muslim is all about."

Tariq took another bite and belched. "Hey, brother, if you haven't figured it out yet, I don't give a shit about your sister."

Farid finished his Coke, stood up, and crossed over to the other side of the hard plastic table. The other young man just looked at him with sleepy eyes. Farid grabbed him by the shirt, lifted him halfway out of his seat, and punched him in the jaw. Or tried to—the punch barely grazed the other man's cheek. Shrieking wildly, like a hungry hyena moving in for the kill, Tariq fought back. He landed a couple of punches on the side of Farid's head, hit him in the stomach, and kicked him when he was down. After a few more kicks for good measure, he picked up the remaining french fries and poured them all over his fallen friend.

"*Ramadan Mubarak,*" he said while leaving.

\* \* \*

Like the bar, the parking lot was so crowded it was almost impossible to find a space. The detective couldn't believe that a high school production of *Merchant of Venice* could be so popular. After crawling up and down six or seven aisles, he found a narrow spot next to an SUV that had taken all of one space and half of another. But then he remembered that there was a big game that night too. Rouge vs. Noire, crosstown rivals. The cars were for football, not Shakespeare.

But the auditorium was filling up and the play had almost started by the time he found a seat near the back. The principal, a thin, balding man in a baggy suit, came out onto the stage. He acknowledged the play's controversial elements, asked the audience to suspend their judgment, and told them to turn off their cell phones.

The house lights went down, the curtains came up, the stage lights came on. A young man made up to look much older than his years said that he didn't know why he was so sad. Soon the moneylender—Jonathan's friend Zach—appeared and complained about the abuse he customarily received: "You call me misbeliever, cutthroat dog, and spit upon my Jewish gaberdine." Antonio, the melancholy merchant, was unapologetic.

At some point in the second act his son showed up. He looked a lot like himself, except for the sword. It seemed that he was going to run off with the daughter of the "faithless Jew," as Jonathan called him. The detective wondered what the audience—the parents, friends, and non-Shakespeareans who were likely to attend a high school play—thought of these casual slurs. In recent days, at campaign rallies and right-wing demonstrations, old-fashioned bigotry had come back out of the closet. Was the audience making the connection?

By the third act, Shylock was reviewing, once again, the catalogue of abuses he had suffered. The merchant, he said, "hath disgraced me, and hindered me half a million, laughed at my losses, mocked at my gains, scorned my nation, thwarted my bargains, cooled my friends, heated mine enemies." What was Antonio's reason? That he was a Jew. But Shylock had an answer for that: "Hath not a Jew eyes? Hath not a Jew hands, organs, dimensions, senses, affections, passions? …If you prick us, do we not bleed? If you tickle us, do we not laugh? If you poison us, do we not die?"

A wave of emotion seemed to be rippling through the audience. People were actually sitting on the edge of their seats. Kaufmann wondered what Aisha would think of the play. Shylock was portrayed as a stereotypical villain but also as a much-abused victim, even a tragic hero. What if the moneylender were a Muslim? Someone like Dr. Ali, who supposedly lent money at zero interest. Or was that only to other Muslims? Many of the ethnic slurs these days were directed against Muslims. Maybe, Kaufmann reflected, he was wrong to be suspicious of him.

After building up the audience's sympathy, the Jewish moneylender squandered it: "And if you wrong us, shall we not revenge?" Sure, he had a right to feel angry, even to crave revenge, but he wouldn't win many friends in Venice—or in the audience—that way. "The villainy you teach me, I will execute, and it shall go hard but I will better the instruction." Harsh words, to go along with his harsh threat to take a pound of Antonio's flesh. Kaufmann felt a kind of emotional whiplash. Should he sympathize with "the Jew" or disown his anger? Was Shakespeare pandering to his anti-Jewish audience or slyly sneaking in reminders of the Jew's humanity?

When the lights came on for intermission, people rubbed their eyes and rolled their necks to release the tension that had accumulated. He was about to go outside for a breath of fresh air when the principal walked to the front of the stage, his hands shaking, and announced: "Ladies and gentlemen, I'm sorry to tell you that we—unfortunately, we have to evacuate the theater."

Everybody started talking at once, but the principal hurried off the stage and no one seemed to know what was going on. The members of the audience were soon milling about on the edge of the parking lot, speculating wildly.

"A bomb threat?" said an older woman in old-fashioned glasses. "You wouldn't think a four-hundred-year-old play would cause so much fuss."

"It's probably just teenage pranksters," said her companion.

Meanwhile, hordes of spectators were streaming away from the football field. Was the game over already?

He tried to call Jonathan on his cell, but then his son showed up in person, carrying his fake sword. Jonathan said he didn't know any more than he did.

The young woman who played Portia, still in costume and makeup, joined them. After Jonathan introduced them, she touched him lightly on the arm—was there something between them?—and explained that a fight had broken out in the stands at the game.

"And that's why they stopped the play?" asked Kaufmann.

She didn't know.

Soon Zach showed up, accompanied by a girl named Olivia, who played Shylock's daughter Jessica, Jonathan's love interest, along with Olivia's mom. None of them knew anything more about the fight at the football game.

By now the football fans were swarming past the theatergoers, driving some of them along in their wake. There was a lot of pushing and shoving.

Eventually the principal came out to the parking lot and addressed the thinning crowd. "I'm sorry," he said, shivering slightly in the cool night air, "but I'm going to have to ask you all to go home. Emotions were running high at the game, and things got out of hand. We cannot guarantee the safety of all concerned, especially our guests from Terre Rouge High School. Both the football game and the play have been suspended. It remains to be seen whether the rest of the game will be played at a later date or the current score will stand. For those of you who weren't there, Rouge was leading, 13-10."

The parents, the friends, the actors, the crew, the supporters of both football teams, and the players who had managed to shower and dress and make it out to the parking lot started buzzing once more.

He asked his son if he wanted a ride home.

"Thanks, Dad, but I'll catch one with Zach or Becky."

* * *

There was a bar twenty miles away where no one knew them. Actually, the bartender and a few regulars knew them, but the regulars minded their own business and he gave generous tips to the bartender to forget they had ever been there. He liked to meet Samantha for a drink before heading back to her apartment for a…nightcap.

"Cheers," he said to her over gin-and-tonics.

She was twenty-nine, blonde, taller than he was, with bright red lipstick and makeup artfully applied on her cheeks and around her eyes.

"You know Muslims invented algebra," he told her. "It's an Arabic word."

"I thought it was the Babylonians. Or maybe the Indians." She had a degree in finance and knew a thing or two about numbers.

"Well, the Arabs developed it. Algebra would not have become what it is today if not for the Arabs."

"So they conquered the world with x's and y's? Or whatever the letters are in Arabic."

"Something like that. They invented zero too."

"Zero? But that's nothing," she teased.

"They created something from nothing. That's a lot."

She leaned over and kissed him. "You're too clever for an old man, Ahmed."

He swatted her on the behind and said, "We Muslims invented hospitals and pharmacies. It doesn't matter if you grow older as long as you take care of yourself and live a virtuous life. *Inshallah*, I will live to a hundred."

"But will you still be able to—"

"*Inshallah*."

163

\* \* \*

A man in a badly-fitting gray-green sports jacket came up to him after the play and asked him if his name was Jonathan Kaufmann. He said it was. Then he noticed a uniformed policeman at the edge of the stage, a younger man with short blond hair, faint eyebrows, and puffy cheeks.

"You need to come with us," the first man said.

"What are you talking about?"

"Police." The man, pale, with circles under his eyes, flashed a badge. "Detective De Sousa."

Zach and Becky were watching the little drama unfold.

"What do you want?"

"Don't worry. It's routine. We have some questions for you."

Questions? What questions? Like why didn't you help your mom when she was suffering? Why did you refuse to believe she was dying? How could you have been such a jerk?

"But I—I'm in a play."

The man glanced at all the spectators and stray actors milling about. "Really?"

Jonathan asked Zach to call his dad and tell him what had happened. He started walking across the parking lot with the two police officers when the plainclothes one pointed to the sword and said, "Better leave that here."

\* \* \*

Driving home in the car, Kaufmann kept thinking about what he had seen. He wondered what was going to happen to Shylock—and Antonio. He had a vague knowledge of the play, but the details escaped him. Would the ships return safely? Would the moneylender try to extract his pound of flesh? Would he get his revenge, or would the Christians get their revenge on "the Jew"? He had a feeling things wouldn't end happily.

Then he started thinking about the young woman who played Portia, the one who was leaning on his son's arm. Why didn't Jonathan tell him anything about his personal life? Of course, he didn't tell Jonathan anything about his. It was a raw and sensitive subject. One thought led to another, and an image of the woman with salt and pepper hair, the one who was sitting by herself and reading a book in the restaurant, flashed into his mind. He suddenly realized who she was. The clerk at police headquarters who transcribed statements, filed reports, and generally kept the place running. Or buried reports so deeply that no one could ever find them again, making sure that nothing was ever accomplished. What was her name again? Jane? Janet? Marjorie? So she was the mysterious *ftirl*? He knew he was being unfair, but the thought depressed him immensely. His own ridiculous fantasies depressed him even more.

* * *

The police department building was full of gray metal desks and light bulbs whose illumination managed to be both dim and harsh at the same time. He had been there several times with his dad, but now the officers hustling drunks and drug addicts down a seasick-green corridor made him feel like he was one of the junkies.

The two cops led him to an unused conference room and asked if he wanted something to drink. He shook his head. Without his fake sword, he felt naked.

"So you play football?" De Sousa wondered. He was still wearing his jacket, but he had loosened his tie.

"Yeah."

"Coach says you didn't play tonight."

"That's right."

"Why not?" asked the uniformed officer, the one with the short hair and the full face.

"The play. Tonight was opening night."

"But today was the big game. Rouge and Noire. Crosstown rivals and all that."

Jonathan blinked. "I don't understand what—"

"Tell us about the party. Last Saturday night."

The detective lit a cigarette, and Jonathan found it hard to breathe.

"What about it?"

"Pretty wild, wasn't it?"

"Well—"

"Are you sexually active, Mr. Kaufmann?"

"Why are you—"

The two of them just stared at him. The detective smoothed the front of his shirt.

"Well, it depends what you mean by active."

"Let me put it this way," said the detective, pushing his chair closer to Jonathan's, practically blowing smoke in his face. "How long have you known Yasmin Ali?"

"Yasmin? I just met her last week. After the game."

"But you said you didn't play last week. You were rehearsing."

"What? No. Did I say that?" It was late, and Jonathan was getting confused.

"You saw her again at the party, didn't you?"

"Well, yeah."

"And you took her into a bedroom and had sex with her, didn't you?"

"No."

"Did you force her to have sex with you, Jonathan? Was she a virgin?"

"No, of course not."

"She wasn't a virgin?"

"It wasn't my fault. She came on to me."

"You want us to believe that?" said the younger cop, his face reddening. "A fourteen-year-old girl. Religious too, if you can call that shit a religion."

"Fourteen? Jesus."

"But you fucked her anyway, didn't you? Did that give you a special kick?"

"No! It wasn't that way at all."

"Kaufmann. You're a Jew, right? Did you tell her that?"

"What do you mean?"

The cop put his hands on Jonathan's chest and gave him a shove. "Maybe," he continued, "she didn't want to go into the bedroom, so you suggested you go out for a little ride. You found a secluded spot in the hills, fucked her, strangled her—and left her body in the woods."

"You found her body?" he gasped.

"Maybe you'd like to show us where it is," the detective suggested. He blew out more smoke.

Jonathan's head was throbbing. He felt he was going to throw up.

"Can I have that drink now?"

"There's no point in covering things up," said De Sousa. "We have pictures. They tell the whole story."

\* \* \*

Kaufmann had just opened a bottle of beer when the phone ring. It was Zach, who filled him in.

"What the hell?"

He got back into his car and drove downtown. A lot of other cars were going somewhere, slowly, and the lights seemed timed to turn red whenever he got near them. Once there, he stormed past the duty sergeant, barreled down the hall, and threw open the door of the first interrogation room. It was empty. He was about to open the next door when Captain Schroeder—broad shoulders, big bosom, and all—emerged from her office and headed him off.

"We just need to ask him some questions," she explained.

"Questions! What are you talking about?"

"Didn't Sergeant Khoury tell you?"

"Tell me what?"

"We have photographs. Of your son and the Ali girl in, well, compromising positions."

Kaufmann was speechless.

"We have to touch all the bases."

"What do you mean—compromising positions?"

"Her head in his, uh, lap. I mean, I know it was a party. I know they're experimenting at that age. But…"

"Jesus," Kaufmann muttered, under his breath. "How long is this going to take?"

Schroeder looked him in the eye. "You better go home and get some rest, Ezra. We'll call you when we're through."

The detective stared back. "Fuck that. I'm not going anywhere."

# Saturday: Vows

*The woman was dressed in a simple dress and her head was covered by a scarf. Only her face was visible, and the look on her face plainly indicated she was frightened. Numerous onlookers were standing about, waiting for the ceremony to begin. Some of them were old, some young. Some wore long dark robes, others sweatshirts and jeans. One of them looked like Dr. Ali. He was smoking a cigar. All of the onlookers were male.*

*Two bearded men were gripping the woman's arms and shoving her to the ground. Then the man who looked like Dr. Ali started lashing her back with a heavy bullwhip. The woman was screaming, but no sound came out.*

It was then that Aisha realized that she was the woman. She was screaming without making a sound, but at the same time she was looking down on the ghastly scene from far away, as if from a helicopter or even another planet. What had she done to trigger such a punishment? *Blood started flowing. The onlookers were jeering now.* Aisha watched them from a distance. What had turned them into such jackals? Religion? Centuries of colonial humiliation? A need to control their wayward wives and daughters? Fear of their own sexual urges?

But now she was back inside the woman's body. She was the woman. *Every stroke of the whip caused her to recoil in pain. Her back was completely bloody. She was losing consciousness. She was going to scream. Or die first.*

She sat up in bed, screaming noiselessly, unable to breathe. But at that very moment she heard the steady, rhythmic percussion of the Ramadan drummer. It was reminding her to wake up, eat something for the *suhoor* meal, and say the *fajr* prayer. Only this time the drum seemed to be accompanied by a gentle, melodic oud. She imagined that the drummer was a man and the oud player a woman. The music they made together was surprisingly beautiful. Was the beautiful harmony of male and female musicians a harbinger of better things to come? The air entered her lungs, and gradually she began to breathe again. But the fear and pain took a long time to go away.

\* \* \*

Kadiye roused Jamal and led him downstairs, still hooded, to a car. It was raining. The young guard pushed Jamal's head down, and Jamal stumbled into the back seat.

The car pulled away from the curb with a wet screech, and that was the last sound he heard for a long while except the steady drumbeat of the rain on the roof and the swish-swish of the wipers on the windshield. Traffic was light at that hour, and they followed what seemed to be a zigzag route of many left turns and a few right ones. He thought he caught a blurry glimpse of used auto dealerships and fast food franchises through the heavy fabric of his hood, like a blind man picking out shadows in the half-light.

Eventually, Kadiye spoke. "You can take off your hood now."

He seemed calmer this morning.

"I can't. My hands are tied."

"Hmm. I guess you'll have to wait."

The windshield wipers continued to make their racket. Occasionally a car horn sounded or brakes squealed. Every so often they stopped at a red light.

"Where are you taking me?"

Kadiye didn't say anything.

"Where?"

"It doesn't matter."

"What do you mean it doesn't matter?"

Kadiye didn't answer. The car skidded along the wet streets. He could feel every pothole. His captor turned on the radio and cycled through a number of stations until he found a religious one. The announcer talked about Ramadan and the upcoming celebration at the end of the holiday.

Finally, Kadiye pulled off the road. He parked the car on the shoulder, turned off the engine, and walked around to the back seat. The hood came off and then the rope.

Jamal stretched his neck and flexed his sore wrists.

"Get out," said the guard.

Jamal climbed stiffly out of the car. The sky was gray, the rain still falling in a cold drizzle. Cars and trucks whizzed past the empty fields.

Kadiye climbed back into the car and turned on the ignition. The Islamic station came back on.

"If anyone asks," he called out the window, "say I was at Friday prayers." Jamal stared at him blankly. He was too worn out to think. "But—"

"Go on!" he shouted. "Get out of here! If Allah gives you opportunity, take it!"

The young guard pulled back into traffic, sending pebbles flying.

"Hey, where am I?" yelled Jamal, but the car was gone.

A grain silo and a billboard advertising a feed and seed store loomed in the distance.

\* \* \*

Already fifteen or twenty people had gathered in the park, though it was still drizzly and overcast. Aisha surveyed the crowd. Men, women, young, old, even a few children. Some women were in *hijab*, while the young men wore the usual uniform of faded blue jeans, torn tennis shoes, and random baseball caps. The onlookers talked and joked among themselves, but it seemed to her that they joked too much, talked too fast. There was an undercurrent of tension.

Still a reporter covering a story, she took out her notebook and approached a couple of teenage boys. One of them was carrying a football.

"Hey, guys. Can I ask you a few questions?"

They looked puzzled but didn't say no.

"So why are you here?"

They looked at each other and snickered. "Just curious," said the one with the football, a beefy kid who was probably sixteen or seventeen. The other one, probably younger, said nothing.

"Curious about what?"

"You know."

"So what do you expect to see?"

The younger one shrugged and said, "I dunno."

She asked them if they were in high school.

"Yeah," said the older one, the one with the ball. "Rouge."

She thanked them for their time and moved on to a young woman in stretch pants who wasn't wearing a headscarf.

"Do you mind if I ask you some questions?"

After Aisha explained that she worked for the local newspaper, the woman said she didn't mind. The reporter asked her where she had heard about the proposed punishment.

"Facebook. All my friends are talking about it. But they're horrified."

"May I ask what kind of job you have?"

"I'm a stylist at a salon downtown." Her own hair was short, wavy, dyed blonde.

"So why do you think the girl is being punished?"

The young woman shook her head. "I don't know. Wearing too much makeup? Getting too free with boys? Whatever it is, I think they should leave all that to the parents. It's not their job to keep kids in line."

"Who are *they*? Who do you think is behind it?"

"I don't know. Some strict religious types who've gone off the deep end."

Aisha wrote it down.

"If you don't mind my asking, are you a Muslim?"

"Yes, I am. At least my parents brought me up that way. But I don't pray much anymore."

"Are you fasting?"

The woman laughed. "Do I have to answer that?"

"No," she said, smiling.

There was a break in the clouds, a patch of blue sky appeared, and the sun started to come out. She spotted Ezra at the park entrance, near some trees that were beginning to lose their yellow leaves, and waved.

* * *

"I'm going to the *masjid*," Ali told his wife. "If anyone calls, just tell them I'm not home."

"What about this craziness in the park?" said Mariam. "We can't let this happen."

She was washing the counters of their gleaming, modern kitchen, hours after their predawn breakfast.

"That's just hot air. I don't think they're going to go through with it."

"Why do you say that?"

He reached out and touched her wet hand. "If they did, they'd be arrested. They may be crazy, but not that crazy."

"I thought you didn't trust the police."

"I don't. But if it's one thing they're good at, it's cracking down on Muslims."

Mariam removed her hand and continued wiping down the granite counter. She suspected that her husband was going to the park after all, but she wasn't taking any chances. She had already called the chief and asked him to take the necessary steps to protect her daughter.

\* \* \*

Tariq paced back and forth across the hard concrete floor of the warehouse, yelling at his young follower.

"How could you fuck up the one job I asked you to do? Losing the two prisoners you were s'pose to keep an eye on and one of them just a ten-year-old kid."

"I told you," said Kadiye, who was sitting on the green sofa with the Qur'an in his hand, "they escaped while I was at Friday prayers."

"Who said you could leave them alone?"

"It is incumbent upon good Muslims to pray together."

Tariq muttered a few curses under his breath. "Friday prayers are on Friday. Yesterday. When were you going to tell me?"

"I—I was afraid to."

Tariq continued to pace. "Why the fuck did you come here anyway?"

"My father was killed, my mother was raped, my two sisters—well, I don't know what happened to them. It's not safe in my country."

"At least they don't have fags in your country."

The young man didn't seem to know for sure what fags were, but he said, "We do, but…they don't last long."

\* \* \*

A boy was flying a kite. Two men were sitting on a bench and playing chess. Aisha snapped some pictures with her cellphone. More people were streaming into the park—couples towing little children, cyclists riding by, old people out for a bit of sun before the rains returned—but that wasn't unusual; it happened every Saturday.

"What do you think's going on?" Kaufmann asked her.

"I don't know. False alarm?"

"Better than the real thing, anyway."

"But now we're back to square one."

Those who had gathered in hopes of witnessing the promised spectacle were starting to drift away.

It had been a long night for the detective. By the time his colleagues had finished with Jonathan, it was four in the morning. He knew De Sousa as a grumpy veteran who was not above dirty tricks, but what was that rookie cop doing there? Jonathan said he had made some odd comments about virgins and terrorists, Muslims and Jews. What was going on?

And what about his partner?

Kaufmann had left an angry message on Khoury's phone, asking him why he had implicated his son without even letting him know. A few hours later Khoury texted back, saying, "Sorry, boss. I thought I needed to go through channels." Boss!? Channels? If he was Khoury's boss, or even just his partner, why had Khoury cut him out of the loop? Well, they would settle their scores later.

Now Aisha looked over his shoulder. "Do you hear that?"

A siren, coming closer.

"Fire? Ambulance?"

Suddenly, a police car with flashing blue and red lights drove right up onto the wet grass at the edge of the park. The first car was followed by two more. Four or five uniformed policemen jumped out of the cars and immediately began swinging their nightsticks. They seemed to be making a sweep through the crowd.

Through a megaphone, one of the officers ordered everyone to disperse. The chess players grumbled but packed up their set. Disappointed and bewildered, the young kite flyers reeled in their kites and wandered off. The twenty-something parents took their children's hands and hustled them to safety. The would-be gawkers muttered to themselves but didn't protest.

Where was Aisha? Kaufmann had suddenly lost sight of her.

But he spotted two men in dark blue uniforms, near the swing sets, beating a slight, middle-aged man in traditional Middle Eastern robes. One of the policemen wrestled him to the ground, and the other beat him with his stick. Perhaps they thought he was involved in the rumored punishment. The man was trying to fight back, but the police officer kept pommeling him. Someone else seemed to be intervening, trying to help the man. From a distance, it looked like Dr. Ali.

He attempted to get closer but was able to take only a few steps before he was handcuffed and shoved into the back of a police van. He tried to show his badge, but in the confusion no one paid any attention. In a few minutes, he and several other suspects were whisked away.

* * *

**Sorry, brother,** Tariq had texted. **No hard feelings.**

**Where r u?** Farid had texted back. He had slipped out of the house after early prayers and was working on a paper for school at the local library.

**Why?**

Farid called him directly. "I want to talk to you," he explained.

"So talk."

"Face-to-face."

His friend, or ex-friend, told him where he was, and Farid had taken two buses to get there. It turned out to be a rundown industrial building in a neighborhood of old furniture factories, dive bars, and train tracks that seemed to lead nowhere. A few out-of-the-way stores and offices were closed for the weekend. A homeless man was sleeping in a doorway. The near-empty streets looked grimy and full of potholes, but now the sun was out and the oil-slicked puddles gleamed in the light.

"What is this place?" he asked Tariq, apparently alone, his head still covered by the red *kufi.*

"A warehouse. Used to store parts of some sort. I'm not really sure."

"So what are you doing here?"

Tariq shrugged.

Farid took a look around. The windows were cracked and dirty; a cool breeze blew right through the cracks. A moss-green sofa was planted incongruously in the middle of the room. A dark closet in the back—he pulled the dangling cord to turn on the light—was full of shelves, and some of the shelves housed little boxes containing nails or screws of various sizes.

But there was no sign of Yasmin.

"Where's my sister?" said Farid.

Tariq shook his head wearily. "I told you, brother, I have no idea."

"You're not just messing with me?"

"I—I'm sorry for what I said. Of course I care about your sister. I just don't know where she is."

Farid didn't know what to think.

"Like I said, all this fasting makes me crazy. I know it's a good thing. I know it should bring me closer to Allah. But…I've been under a lot of stress lately. My girlfriend left me. I don't have my meds. My head's messed up."

Farid nodded.

The other man continued, "I know that, in Ramadan, you're supposed to be kind and compassionate. Like, forgiving people for things they did to you."

"Mnn."

"Can you forgive me, brother? I'm really sorry."

He opened his arms to Farid, and Farid, still sore from the night before, reluctantly returned his hug.

\* \* \*

After thumbing a ride with a passing truck driver, Jamal had managed to make his way home. He entered the apartment building and slowly climbed up the stairs. He met a neighbor whose name he had forgotten. They exchanged perfunctory greetings.

When he opened the door to his apartment, he found Muhammad sleeping on the bed. He looked as if he had lost weight.

"Poor Muhammad! Poor little cat!" he said, stroking the animal's bedraggled fur.

Muhammad purred and made a few squeaky sounds.

"Here, let me give you some food."

He went into the kitchen. Muhammad followed, pulling an invisible ribbon around and between Jamal's legs, rubbing his fur against the wrinkled pants his master had slept in for three straight days. Surprisingly, there were some kibbles in the cat's bowl. He wondered whether it was a Ramadan miracle, but then he discovered Aisha's note. He needed to call her.

But first he called the dispatcher at the taxi company.

"Where you been?" said the man on duty. "We almost sent out a search party."

"Why didn't you?" replied Jamal.

"We figured you'd turn up eventually. Especially after your taxi showed up."

"What?"

"Yeah, someone dropped it off in the middle of the night. Good Samaritan, I suppose."

Jamal shook his head, silently. "I'll come in later today," he said.

"No need," said the other.

"It's okay. I just need a few hours to rest."

The sunlight filtering in through the kitchen window seemed to be making him sleepy.

"Take as long as you want, my friend. Don't matter no more."

"What do you mean?"

"The boss wasn't happy. I guess you're fired."

"It—it wasn't my fault. I was kidnapped."

"Sorry, man. The wheels keep turning."

"What does that mean?"

"Lay low. Try again in a few months. You never know."

There was a click at the other end of the line. Muhammad looked up and purred.

\* \* \*

Jonathan and Zach burst into the warehouse like the Hardy Boys on a mission. Zach, who had followed Farid from his house to the library, called his friend—still asleep—when Yasmin's brother made another move. The two of them trailed him to the quiet, potholed industrial district where they found themselves now.

"Who the fuck are you?" demanded the tall young man with the red cloth head covering.

"Where's Yasmin?" demanded Jonathan in return.

"Do you know who these clowns are?" the tall one asked Farid.

Yasmin's brother shook his head.

Jonathan turned to him. "Your sister. Where is she?"

"I wish I knew."

Jonathan looked at Zach, then turned back to the other. "Aren't you worried?"

"Of course I'm worried!" Farid shouted. "She's my little sister!"

\* \* \*

Hanan was reading a Harry Potter book when Aisha arrived at Henry's small but nicely-decorated apartment. A chipped glass coffee table anchored the living area. There were abstract prints on the wall and green plants on the side table.

"So how was the rally?" asked Henry.

Aisha turned to her daughter. "Sweetie, would you mind going into the bedroom while I talk to Henry?"

After Hanan left, she replied, "It wasn't a rally. More like a public stoning." Images of the previous night's dream flashed into her head.

"What do you mean?"

"They were threatening to flog a young woman for bad behavior, but the police arrived before the girl or her captors showed up."

"Thank God for that."

Aisha nodded. "But the girl is still missing."

Henry asked her if she would like some tea.

"It's not yet sundown."

"Sorry. Do you mind if I make some for myself?"

She shook her head. While he was in the kitchen, she went into the bedroom and asked her daughter how the morning had gone.

"Great," said Hanan. "I like Uncle Henry."

Aisha smiled. "Good. We'll go home soon."

When she came back into the living room, Henry had returned with his tea. She asked him whether he had heard from Jamal.

"I don't think we're on speaking terms."

She told him that Jamal's apartment was empty and the cat seemed to be starving.

Henry frowned. "That doesn't sound like him."

"I'm really worried. Where could he be?"

"Have you tried the taxi office?"

"No."

Henry took out his cell phone. The dispatcher didn't want to release any information, even after Aisha came on the line and said she was his ex-wife, but eventually he gave her a few crumbs.

"He missed several shifts—we didn't know where he was—but he called in today."

"You talked to him?"

"That's right, ma'am."

"Did he say what happened?"

"Not really."

"Is he all right?"

"I couldn't say. You'll have to ask him."

After relaying the news to Henry, she called Jamal's home number one more time. This time he answered.

"Where in the name of Allah have you been?"

"Oh, took a little vacation."

"Be serious. I was worried about you. We both were."

"Anna?" He preferred to use the American name for their daughter.

"Not Hanan. She doesn't know you were missing. I meant Henry."

"Hmm."

"I fed Muhammad."

Jamal's tone seemed to soften. "I know, Aisha. Thank you for taking care of him. The poor guy had to suffer because his Muslim brothers held me captive."

"What are you talking about?"

"The morality police. The God squad. I'll tell you about it tomorrow. Shall I pick Anna up as usual?"

Was tomorrow Sunday? It was hard to keep track. "Yes, okay. Do you want to speak to her?"

"Of course."

"We're at Henry's apartment. You want to speak to him while I get Hanan?"

Jamal didn't say anything. Aisha handed the phone to Henry.

"Are you all right?" asked Henry.

"I'm okay. Just tired and angry. You were right: they don't like people like you and me. Or at least me. They don't want gay Muslim poet taxi drivers on their recruiting posters."

Henry laughed. "Maybe you should move out of the neighborhood."

"I may have to. I think I'm being evicted."

"Jesus, I'm sorry. You, uh, know you can stay here if you need a place."

"Listen, Henry—"

Hanan ran out of the bedroom and grabbed the phone. "Hi, Daddy!" she squealed.

"How are you doing, little one?"

"Fine. I was reading Harry Potter. Uncle Henry watched me while Mom was away."

"Uncle Henry is a good uncle, isn't he?"

Hanan smiled. "Yeah, he's great."

"Well," said Jamal, "I'll see you tomorrow morning. Think of some fun things to do."

\* \* \*

*Hot, cold, hot again. Neck hurts, shoulder aches.* Peering down at the torn, creased page, she started to cry. *I'm not going "home." It's not my home! They kill girls there. Honor killing. Honor? Do they kill girls they find on slut lists?* Despite the late afternoon heat, she shuddered.

\* \* \*

The only light was that which came through a small barred window near the ceiling of the holding cell on the fourth floor of the police building, so Kaufmann wasn't sure whether the sun was out or the drizzle had returned.

He shared the cell with five other people—two men in warmup suits and tennis shoes who looked as if they had never seen the inside of a gym, an older woman in *hijab*, an African American teenager, and a young woman in tight jeans, perhaps Indian or Pakistani. The two men whispered to each other; the teenager listened to music through headphones which, surprisingly, the arresting officers had not taken from him; the woman in the headscarf just sat there with a glum look on her face. The young woman looked at him; he shrugged and shook his head.

His thoughts strayed to the unsolved shooting of the three-year-old boy. The police were there that day. They had weapons. Lightweight, semiautomatic pistols, as a matter of fact. If it wasn't the work of Islamophobic "Christians" or radical Muslims or an angry wife or some other disturbed and alienated individual who had reached the end of his or her tether, maybe the culprit was a rogue cop. Richter, the rookie? He seemed to have a thing about Muslims. Despite all their training on positive community relations and the proper use of force, some cops did crazy things. It was known to happen.

But if that was the case, why hadn't anyone found traces of the shooting? Kaufmann had worked with Rudnitsky, the Forensics lead, for over ten years. There had never been any problem. But maybe some other investigator was covering for a fellow officer. Maybe the cover-up went even higher. The Thin Blue Line and that sort of thing.

Looking around, Kaufmann noticed some graffiti on the concrete wall behind him. Crude sexual drawings. A few phone numbers. Not far away, the phrase *Black lives matter*. Below that, *Muslim lives matter*. Below that—*Muslim women's lives matter too*. Can't argue with that. He wondered what had happened to Aisha.

They heard footsteps. A guard, accompanied by a broad-shouldered African American woman, approached the cell door and opened it. Not just any African American woman—Captain Schroeder.

"Sorry, Ezra. A mix-up."

"Jesus," he said, shaking his head again. "First my son, then me."

"We just asked him some questions."

"All night?"

"You know how it is," she said.

"Yeah. Right. How it is."

They were walking out of the jail and into the part of the building devoted to police department offices.

"Captain," he continued, "who is this kid Richter?"

"Richter?" She paused to reflect. "A good man. Served in Afghanistan. A bit too gung-ho, maybe, but he'll settle down."

Kaufmann didn't say anything.

At the end of the corridor, the captain repeated her earlier apology. "I'm sorry. The city's on edge. We need to solve these cases. Now."

* * *

180

Becky's text came in as he and Zach were sitting in Zach's bedroom, doing math homework and listening to Bruce Springsteen. A ten-pound mathematics textbook lay open on the desk, and graphs of ellipses and hyperbolas lay scattered on the bed.

**I've found her!!!** Becky wrote. **Call me soon as u get this.**

Zach stopped the music, and Jonathan called Becky.

"Where are you?" he said.

"Two blocks from Haniya's house."

"Haniya?"

"Yasmin's friend. From middle school. She's hiding Yasmin in her attic."

"You're kidding. What do Haniya's parents say?"

"Nothing. They don't know."

Jonathan whistled. "So no one, like, kidnapped her?"

"Right. She just ran away."

Zach was gesturing at him, and he paused a moment to fill Zach in.

"But why?" he asked Becky. "Why is she hiding in someone's attic?"

"Apparently, she got into a fight with her father."

"Christ. I better tell my dad. I think he's looking for her too."

"No," said Becky. "You can't tell anyone. She doesn't want her parents or anyone else to know where she is."

"But—but she's all right?"

There was a long pause. "She's afraid to go home. But I don't think that's the whole story. Like you said, maybe she's feeling ashamed about the party. The slut list."

"Why do you say that?"

"That's the impression I got from talking to Haniya. She didn't just run away. She wants to, like, disappear."

"She can't hide out in someone's attic forever."

"Maybe you should talk to her."

Jonathan didn't know what to say. "Me?"

"Yeah. You."

\* \* \*

Kaufmann checked his messages. There were several from Aisha. She had been swept out of the park by the police. He called her, and when she didn't answer, he left a voice mail telling her he was all right. He walked a few blocks in no particular direction before remembering that he had left his car near the park.

He hailed a cab. There was a dog on the floor of the passenger seat.

"Do you take him with you everywhere?" he asked the driver.

"Anton is good dog," the man said with a Russian accent. "No bother anyone."

The sun was setting, and the evening breeze was getting colder. Kaufmann closed his window.

"Where you go?" said the cabbie.

He recited his home address, then changed his mind and gave another location. "It's a church, really, but they're holding Jewish services there tonight."

The streets were still slick, and the heavy vehicle bounced along them like a clumsy seal.

"Services?"

"It's the beginning of Yom Kippur. The Day of Atonement."

"I am Jewish too, but we don't practice Jewish in Soviet Union." The cab hit a pothole, and the dog lifted his head. "Tell me, what is this Day of Opponent?"

"Atonement," said the detective. "Making amends, trying to repair the damage you've done."

Speaking of which, should he fast this year? Do some serious soul-searching? Repair the breach with, for example, his son? The sun had definitely set now, and the buildings along the street were cast in a gray pall.

"Hey," said Kaufmann, "maybe you'd like to come to *Kol Nidre* with me tonight."

Anton adjusted his position on the seat.

"What is Cold Knee Day?" said the driver.

"The first words of the prayer. They mean 'all vows.'"

"Vows? What vows?"

The detective took a deep breath. "You know that in Spain around the time of Columbus—the time of the Inquisition—Jews weren't allowed to practice their religion either?"

The cabbie looked into the mirror and shook his head.

"Yes, they could be killed if they didn't convert to Christianity—or at least pretend to be Christians. I think the *Kol Nidre* prayer is actually older than that, but the *conversos*, the secret Jews, used the prayer as a way of asking God for forgiveness—for the false vows they had to make to a different religion."

The cabbie appeared to ponder this history lesson, and the detective took the opportunity to send a text to his son.

**Hey, Jonathan. Hope ur all right after long night. I'm in cab on way to High Holiday services. Wanna meet me there?**

After a few minutes, the taxi driver deposited him in front of a plain white wooden building with a modest steeple on a quiet but windy street. Fifteen or twenty people, some dressed up in suits and fancy dresses, others in very casual shirts and pants and shoes, were streaming along the street on their way to services. Some carried blue velvet *tallit* bags; others checked their cell phones as if they had other things on their minds.

"You sure you don't want to come?"

The dog craned his neck toward the departing passenger.

"No, no, I have Anton," said the driver. "But one thing I am not understand."

"What's that?"

"What if God make false vow? Cancel promise. What if he promise something, then take away? Tell me, this is all right?"

The cool breeze caused a few leaves to flutter and fall from a nearby tree. False promises, false hopes.

"I don't know," said Kaufmann. "Maybe you should ask the rabbi."

He paid his fare and went inside the church.

\* \* \*

Brodsky switched on the car stereo and played an old tape of emotional Russian songs. The dog seemed to like it. He poked his head under Brodsky's hand, wanting it to be rubbed.

"Soon, Anton. Go home soon."

He and Elena had started bickering about insignificant things, and then one day as she was preparing dinner she suddenly turned to him and said, in English, "If you didn't steal bicycle—"

"B—but he want bicycle. You said we should get him bicycle."

She raised her voice. "I didn't say to steal it."

"But we have no money," he shouted back.

"We could have manage. It's always same," she said bitterly. "You take something good, something happy, and ruin it. "

Brodsky started to answer and then just gave up. The whole thing was too painful. They were living in another city, another state, and the next day he dragged himself to the Greyhound terminal and left.

But maybe it was time for him to go back, give it another try. Things were hard on her too.

Brodsky pulled over to the curb and parked the hulking cab. After making sure that the window was open a crack, he stepped out of the car.

"Be good dog," he said. "I come back soon."

The cabbie walked up the block and opened the door of a hole-in-the-wall bar with a flashing neon sign in the window. There were only a few customers in the place, but the burly bartender was lining up glasses and dropping olives into them as if expecting a big crowd to show up at any minute.

"What'll it be, pal?" he said.

"Stolichnaya. Over ice."

"You got it."

An American football match was playing on the television set above the rows of bottles. Big men in colorful uniforms smashed into each other on a brilliant green field. Brodsky felt tired just watching them. His head ached.

The bartender brought him his drink.

"Are you all right?"

Brodsky shook his head.

"Relax, pal. Everything's cool. Watch the game."

Actually, everything wasn't cool, and he didn't like American football. The bartender gave him a puzzled look, then strolled to the other end of the bar, where two young women in bright red lipstick were requesting refills.

Brodsky finished his drink, left some money on the bar, and headed out into the night.

* * *

The service began with the traditional plaintive melody, beautiful but melancholy, played on a single cello by a woman sitting by herself on a simple, straight-backed chair. Young, attractive, and serious, she reminded Ezra of his wife Rachel when they had first met.

During the playing of the music, he thought about the marriage vows he had made to Rachel. I am my beloved, and my beloved is mine. Would it violate those vows to see other women, to develop a relationship, even an intimate one? What would Jonathan think? Maybe the anonymous letters were God's mocking comment on his inner struggles.

He remembered the week when Rachel's illness was first diagnosed. She had been having stomach pains, so he dropped her off at the gastroenterologist's office and went to work. When he went back to pick her up, she was no longer there. Someone referred him to the emergency room, where he tracked her down.

She had become disoriented, delirious, from a chemical imbalance caused by the disease. They moved her to the ICU and determined what the problem was. The news was not good.

He remembered the tearful conversation with Jonathan, younger and less guarded then; the consultation with the young specialist at the research hospital, who told her point blank that she had no chance of survival and explained that he believed in being honest with his patients; the crocodile tears of the radiologist, who said, feebly, "I wish I could help you"; followed by the emergency trip to the rabbi for spiritual reassurance, the very same rabbi who was now sitting quietly in his white High Holiday gown listening to the mournful sounds of the cello.

"Now?" he had asked her.

"Yes, now. Right now."

Her face looked stricken. They drove over to the rabbi's office and asked the receptionist if they could see him. She asked them, politely, to wait a minute. They waited. The rabbi ushered them into a small study, where they talked about life and death, with something about God thrown in. "Think of a butterfly," said the rabbi, who was younger than they were. "When the caterpillar is transformed into a butterfly, she doesn't know what is happening to her. She thinks she is dying. But in truth she is metamorphosing into a serene and beautiful new creature."

Hmm. Right.

He remembered the ups and downs. The trips to the emergency room in the middle of the night. The regular outpatient visits, brightened by the smiles and banter of the nurses. The oversized get-well card from her young ex-clients. The pain, the vomiting, the taking of blood, the IVs, the radiation and chemotherapy, the shrinking of the tumor, the stable blood markers, the emaciated body, the modest weight gain. The steady stream of friends and acquaintances bearing frozen casseroles. The trip to see the sold-out musical fresh from Broadway. The fear and hope. The meditation tapes. Acupuncture. The medical miracle books. The return to work. The flurry of client visits, the ambitious plans, the burst of activity. The turn for the worse. The last visit to the doctor. The counselor from the hospice.

The cellist finished her piece, and the cantor, a round-faced man with a round belly, began to recite the *Kol Nidre.*

What about the vow that God had made to her? The taxi driver was right. Surely He had promised human beings something when He had created them—and the heavens and the earth and everything else—out of nothing. Surely there was some point to it all. Were they supposed to forgive the Big Guy for reneging on his promises? What could God do to make amends?

Of course there was no Big Guy in the Sky. That much was obvious. If God was anything, it was the mystery behind or within or amid everything. The last piece of a puzzle that included black holes and dark energy and semi-intelligent creatures bent on destroying themselves but capable of discovering or inventing things like black holes and dark energy. That God didn't make any promises. That God didn't know or care about two-legged earthlings who liked to talk to themselves and attribute the mumblings to "God."

Yet humans hungry for meaning kept imagining their god was telling them to do all kinds of horrible things. Wasn't that what had happened to the boy in the park and the young girl who had gone missing? Hadn't they run into one or more overeager God-zealots? The cases were still unsolved. He needed to go back to Forensics. He needed to check out the rookie cop. And he needed to find the still-missing girl. Speaking of making amends, he needed to patch up his differences with his partner. It wasn't Khoury's fault that Jonathan had gotten mixed up with the girl at the party. Hey, Jonathan! What really happened? Do you want to talk about it?

The cantor finished the third and final repetition of the *Kol Nidre*, and the rabbi—sneakers peeking out beneath his silky white robe because real shoes were too extravagant for a day of soul-searching—began to lead the congregation in the old chants and prayers.

\* \* \*

"You sure you want to come?" he had said.

"Yes, of course I do," Becky had insisted.

The Saturday night performance of the play had been canceled—belatedly—because of the Jewish holiday, but there would be another performance Sunday night.

"It's just a lot of dirt and dead leaves."

"I get it. I've been to cemeteries before."

They had hopped on a bus and walked the last six or seven blocks under a silvery moon. A text from his dad had appeared on his phone. Jonathan texted something back.

Becky asked him if they had a good relationship.

Jonathan shrugged. "It's hard to, like, open up."

"What about Yasmin? Have you thought about talking to her?"

"What can I say?"

"Make her feel that she's not, you know, a slut."

The cemetery was located on a hillside overlooking the city, whose lights sparkled beneath them like distant stars. They wandered around for a while before finding the grave. The wind whistled through the half-bare trees, and a few more leaves fell on the graves in the time they were there. A curious owl hooted from a distant branch.

"Here it is," said Jonathan. "I haven't been back since—"

A simple stone slab inscribed with a star of David and his mother's name and dates.

"Do you want me to leave you alone?"

Jonathan shook his head. He stared at the headstone for a while, then sat down on the damp earth beside the grave. Becky sat next to him.

He buried his head in his hands. Becky thought he might be crying, but after a minute he raised his fists, opened his mouth, and howled. The sound seemed to rip through his chest. Becky jumped back.

"Are you all right?"

"Yeah, fine," he muttered, through his tears. "I'm fine."

The owl continued to hoot high up in the tree.

"I was just remembering the hour she died," he explained. "It was late in the afternoon. I was upstairs listening to music. My dad said to come down quickly."

Becky put her arm around Jonathan's shoulder.

"Tell me about it," she said.

\* \* \*

Anton was waiting for Brodsky in the cab.

"Good boy, Anton. Good boy." The dog licked his hand as he ruffled the animal's fur.

Brodsky sat down in the driver's seat and gripped the steering wheel without turning on the ignition. Every so often he had tried to talk about the terrible thing that had happened, but either he couldn't say anything or the other person didn't want to listen. Now with the sun down and the temperature dropping, he turned to the dog.

"You remember Sasha? Throw ball, scratch tummy?"

Anton looked up at his master, trying to grasp the meaning of the words.

"Killed," said the cabbie, switching to his native Russian. "Riding his bicycle. Do you understand, Anton? Run over. He was only ten."

Brodsky scratched Anton between the ears. The dog murmured happily.

"It wasn't an illness," he continued. "Or a gang shooting. Or a terrorist attack. He was just...run over. A car spinning out of control. A stupid, senseless accident."

Anton growled mildly, as if trying to respond to Brodsky's lament.

"Tell me, Anton," he said in English, "how it is possible? How it is possible?"

The dog continued to look into his master's face, trying to understand what he was saying.

\* \* \*

Aisha peered inside the refrigerator.

"You're in luck, Hanan. We're having your favorite meal."

"Banana muffins?" she asked archly.

"No, not banana muffins. Falafel with tahini sauce. Not too spicy. The way you like it."

Hanan grinned. "Thank you, Mom."

First they would thank Allah for his blessings. Then they would eat. And after that she would call Ezra to make sure he was really all right—and to figure out what either of them might do to solve the disappearance of the girl. And the shooting of the little boy. Of course, she was a reporter and he was a cop, but no one said they couldn't talk. She knew that that night was the beginning of an important fast day for observant Jews, and in that spirit, she wanted to take advantage of the near-coincidence of the two holidays and ask him if he would like to celebrate Eid al-Fitr, the upcoming end of the Ramadan fast, with her.

\* \* \*

Having fed Muhammad, Jamal made a simple dinner for himself. He sat down at the kitchen table with food in front of him and the cat in his lap and took out his poetry notebook. He turned to the poem he had started writing about being evicted, and after thinking about it for several minutes he revised a few words, added several more lines, and gave the poem a title: "Eviction Notice."

*When they come to evict me*
*I will steal one last glance at the lemon tree*
*and I will remember the other times they came*
*to evict us*
*first the beautiful white house with the courtyard*

*and the light in the afternoons*
*and the lemon tree there too*
*then the concrete hovel in the camp*
*without running water or electricity*
*without a tree of any kind*
*just starving dogs running wild barking*
*naked children laughing and crying in the sun*
*so-called freedom fighters brandishing heavy weapons*
*smoking ashen cigarettes*
*and this time I will*
*drink a cool glass of water from the tap*
*collect my furniture*
*arrange it on the sidewalk*
*prop the bed frame against the kitchen table*
*a matchbook under one of its feet*
*the poetry table I call it*
*where my best writing gets done*
*and the nightstand with the books of poetry on it*
*more poetry to warm the soul and ward off doubt*
*not to mention the mattress sticky with love*
*and when I put a bowl for the cat down*
*on the street corner*
*I will say*
*there is no God but God*
*and you Muhammad are his prophet*

Jamal stroked Muhammad's warm fur and ate a forkful of rice.

* * *

In the middle of one of the prayers, Kaufmann glanced toward the front of the makeshift Jewish prayer house. He caught a glimpse of the cello player with her wavy, chestnut-brown hair. The one who reminded him of Rachel. He rubbed his eyes, tried to focus more clearly on the woman's face, lost his place in the prayer. He flashed back to Rachel's last day.

It was late afternoon; the blinds were half-drawn and the light was fading. She had stopped eating. She had lost the ability to speak. Her body was shutting down. He had been giving her morphine to lessen the pain and help her sleep. But she didn't sleep. She breathed slowly, intermittently, with great difficulty. She tried to blink her eyes. She seemed to be trying to lift her head to indicate something above them. Jonathan was playing some music in his room; they could hear the sounds above them. He ran upstairs, knocked on the door, and told Jonathan to come quickly. The two of them sat by her side. He held her hand and told her he loved her. It's okay, he told her, trying to ease her mind, even though it wasn't. She fluttered her eyelids, tried to breathe, struggled very hard to breathe. Stopped breathing.

Soon afterward the rabbi came. He gently checked her eyes and breath to make sure she was dead, recited a traditional passage about the worth of a good woman, her price above rubies, and led them in the singing of the most famous Jewish prayer, the *Shema*, the one that called on the Jewish people to recognize the Oneness of God. The Godness of God. Not this or that deity but…God. Yet when he tried to sing the prayer, he found that he couldn't do it. He couldn't carry the tune. All that came out of his mouth were discordant bleats and wails.

But now, perhaps, it was different. Somehow the cello music—mournful, plaintive, heart-wrenching, yet beautiful—had replaced the broken sounds. Of course she was gone. But not entirely gone? Some part of her still flickering somewhere in the universe? Didn't the physicists say that nothing was ever really lost, just transformed into something else? Silently, wordlessly, half-unconsciously, he asked her for permission to see more of the lovely, caring, strong-willed reporter in the headscarf. He was eager to know her better.

**The End**

# Acknowledgments

I'd like to thank the editors of *Ducts*, *The Milo Review*, and *JewishFiction.net*, in whose pages stories adapted from this book appeared. Thanks also to Jesse Coleman, Caroline Leavitt, and Rachel Schoenbauer for their editorial suggestions. Thanks, as well, to Zara Kramer and the rest of the Pandamoon team for their guidance and support. Thank you to Anton Chekhov, whose moving story "*Misery*" inspired one of the threads of this novel. I'd like to thank Len and Libby Traubman for creating the Arab-Jewish Dialogue Group in which I participated. I'm grateful to Rabbi Michael Lerner and, more recently, Cat Zavis for the deeply empathetic understanding expressed and embodied in *Tikkun* and the Network of Spiritual Progressives. Finally, I'm grateful to Jenny and Jocelyn for being the two best daughters in the world and to Margo for sharing her life with me.

# About the Author

Randolph Splitter graduated from Hamilton College, earned a Ph.D. in English from the University of California, Berkeley, and taught at Caltech and De Anza College. He is the author of two previous books, Body and Soul (fiction) and Proust's 'Recherche': A Psychoanalytic Interpretation. With two grown daughters and three grandkids, he currently lives with his wife in Portland, Oregon.

Thank you for purchasing this copy of *The Ramadan Drummer.* If you enjoyed this book, please let the author know by posting a review.

**Growing good ideas into great reads…one book at a time.**

Visit www.pandamoonpublishing.com to learn more about other works by our talented authors.

**Mystery/Thriller/Suspense**
- *A Flash of Red* by Sarah K. Stephens
- *Evening in the Yellow Wood* by Laura Kemp
- *Fate's Past* by Jason Huebinger
- *Graffiti Creek* by Matt Coleman
- *Juggling Kittens* by Matt Coleman
- *Killer Secrets* by Sherrie Orvik
- *Knights of the Shield* by Jeff Messick
- *Kricket* by Penni Jones
- *Looking into the Sun* by Todd Tavolazzi
- *On the Bricks Series Book 1: On the Bricks* by Penni Jones
- *Rogue Saga Series Book 1: Rogue Alliance* by Michelle Bellon
- *Southbound* by Jason Beem
- *The Juliet* by Laura Ellen Scott
- *The Last Detective* by Brian Cohn
- *The Moses Winter Mysteries Book 1: Made Safe* by Francis Sparks
- *The New Royal Mysteries Book 1: The Mean Bone in Her Body* by Laura Ellen Scott
- *The New Royal Mysteries Book 2: Crybaby Lane* by Laura Ellen Scott
- *The Ramadan Drummer* by Randolph Splitter
- *The Teratologist* by Ward Parker
- *The Unraveling of Brendan Meeks* by Brian Cohn
- *The Zeke Adams Series Book 1: Pariah* by Ward Parker
- *This Darkness Got to Give* by Dave Housley

**Science Fiction/Fantasy**

- *Becoming Thuperman* by Elgon Williams
- *Children of Colondona Book 1: The Wizard's Apprentice* by Alisse Lee Goldenberg
- *Children of Colondona Book 2: The Island of Mystics* by Alisse Lee Goldenberg
- *Chimera Catalyst* by Susan Kuchinskas
- *Dybbuk Scrolls Trilogy Book 1: The Song of Hadariah* by Alisse Lee Goldenberg
- *Dybbuk Scrolls Trilogy Book 2: The Song of Vengeance* by Alisse Lee Goldenberg
- *Dybbuk Scrolls Trilogy Book 3: The Song of War* by Alisse Lee Goldenberg
- *Everly Series Book 1: Everly* by Meg Bonney
- *.EXE Chronicles Book 1: Hello World* by Alexandra Tauber and Tiffany Rose
- *Fried Windows (In a Light White Sauce)* by Elgon Williams
- *Magehunter Saga Book 1: Magehunter* by Jeff Messick
- *Project 137* by Seth Augenstein
- *Revengers Series Book 1: Revengers* by David Valdes Greenwood
- *The Bath Salts Journals: Volume One* by Alisse Lee Goldenberg and An Tran
- *The Crimson Chronicles Book 1: Crimson Forest* by Christine Gabriel
- *The Crimson Chronicles Book 2: Crimson Moon* by Christine Gabriel
- *The Phaethon Series Book 1: Phaethon* by Rachel Sharp
- *The Sitnalta Series Book 1: Sitnalta* by Alisse Lee Goldenberg
- *The Sitnalta Series Book 2: The Kingdom Thief* by Alisse Lee Goldenberg
- *The Sitnalta Series Book 3: The City of Arches* by Alisse Lee Goldenberg
- *The Sitnalta Series Book 4: The Hedgewitch's Charm* by Alisse Lee Goldenberg
- *The Sitnalta Series Book 5: The False Princess* by Alisse Lee Goldenberg
- *The Wolfcat Chronicles Book 1: Wolfcat 1 by* Elgon Williams

**Women's Fiction**

- *Beautiful Secret* by Dana Faletti
- *The Long Way Home* by Regina West
- *The Mason Siblings Series Book 1: Love's Misadventure* by Cheri Champagne
- *The Mason Siblings Series Book 2: The Trouble with Love* by Cheri Champagne
- *The Mason Siblings Series Book 3: Love and Deceit* by Cheri Champagne
- *The Mason Siblings Series Book 4: Final Battle for Love* by Cheri Champagne
- *The Seductive Spies Series Book 1: The Thespian Spy* by Cheri Champagne
- *The Seductive Spy Series Book 2: The Seamstress and the Spy* by Cheri Champagne
- *The Shape of the Atmosphere* by Jessica Dainty
- *The To-Hell-And-Back Club Book 1: The To-Hell-And-Back Club* by Jill Hannah Anderson
- *The To-Hell-And-Back Club Book 2: Crazy Little Town Called Love* by Jill Hannah Anderson

CPSIA information can be obtained
at www.ICGtesting.com
Printed in the USA
LVHW082357300522
720046LV00014B/1360

9 781945 502781